THE
UNINVITED

THE
UNINVITED

PAUL CORNELL

Virgin

First published in Great Britain in 1997 by
Virgin Books
an imprint of Virgin Publishing Ltd
332 Ladbroke Grove
London W10 5AH

Cover photographs and all internal photographs by
Stephen Morley

ISBN 0 7535 02208

Typeset by Galleon Typesetting, Ipswich
Printed and bound in Great Britain by
Mackays of Chatham PLC

1

THE VICTIMLESS DEATH SYNDROME

The sun rose from the deep blue into the black, and was obscured by it, its topmost edge encountering a dark mass of distant trees on the horizon. A flock of birds flew under it.

Steve Blake looked up from the inverted image in the viewfinder of his Hassalblad camera and waited for the birds to pass. He'd chosen this setting as part of an exercise on colour for the photography class he taught, but it wasn't turning out the way he'd imagined it when he'd set out. The sunset he'd had in mind had been brighter, more vivid. Like the sunsets of his childhood. The sky over the seashore here at Scrane End seemed a pale imitation of what it should have been. What should have been velvet blue was washy. What should have been a deep orange was blanched. And what should have been peaceful seemed . . . ominous. It was because of either pollution or nostalgia. Or maybe what was happening in your own life had a big effect on what sort of sunset you saw.

He bent to examine the view again, took a deep inhalation of Norfolk air. And coughed. Well, clean air was a relative concept. And it probably didn't help that he'd tried to smoke and drink as hard as any other photojournalist in those days when he was one. He clicked the shutter and stood straight once more, trying to luxuriate in the quiet and the distant bird calls on the breeze. Whatever industry was doing to the atmosphere, you at least ought to be able to enjoy the silence.

But he couldn't.

1

He separated the camera from its tripod and took them both back to the battered MG that was parked on the gravel path nearby. A chill passed through him as he opened the boot, and he puffed his cheeks out and thought about pub grub in the village. There had to be something that would put warmth in him again. A shield against the cold. And against the thought of what had happened to those better sunsets.

The Jaguar slid up to the gates of the power plant. With a cheerful goodnight, the security guard moved swiftly to the controls of the barrier, allowing the car to pass out into the gathering twilight.

James Wilson hummed to himself as he changed gear and accelerated away from the lights of the plant behind him. There was something comforting about the interior of his car. It was as if being insulated from the noise of the engine insulated you from the cares of the day as well. And today he needed a little insulation. Partridge and his bureaucracy! Endlessly debating the new national grid protocols. Sometimes he felt like just dropping his briefcase on the table, and saying: 'I'm the energy council commissioner and you're not. So just do what I say and be done with it.' He chuckled at the thought, relaxing a little. He'd have a really long soak when he got home, and then call Ginny and ask to speak to young Ben. See what the lad wanted for his birthday.

Above the woods, the first stars were coming out against the dark blue. James flicked the button on his CD player and hummed along to Mozart as he negotiated the familiar country roads, feeling himself sinking into the upholstered seat.

His hum cut off suddenly as the music did. Silence. Oh no, not this above all else. A fault in his wonderful comfortmobile. Glancing at the road in front, he pressed a few buttons at random, but still no go. The thing was completely dead. A matter for that nice little garage down the road from his home, then. That'd be all right. Almost a pleasure to have

2

to visit it. The owner took pains to explain every repair he'd made, enjoying James' interest in all matters mechanical. People like that were the best thing about industry, the sort of people he enjoyed having in his boardrooms. The sort of people he enjoyed introducing the younger employees to. There was no reason why any industrial process, even the nuclear one, had to be aloof and mechanical. All you needed were the right people.

He returned his attention to the road with a little sigh, and placed his left hand back on the steering wheel in anticipation of a sharp bend ahead.

But just as he did so, the wheel moved. Against the pull of his right hand. Only a touch as he turned the bend, but almost as if the car wanted to make the turn in its own way. The door locks started to pop up and down, as if a playful child were hitting them. The light behind his dashboard started to flicker on and off.

Instinctively, he tried to change down and brake.

The gear lever wouldn't move, the brake pedal was a solid block under his foot.

James realised that he was breathing fast, in accident mode, waiting for the impact.

But, incredibly, the car smoothly took the bend, moved into the open stretch of road beyond, and, as James desperately tried to slow it down . . . accelerated.

Blake was humming one song after another as he drove, not quite settling on anything. He'd given up on the radio after a meaningless swirl around the dial. His humming stopped when he noticed the Jaguar headlights in his rear-view mirror. They were growing larger far too fast, gaining on him with a predatory speed.

He shook his head in resignation and waited for the car to pass.

James Wilson had his teeth clenched, his palms burning on the wheel as it turned back and forth against his strength. His mouth was moving in random patterns of horror. The figures on the dashboard clock had started to spin like an LED fruit machine. There seemed to be a terrible pressure inside the Jaguar, as if the windows were going to burst outwards. James felt that this was the force moving the wheel, a sort of invisible ghost that flowed all around his body, that could have crushed his head had it wanted to.

The car in front was a welcome sign of fellow humanity amongst this horror. Until the front of the Jaguar stabbed purposefully forward and nudged it. It was as if the force were playing with the cars.

'Stop!' James cried out. 'Please . . . Stop!'

Blake slammed forward in his seatbelt, and yelled over his shoulder at the terrified-looking middle-aged man behind him, 'What are you trying to do?'

Ahead was a grassy verge. He swung the steering column and braked, sending the MG skidding on to it.

The Jaguar shot past. He glimpsed the face of the man again. He was terrified. Blake thought he even made out the words he was shouting: 'Help me!'

The Jaguar shot straight across the next bend and off the road. It burst through the fence like a bullet.

The camera was in Blake's hand before he even thought about it. Straight out of the glove compartment. A single lens reflex. In the second that it took for him to drop it again and open his door, Blake caught the irony of that phrase.

Those reflexes were never going to leave him. Despite all his efforts.

He ran across the road towards the jagged gap in the fence. There was already a whiff of smoke in the air.

The Jaguar was lying in a crumpled heap in a little wooded valley beside the road. It had evidently landed nose first. Flames were blossoming from underneath. Inside, Blake saw the familiar middle-aged man he'd

4

glimpsed in his rear-view mirror. He didn't seem to be trapped, but he was hardly moving. His shoulders were set like they were in a vice. Only his head turned to look at Blake, and that seemed to strain every sinew in the man's neck.

As if his whole will was required for the task, the man mouthed two words to Blake. The same words as before.

'Help me.'

And then the car exploded.

Blake was shoved off his feet by the wall of hot air, the light of the blast filling his eyes as the sound burst over him. The trees sliced shadows across the road as the illumination filled the entire sky. Lightning, Blake's brain scrabbled for the thought, we've been hit by lightning. The light and the sound were too much for an ordinary explosion. And it seemed to go on and on, fire rolling from the wreckage of the car in waves that made him instinctively scramble backwards to the road, hiding his head on the ground to preserve himself from this terrifying thing above.

It might have been seconds or minutes before the thunder subsided. Blake finally raised his head from the tarmac and looked back into the furnace in the valley. He realised that the heat had died away into a twisted, blackened shape and a shroud of oily smoke.

He staggered up, and took a couple of stumbling steps towards the mess. Then stopped and sat down, realising that there was absolutely nothing he could do.

The taste of the smoke was weird and oily, full of the smell of flesh and leather. Steven Blake felt very sick. He knew that smell so well it was like a call from an old friend.

The first police car had arrived before Blake had thought about using his mobile. Now, the night was filled with the clip and fuzz of walkie-talkies, an ambulance and fire engine were in attendance, and the charred remains of the

5

Jaguar were illuminated by an arc light. Insects had filled the air between that light and the car.

Blake and a police superintendent who'd identified himself as Ferguson stood watching as a paramedic and a fireman struggled to open the blackened door of the car with a range of tools. Suddenly, the door gave way, and a curled bundle of flesh and cloth was revealed, melted against the steering wheel.

Brake turned away quickly, not trusting himself.

Ferguson turned more slowly. Professional distance, Blake thought, lowering his head and putting his hands on his knees. That's what he'd call it. It doesn't disturb him.

'You sure he wasn't swerving to avoid something?' Ferguson asked. 'An animal? Anything?' He had a face like that of a stand-up comedian from the club circuit, or a sitcom bank manager. But the funny man was definitely playing a serious role. The eyes that might have twinkled were like little stones.

'I've told you. He was driving like a maniac.'

The policeman actually managed a smile. 'I think we can tell that much by how he ended up.'

Blake tried not to look irritated at Ferguson's composure. He'd turned away a moment ago not because he wanted to miss the sight of the blackened corpse, but because he was aware of the opposite reaction inside him. The reaction that he'd spent this latter part of his life fighting.

He'd wanted to stare.

He'd wanted to take a photograph.

He sighed. 'I don't know what else to say. It isn't as if he didn't know the road. He drove up and down it often enough.'

'You know him?'

Blake had figured it out as the emergency services arrived. Where he'd seen that frightened face before. On the television, several times that week, in a series of cuddly adverts for British Nuclear Fuels. There'd been quite an uproar in the broadsheets about them. A kindly management type and his nephew were seen making sandcastles on the beach, next to the nuclear plant in this area. He couldn't remember the name that had flashed up at the start of the commercials, but he could remember the tag-line: 'I live with nuclear power on my doorstep. That way, I don't have so far to drive.' Nice laugh the man had. Did have.

'Not to talk to,' he told the policeman. 'I know who he is, though. Some bigwig in British Nuclear Power, wasn't he?'

That cold smile again. 'Pretty suitable death, then. He's practically deep-fried the whole place.' Ferguson moved off to supervise the stretcher party that had arrived from the ambulance, taking his emotional detachment with him.

Blake sighed, and idly reached up to pluck a desiccated leaf off a nearby tree. The whole sweep of plant life had been blackened and shrivelled by the explosion. He broke the leaf in two and sniffed it in his palm.

Then he closed his eyes. He should have known better.

That smell again. The smell of chemical explosives. The smell that took him back to a place he didn't want to be.

Blake woke the next morning feeling OK. He was sure he'd had troubled dreams, but now the first things in his mind were breakfast and work.

That was not good. He'd seen a man burnt to death and here he was thinking of bacon.

But he made his breakfast, ate it, and went to work.

Because he was OK. He had to be OK.

Life went on, didn't it?

His tutorial group were surprised at the photos he handed to them that morning. They were expecting colour

7

compositions, that sunset he'd talked about capturing. What they got was a collection of images from contemporary warfare. Dead soldiers lying in awkward neglect. Upturned vehicles and houses. Burning peasants. He made up something appropriate as he went along. This was the first time a lot of them would have heard about what he used to do. About the sort of person he used to be.

'A lot of people don't believe in it,' he found himself saying as he placed another horror on another lap. 'Instinct. Hunch.' He swung round to address the whole group and tapped the photo in his hand. It was of a gang of civilians, many about their age, turning over a jeep with soldiers inside. 'Neither did I until I came across this jeep. I found it down a side street. I went down there just because I felt there was going to be something worth taking.'

'What was going through your head when you were taking it?' a student asked. Robert, the bald Scottish one with the goatee. He always asked the tough questions.

'The usual stuff. The light. Depth of field. Focal length.' He paused, biting his lip. He remembered that smell, the crushed leaf. 'Mainly the light.'

'No. I mean . . . your feelings about what was going on.'

He took another sheaf of photographs from his desk and started to distribute them. *Charred Corpse Eight*. When he heard his voice, he was surprised that it sounded apologetic. As if he was making excuses. 'I was . . . there to take photographs. If I'd have let anything else in, I'd have been lost. All I cared about was what I could see through the lens.' He looked at his student imploringly, almost questioningly. 'That's the only way I could do it.'

'Was there ever a time when you couldn't do that?'

'Not until much later.'

'What changed?'

Blake found that he was staring at the little black dots which made up *Charred Corpse Eight*. 'I did,' he said. And

8

then, suddenly, he felt very angry with himself. He'd done this instead of doing the thing that he really should have done. The thing that a civilised human being ought to do. He looked up at his class. 'Look, I'm afraid we have to finish here. There's somewhere I have to go. Could you make sure all this stuff is put away? Thanks.'

And he walked away.

He could hear them starting to talk about him as he left the room.

James Wilson, that was the name, as a call to a friend confirmed. And James Wilson's house, as a second call indicated, was, just like the adverts said, not very far from his favourite power station. It was a large manor house, surrounded by an eight-foot-high wall. The entrance was protected by a pair of vast metal gates.

Blake got out of the MG and pressed a button on an intercom. 'It's Steve Blake here. For Mrs Wilson.'

'Who?' The female voice sounded mightily distracted. As well it might.

'Steve Blake. She doesn't know me. I was there when her husband had his accident. I thought I should come. I understand if she doesn't want to see me.'

There was no reply. Just when Blake thought he'd been given the cold shoulder, there was a click, and the gates began to swing open.

One drive down the longest gravel driveway in the world later, Blake rang the doorbell of the manor house. It was answered by an attractive, distracted-looking woman in her mid-forties.

'Mrs Wilson?' Blake began. 'It's about your husband.' He saw that she was staring at him and suddenly felt very stupid and selfish and inappropriate. 'I'm sorry, I'm probably the last person you want to see right now.'

'Are you a friend of my husband?' she asked, almost pleadingly.

9

'No, not really. It's just — I was there when it happened.'

'He's . . .' She stopped, searching his face with her eyes. 'There's something wrong. Maybe if you talked to him . . .'

'Talked to him?' The insane thought flashed into Blake's head that maybe nobody had told her. 'How do you mean?'

'This might sound odd, but I —'

A voice interrupted her. A voice familiar to Blake from a week of advertisements. 'Darling, who is it?'

James Wilson stepped into the light, out of the darkness of his hallway. He peered at Blake like the total stranger he was, as his wife fell silent.

'Can I help you?' he asked.

2

F FOR FAKE

Blake reached for the glass of whisky that his gracious host was holding out to him, and, after a moment where he realised that he was still staring, took it. Wilson moved from his drinks cabinet, watching him, an awkward smile flashing at Blake briefly.

'I was so sure it was you,' Blake told him, floundering. He'd come here to do the decent thing, only to find that no decent thing needed to be done. 'I saw you.'

'What you saw was my car.' The voice wasn't as reassuring in real life as it was on the telly. 'It's my belief that your imagination did the rest. Filled in the blanks, so to speak.' He sat down, and Blake did also.

'So have they found out who really was killed in your car?' He could find whoever it had been. Do this business for real.

Wilson snorted. 'Not much hope of identifying him from the remains, apparently. It'll be some local yob.' He seemed to savour the word. 'A joyrider.'

'Is that what the police think?'

'What else is there to think?'

'Well, if he was young, he'd have been missed by now, wouldn't he?'

Wilson laughed bitterly. 'Most parents don't know where their children are from one day to the next these days. Stupid bastard, whoever he was.'

Blake was starting to get annoyed on behalf of whoever had been in the car. He couldn't keep the sharpness out of his tone. 'And he took the car from the pub car park?'

11

Wilson nodded.

'Must have been a pretty sophisticated joyrider. The security on Jags these days . . .'

'These people don't see security as a deterrent, Mr Blake. They see it as a challenge.'

'But you were in the pub . . . And you didn't hear an alarm or anything?'

Blake wanted to get up, get out of here, but these answers he was getting weren't going to lead him to where he desperately wanted to go. It was as if Wilson was just flinging back the first thing that came into his head. He didn't seem at all concerned for the fate of that curled up cinder that had been a human being.

'Perhaps the man was just an experienced and deter-mined car thief. Stealing to order. Happens all the time.'

'So . . . why was he driving like a maniac?'

'Who knows? A car with that power in the hands of some spotty youth is a dangerous beast.'

'No . . .' This was insane, but Blake couldn't let it go. All he wanted was sense, closure, and Wilson's answers were making him more and more uneasy. 'No. I saw the man. He was older.'

Wilson sighed, bemused. 'Mr Blake, you came to my house because you thought I was dead. I hardly think you're a great judge of what does and does not make sense.' He stood, indicating that the interview was over. 'Now, as diverting as this has been, I have a very demand-ing schedule.'

Blake stood, feeling suddenly awkward as Wilson led him from the room. The man was right. He was battering away at nothing, trying to find some sort of peace for himself in an affair that, in the end, was nothing to do with him.

'I'll see myself out,' he told the executive's back as it vanished into the interior of the house.

He nodded to Mrs Wilson as he passed her at work

in the kitchen. She looked up briefly.

And that pleading look was still in her eyes.

The crash site had been taped off by the police. Blake got out of his car, feeling like a ball in a game of emotional pinball. He'd been intending to go back to college, or to go home and throw out his combat photos, but instead he'd come back here. Despite himself, he felt all Jeepy. That sense that had taken him down that side street to find the overturned Jeep. It felt like there was something down this street worth taking.

Of course, that was how it had always started. But then there came the blood and the bullets and the dead women and the almost certain untreated post traumatic stress syndrome and for God's sake Steve go home.

He slipped his smallest camera from his pocket and snapped a few shots of the police officers in all-concealing white suits collecting evidence around the site below.

Framed in his field of view, Superintendent Ferguson marched up the bank, waving his arms. He was in his shirtsleeves. As if he'd been doing some messy and private task. 'I'm sorry, sir,' he called. 'You can't do that here.'

Blake lowered his camera. 'I'm sorry. I didn't realise. How's it going?' Ferguson ignored him as he took his uniform jacket from his driver. 'Steve Blake. I was here last night. I witnessed the accident.'

'Of course,' Ferguson said, preoccupied. 'Of course you did. You've already made a statement, haven't you?'

Blake nodded. 'Funny business, eh? It not being James Wilson in the car after all. What's your theory? Was it a joyrider?'

Ferguson finally paid attention, giving Blake an appraising glance. 'In my job it never pays to jump to conclusions too soon.'

'So how do you go about finding out who it was? Dental records? Mr Wilson told me that the remains were too burnt to identify.'

13

Ferguson looked casual. 'You were closer to the explosion than me. You felt the heat. There was nothing left.'

The policeman turned to head for his car. But Blake followed.

'I know these cars have big petrol tanks, but I was wondering if something else could have caused the explosion?'

'That has occurred to us, Mr Blake. We've got a couple of explosives experts coming over. I suspect they have slightly more experience of these things than you do.'

Blake refrained from saying that was probably untrue. 'So you think something odd might have been going on?'

'I don't think anything,' Ferguson purred patronisingly, 'until I've got the evidence.' With another significant look, he climbed into his car and shut the door on Blake.

Blake watched as the police driver took the car around the bend in the road. Although Ferguson sat rigid in his seat, he couldn't get over the feeling that the policeman's whole attention was still on him.

Jeepy. Very, very Jeepy. Damn it.

Blake got back in time to take his second tutorial group of the day, but he was preoccupied. Once again, he let the lesson plan go to the wall as he fished in his files for his favourite set of photos. The safe ones. The fakes. He distributed them to the students, and hoped that the morning's group hadn't told this lot that he was losing his marbles. The Cottingley fairies; Trotsky on the balcony in Red Square, before and after he was airbrushed out by Stalin; the famous shot of a government soldier from the Spanish Civil War, caught in the moment of death as he fell, dropping his rifle. Robert Capa, the photographer, had always maintained that the shot was real, but, as it had come to represent the horrors of that conflict, various authorities had cast doubt on it.

'The moment of truth,' Blake said to the young people sitting around him. 'Was he dead, or was he faking?' He wondered if they would ever see a real corpse at any point in

14

heir lives. 'Was the photographer lying to prove a bigger ruth? I want you to think about the relationship between he truth and an image of it. Do you see what you want to ee, or what the photographer wants you to see?'

He stopped at the thought. He was no longer a journalist. He didn't have to get involved in the messy business of nterpreting the truth any more. And yet his instincts were creaming at him to do just that. To frame things again. To ut them in context and sort them out. Not for his own oor, tormented, brain's sake, but for the sake of some poor nknown sod who had taken a very heavy fall for reasons as et unknown. 'Where's the truth?' he whispered.

He glanced up from his reverie and realised that his utorial group were all looking at him rather than at the hotos.

Norwich Coroner's Court was in session in a small, draughty hall in the magistrates' courthouse. Blake had roned his suit for the occasion, wishing he'd had it dry-cleaned. He'd been surprised to see, amongst the handful of people in attendance, James Wilson, and had been tempted to go up to the man and poke him to see if he was solid. Wilson's presence, at what Blake still couldn't help but think of as Wilson's own coroner's inquest, was like something out of *Randall and Hopkirk*. Ferguson was there too.

'What sort of speed would you say the victim was travelling at, Mr Blake?' the coroner, an elderly, precise-looking man, asked when it was Blake's turn to give evidence. 'Approximately?'

Blake's eyes couldn't help alighting on Wilson. 'I think eighty, maybe ninety miles an hour. Then Wilson . . .' He looked quickly back to the coroner. 'Well, I was certain at the time it was James Wilson at the wheel.'

The coroner nodded to Blake and smiled in a way he didn't really like. 'But that information was in fact incorrect?'

Blake paused. Wilson had seemed to smile at that moment too. The smile of a man who had completed a brilliant piece of fakery. Ta–dah!

'Yes,' he concluded. 'It would . . . appear so.'

The coroner dismissed him with another of those little smiles. 'Thank you, Mr Blake.'

The presentation of evidence took most of the day. What Blake had feared would happen, did. Photographs were shown. Obscene blow-ups of the car's interior, with trimmings of man. Nice compositional style on some of them. Very good light.

He made himself concentrate on the pathologist, who identified herself as Dr Sarah Armstrong, as she began to speak. She was a studious-looking black woman, whose braided hair spoke of her being more fun in her social life than her sensible spectacles would indicate.

'The remains of the victim were so damaged that, practically speaking, there was nothing to do a post-mortem on. Unusually, even the victim's teeth were destroyed by the severity of the blaze.'

Blake glanced past Dr Armstrong at the sound of the door behind her opening. An extraordinary man had just entered the building and was taking his seat. He wore the uniform of a very high-ranking police officer. Detective chief superintendent, Blake decided. He had a hawklike, haunted face, a face that had seen some terrible things. But that wasn't the startling thing about him. He had entered the building as if he literally owned it, and was looking around as if he were considering redecoration.

As the man took his seat behind him, Blake realised that he had been staring, and turned back to what Dr Armstrong was saying.

'I would like, however, to comment on the degree of burns suffered by the victim. These were so exceptional that I asked the forensic scientist on the case to account for the heat at what was, basically, a car accident. With your permission, I will read his comments.'

The coroner nodded for her to go ahead. Blake glanced behind again. The new arrival had leaned forward in his seat, listening intently as he exchanged an expectant look with Ferguson.

' "To generate the degree of destruction that I saw at the accident site," ' Dr Armstrong read, ' "you would normally need the sort of heat generated by a bomb or volcanic rock. I can only conclude that the victim's car had, in some way, been exposed to as-yet-unidentified chemicals or explosives." '

'Thank you.' The coroner made a note as Dr Armstrong stepped down, then glanced across to Ferguson. 'Superintendent Ferguson? Anything more to add?'

Ferguson stood. 'Just that we are conducting rigorous enquiries into the possibility that Mr Wilson's car was exposed to some sort of radiation at the power plant where he is based —'

Blake stopped himself from sighing out loud. Radiation? They really were trying to fit the evidence to the situation. Just because Wilson worked in the nuclear industry . . . He glanced over his shoulder and saw that the new arrival was watching Ferguson's speech closely, as if ready to prompt.

'Or that the person who stole the car was carrying substances that may have exacerbated the petrol tank explosion. So far, I'm afraid our investigations have proved fruitless.'

'And in your considerable experience,' asked the coroner, 'is such evidence likely to be forthcoming?'

'Frankly, no. The incident was unusual, but accidents are by their nature unusual. Although we can only speculate, it is my personal belief that this was the work of another so-called joyrider.'

Blake bit his lip at that. He glanced between Ferguson, Wilson, and the new arrival. Their body language was all the same. One goal up with thirty seconds to play. We're about to get away with this. He stopped himself. That

17

was ridiculous. He was making conspiracies up out of nothing.

'Thank you, Superintendent,' said the coroner. And that was that.

Blake caught up with Dr Armstrong as she left the hall. ' "Open verdict"? What's that supposed to mean?'

'What it says.' She dealt with him as calmly as she'd dealt with the dead man. 'No conclusions can be drawn.'

Blake shook his head, insistent. He needed this. He needed to know the name of the man he'd seen die. 'I saw that car go over the edge. The driver was a middle-aged man in a suit. He didn't look much like a joyrider.'

Dr Armstrong smiled gently at him. 'You thought you saw James Wilson go over the edge. That doesn't make you a terribly reliable witness. All the real evidence was destroyed by the blast.'

'Yes.' Blake caught a certain reticence in her eyes: a shadow of a doubt. 'Remarkable, isn't it?'

Blake exited the courthouse just in time to see the mysterious chief superintendent get into his car. He called to Ferguson as he headed for his own. 'Superintendent? Could I have a quick word?'

The policeman looked as if he'd already had enough of Steven Blake. 'What was it you wanted to know?'

Blake made up something that sounded plausible. He just wanted Ferguson to have to deal with this situation for longer than he'd wanted to. 'I just wondered if you'd looked into the possibility of a political attack on James Wilson.'

'A terrorist cell, perhaps?' The knifey smile had returned to the man's face.

'Why not? The director of British Nuclear Power has to have one or two enemies. The anti-nuclear lobby, maybe.'

'Why would a terrorist who successfully breaks into James Wilson's car then settle for driving it off?'

Blake stifled an inappropriate smile. He suddenly felt like he was in *Columbo*, teasing these anomalous details out of the guilty man. In that frame, he already had all the answers, and Ferguson was definitely guilty. That frame felt good, but it was also a fairy tale, and he was starting to become aware of just how much he was getting involved in this particular fairy tale. 'He was driving towards Wilson's house when he died. Maybe he was planning to go there with the car packed with explosives.'

He expected to hear another anomalous answer, one which would once more highlight how bizarre this was all getting. But the policeman did what policemen usually did in grey areas. He reverted to bureaucratese.

'We're already pursuing those lines of enquiry, Mr Blake. An open verdict doesn't mean that our work stops.'

Steve was getting tired of being called Mr Blake. 'You said at the inquest that you thought it was a joyrider. Yesterday, you said you hadn't got the evidence yet. What have you found?'

Ferguson smiled all over his face. 'I'm sorry?'

'When we talked. Yesterday. At the accident site —'

Ferguson shook his head, holding Blake's gaze meaningfully. 'Mr Wilson dying at the wheel of his car, conversations with me that you and I never had . . .' He leaned an inch closer. 'I think your memory is playing some strange tricks on you, Mr Blake.'

Blake took a confused step back, and watched as Ferguson got into his car and was driven away. The fairy tale was true. That had definitely been a threat.

Damn it. Why couldn't his instincts just let him walk away?

When Blake got to the site of the crash, a team of policemen were hauling the wreckage of the Jaguar on to the back of a truck. The ground around the crash site, the seared trees, the charred patch of earth, were soon to be the only witnesses to its presence. In time, nature would deal with those, and a scab would form over the memory. Steven Blake knew how these things happened. All that was left of Deeley Plaza on that terrible day in November 1963 were a few photos, a reel of film played so often that it was now fiction, a movie. He crouched to pluck some grass from the ground. He had to deal with this while it was still real. While it was news rather than an international conspiracy bestseller and a newspaper serialisation and part of the huge realm of half truths that nobody believed enough to do anything about. He sniffed the shrubs, and smelt that horribly evocative smell which wasn't quite napalm, but was enough to tell him that this had been no accident. He popped a sample into a plastic film canister. And though he knew that they added nothing to the truth, that, indeed, these days they made what they saw into somehow more of a fiction, he took photographs.

While he was doing so, he had that sudden human sensation that science had never accepted. The knowledge that he was being watched.

He looked back to the road, and there he was, looking down at him. James Wilson. The man who should be a casualty.

He walked down the bank towards Blake, calling as he came, 'What's your problem, Mr Blake? Is your life really so dull?'

Blake felt something give inside him. He knew, now. He knew from the utter inappropriateness of Wilson's presence that there was a dirty great error in the nature of things standing right in front of him. Wilson had his hands deep in something, and an innocent victim had been killed because of it.

'My problem . . . My problem is that some poor bastard was killed in your car, and nobody cares as long as it wasn't you.'

Wilson sniffed. 'Just how far do you think our sympathy

should stretch? This idiot stole a car. He was probably high on drink and drugs. He drove the thing at high speed along a badly lit road –'

'And left no skid marks when he crashed.'

That line had the desired impact. 'What?'

Blake pointed to the road. 'He lost control of the car, but he didn't brake. Have you had a look at the road? Not a mark.'

Wilson followed Blake's finger to the road.

Blake took a photo of him.

He turned back, holding up a hand in front of his face. The public face of nuclear power, suddenly shy of being photographed. 'Would you stop that please? I'm sure the police will have a good explanation.'

'I'm sure they will. They seem to have an explanation for everything.' He dropped the camera back into his pocket. 'That's why I'm not going to the police with this. I'm going to the press.'

He climbed back up the bank and headed for the road. Glancing over his shoulder, he saw Wilson glowering after him, standing in the middle of what should have been his scene of death.

Joanna Ball sat back in the big chair behind her desk, listening to the messages on her answerphone. She was a sharp-faced, wry-looking woman, who had grown tired of the facial comparisons to Princess Diana by the summer of 1985, and had only just started to outlive them. It didn't help that her mouth was never more than a few milli-metres from a cynical pout. She made a point of not being in on her personal line at work, because it was a way of controlling her social life, because a newspaper editor was supposed to be a hard-bitten bitch and hard to reach, and because listening to lots of messages was usually great fun. It reminded you that you were wanted. This morning, however, all the messages were from the same person.

'I know you have to be there, Joanna,' the voice said. 'I've got to see you.'

Steve Blake. The man whose surname she'd ill-advisedly taken on, and then fought to be rid of after the divorce. It was awful to have made one's reputation with an unwelcome word tagged on to one's life. For Steve to call like this, something was obviously very urgent. One of his cats had probably got stuck on the roof. Or an injured foal had been put down on *Animal Hospital*.

Joanna's secretary, Charlotte, entered, smiling like she'd been left like that by her dentist. 'Was that him again? How many's that?'

'Five.' Joanna clicked the pause button.

'Is he going for some sort of record?'

'Apparently. I suppose I should be grateful for the attention.'

Charlotte cuddled the files she'd brought in. 'Nothing like a sad, burnt-out has-been to make you appreciate how far you've travelled, eh?'

Joanna suddenly found herself to be angry. And angry at being angry. All of which was going to add up to bad news for any PA who tried to be chummy with her today. 'Could you just leave those on the desk, please, Charlotte?' she asked, in a voice that indicated this was a complicated job, possibly beyond the intelligence of the person she was addressing.

Charlotte did so like a shot and left as quickly as she could in those heels. Probably off to gossip about her to the next level of the food chain.

Joanna returned to the answerphone, and played the next message, hoping it was a man. Another man. Any other man.

It was Steve. Message number six.

'It's about business.'

Sure it was.

'It's something I think you'd be very interested in. Here's my number again . . .'

Joanna mouthed along to the phone number. It wasn't as if she'd forgotten. More's the pity.

The reverend stood in front of a conveyor belt with a coffin on it, flanked by a pair of red velvet curtains.

He looked appreciatively at Steve, the only one in the church, as if he was surprised to have an audience. 'For thine is the kingdom, the power and the glory, for ever and ever. Amen.'

The conveyor belt started up. The coffin vanished into the darkness beyond, and the curtains drew closed. Another piece of evidence had moved from reality into the realms of fiction. He'd made himself mark photographic assignments this morning, telling himself over and over that he was a tutor now, not a journalist.

But in between giving marks, he'd kept on calling Joanna.

And then it had occurred to him that if there had been some kid at the wheel of the car, or some older joyrider, or James Wilson's long-lost twin brother, then maybe somebody would care about his death and come to his funeral.

So he'd dropped everything to come here, and found that he was the only person in the world who cared about anything.

'Did you know him?' the vicar asked, his ceremonial duties over.

'No. I saw him die.'

'It was good of you to make the effort to come.'

Blake sighed. He could kid himself, but he couldn't kid anybody else. 'It was the nearest he was going to get to a send-off, wasn't it? Present company excepted.'

The vicar smiled.

'Do you do many of these one man shows?'

'Far too many, I'm sorry to say. Far too many.'

'Maybe I should book you for mine,' Blake muttered.

'I'm sorry?'

23

Blake roused himself. 'Been a bit different if it had been James Wilson's funeral, wouldn't it? You'd have been able to sell tickets.'

The vicar didn't quite seem to know what to make of his tone. There was obviously a pot of tea on for him somewhere. He settled on a truism. 'We're all equal in the eyes of God.'

Blake walked with him to the porch of the church. 'Then how come someone can be killed and not be missed? Just disappear like they never existed? Is it because they're not loved, or is it because they've lost touch with anybody who ever cared about them?' He paused, realising how insane he sounded. 'Or is it because someone powerful wanted it that way?'

The reverend, to give him credit, engaged with the question. But Blake could tell from his tone that he was being quietened down, sympathised with. 'I think this is perhaps a time for acceptance, not questions.'

'That's a "don't know", is it? This man —' he gestured in the direction of the curtains '— he doesn't have a name. He didn't appear to have a life. He hasn't even got a death to call his own.' He was almost shouting. 'He doesn't count, does he?'

The vicar smiled gently. 'Your concern suggests that he does.' He made to head for his vestry, smiling further at the look of revelation on Blake's face. 'If you do find out who he was, you will let me know, won't you?'

And he left.

Suddenly, Blake found that he had something important that he wanted to do. He had had all along. 'Yeah,' he said. 'I'll do that. I'll find out.'

3

THE EX FILES

B lake was sorting out his tutorial photographs when Maggie, his head of department, found him. She'd obviously heard tales in the staff room.

'Steve, are you OK?'

He took *Starving Ethiopian Child Three* from the wall. 'I'm going to take some time off. I've had . . . a bereavement.'

'I'm sorry to hear that. Was it somebody close?'

Blake remembered the heat and the smell. 'Pretty close, yeah. I'm sorry. I know this isn't great timing.' But I've found a quest. I've found a way to get healed. Maybe.

From her expression, it looked as if maybe she understood. 'Take as long as it needs. I'll arrange cover. Anything I can do, just say.'

'Thanks, Maggie. I appreciate that.'

She leaned over to look at the photos that he'd gathered together. 'I didn't know you'd started to use your own work for teaching.'

Blake looked at her for a moment. He felt like he'd given something away. To himself, as well as her. He felt like an alcoholic discussing beer. 'Someone's got to show them how not to do it.'

Thankfully, at that moment bald Robert interrupted and announced that there was a phone call for Steve.

It took him a moment to recognise the voice on the other end of the phone.

'It's Sarah Armstrong. We met yesterday. I was the pathologist on the car crash.'

'Oh.' Blake smiled like it was Christmas morning. 'Hi.'

'Look,' she continued, sounding clipped and swift, like she was doing this while somebody else was out of the room. 'I know you think that there might be some sort of cover-up, and I'm not saying there is, but —'

'You're not happy.' He could hardly prevent himself from smiling. No sooner had he given himself over to this quest than, as if the universe knew it, the floodgates had suddenly opened.

'Just little things. Ferguson let the accident site get infected —'

'Infected?'

'Contaminated with stuff that's nothing to do with the accident. He let that happen very quickly. And I had problems getting access to the body.'

'Could just be the usual, run of the mill, incompetence?'

She sounded tetchy, like she wasn't used to anybody questioning her findings. 'I took some readings. There's no way the body had been exposed to radiation.'

'As if.'

'Yes, I know "as if", but what else do you look for when what happened is impossible? There was no sign of any explosives. Everybody agrees that there was a chemical, but nobody can find a sample to analyse.'

'Are you sure? I think I've smelt it.'

'Well there isn't a sniff now. I've talked to the scene-of-the-crime officers, forensics. Not a thing. That's . . . unusual.'

Blake was grinning to himself. 'Thanks. I take it this is off the record?'

'That's right.'

'Look, I'll be in London in a few days.' He fished for his filofax. 'Where can I get in touch with you?'

A long pause. 'Sorry. This is as far up the plank as I'm willing to walk. I just thought you should know.'

And she hung up. Which Blake probably would have

done too, in her position. But she'd done enough. He now knew exactly what he was going to do next.

Disturbingly, the man who sold the *London Evening Standard* outside Blackfriars underground station recognised Blake immediately. 'Didn't know you were back, Mr Blake,' he called, stopping him in his tracks.

'I'm not back, Harry.'

'Here, have a newspaper.' Harry flashed the headline under Blake's nose.

'No thanks.' Blake raised his hand. 'I'm trying to give them up.'

And before Harry could ask any further questions about Blake's new career and that nice Joanna and if there was any chance of a reconciliation, he was marching swiftly off towards the imposing shape of Cavell House, where Joanna's newspaper lived.

Joanna Ball didn't expect to look up and see her ex in her office. At least, not outside her nightmares. And, in those, her mother and George Clooney were usually also present. The bugger hadn't even had the grace to knock. Not that she was doing anything special. Again, unlike in the dreams.

'How did you get up here?' she asked, trying to sound appropriately peeved as he slopped down into a chair.

He still didn't look at home in London. It was as if he should have mud on his boots. He still had the face of a carer, sweet curls, a rugby player's square-jawed, reliable smile. Two expressions: concerned and hurt. And that uncertain frown always playing about his eyes. He still looked, in short, like he needed a good shag.

Which, after their short but intensive affair-cum-marriage, was downright insulting.

He flicked out a battered old press pass. 'I don't leave home without it.'

'That's three years out of date.'

'Press passes are like people. They gain authority with age.'

Like *some* people. 'You've lost weight.'

'So have you.'

Oh piss off. 'No I haven't.'

'I know, but I thought I'd flatter you.' Disarming grin. 'I need your help.'

'You always did.'

'Can we talk?'

She was going to say something about him stopping being so damn reasonable, when Charlotte entered, and opened her mouth in a disapproving, red 'oh'. Joanna waved airily in her PA's direction.

'Steve, this is Charlotte. She's one of your biggest fans.'

They went to the Golden Star, which, Blake remembered, had been a nasty journo's pub when he and Jo had been together. Now it was wall-to-wall suits and baguettes. Odd that Joanna still came here really. Or maybe she didn't, and that was why she'd led him there.

'So,' she asked, still looking horribly gorgeous and smelling exactly the bloody same as when he'd been able to hug her. 'What's this story that's woken you up? Sheep rustling?'

He refused to be stung. 'More poaching than rustling.'

'Poaching what?'

'Somebody's life. Someone else's death.'

She looked away, haunted. 'You're not still banging on about your photographer's angst, are you? After all this time?'

That would never do, would it? He controlled his expression. 'No. Nothing like that.'

'Good.' She toyed idly with a ring, which was what she always did when she was nervous. 'I thought for a minute you'd come all this way to open up an argument that's way past its sell-by date.'

'Joanna, if I thought anybody else could help, I'd have gone to them like a shot.'

'Thanks, Steve. I'm touched.'

He looked towards the door and folded his arms, on the verge of standing to go.

She laughed. 'OK. What do you want?'

'Wilson, Harold.' Joanna scrolled down the screen of the newspaper library's elegant new Zentex PC. 'Wilson, Jocky. Sorry, went past it. Wilson, James. Here we go.'

'Where are you getting this?' Blake leaned over her shoulder. He hadn't liked the way Joanna had poked her head around the door of the workfloor outside, as if she were checking that Charlotte wasn't about, before leading her biggest mistake through.

'Zentexnet. They've got their own newsgroups, archives, everything. Ideal for businesses. Incredibly fast.' She glanced at Blake's puzzlement. 'Press button. Box make lights.'

He glowered. She grinned and pressed a key. A window sprang up containing the image of a newspaper story. The picture was of Wilson. The headline read: 'Powergen Appoints "Wet"'. At the press of another key, the picture changed. 'Profile: James Wilson: Success Story with a Conscience'.

'Appointed chief executive of BN Power four years ago,' Joanna said. 'A surprise choice as head of the Energy Council early this year.'

'Why a surprise?' Blake asked.

'He's considered quite a liberal.'

Blake raised his eyebrow. 'Not from what little I've seen.'

Joanna made some more images flash by, faster than he could follow. He was amazed that she seemed to be actually reading the text of the nested web pages that sped by.

'Bit unlucky with his cars, your James Wilson, isn't he?'

'What?'

She stopped the flow of information. 'Energy Man in

High Speed Crash.' There was a photo of a sports car crunched up against a tree.

'Three months ago. Hit a tree with his Austin Healey Sprite, near Lincoln. Managed to escape with minor injuries.'

Blake frowned. That made no sense and loads. At the same time. 'What did he say about the circumstances of the accident?'

'Hmm. This is a very short article. "Man Unhurt in Collision with Tree" might be a sassy headline where you live, but –'

'OK . . .' He was struck by a sudden thought. Three months ago there'd been a botched attempt to do . . . whatever it is they . . . whoever they were . . . had just succeeded in doing. Whatever that was exactly. But there was one thing he was certain about. 'Who handled the enquiry? I've got a tenner says it was Superintendent John Ferguson.'

Joanna found the name and smiled. 'Wrong.'

Blake took the tenner from his pocket.

'It was *Inspector* John Ferguson. He's been promoted since then and transferred.'

Blake put the tenner back. 'So what've you got on him?'

'Let's see.' Her hands flashed over the keyboard again, but suddenly she stopped.

A message was flashing on the screen in a small red box. 'System Overload . . . Try Later.'

Joanna sighed. 'Bloody mainframe. What the hell does that mean?'

'I thought you were all powerful?'

'Shut up. I'll get round this. Accounts ignore it all the time. Give me five minutes.' She set about tapping, mousing and occasionally bashing.

Blake watched her, glad that he'd never got the hang of modern life.

* * *

The sign on the desk said DETECTIVE CHIEF SUPERINTENDENT PHILIP GATES. The man behind it was leafing through a file, smiling every now and then at what he saw.

He looked up at a sound from his computer. A Zentex. It had booted itself up, the triangular logo spinning in one corner, and a small red box was flashing on the screen. It contained the words: 'Ferguson File'. Gates' smile faded, replaced by a look of mild concern. He tapped in a series of commands. The lettering in the box changed to 'Access Discontinued'.

Gates picked up his telephone, and dialled a number.

Joanna had eventually got round the problem. She'd tried to tell Blake how, but, like a person given a long and complicated series of directions, he'd started to just nod and make positive noises after the third line. She'd realised that and thwapped him with her mouse mat. Now they were reading the pages she'd located as copies slipped from the desktop printer.

'Superintendent Ferguson grows his own vegetables.' Joanna raised an eyebrow. 'Sharp career rise in last five years. Bright, hard on law and order, hard on the causes of law and order. Transferred to "Central Ops" two years ago.'

'What's that?'

'Comes under the Home Office. Kind of MI5 meets Special Branch with a smattering of Anti-Terrorist Squad. Quango. Wonderful lunches, so my crime man tells me. And at our expense.' She took another page from the printer and glanced at it. 'Here's one from your bizarre lack of death search. Last March some RAF commander was feared dead after a plane crash, but it turned out it wasn't him flying the plane.'

Blake snatched the page from her. 'It's happened before!'

Joanna's hand closed on the corner of the page as she noticed a significant detail. 'Inspector John Ferguson said

31

the police could not identify the pilot because of the severity of the explosion.'

They both stared at the photo at the top of the page. A barely recognisable charred corpse. Then they looked at each other.

Blake spoke with a note of awe in his voice. He knew that they were both feeling the same thing. Pure, unadulterated Jeepiness. 'Another victimless death.'

'Hey, that's my kind of journalism. A snappy headline.' Joanna was deep in thought. 'But factually inaccurate. There *are* victims.'

'But nobody knows who they are! They're never missed. And Ferguson's green fingers are all over every enquiry!' He grabbed another page of printout. 'Look, there's another: nuclear physicist feared dead on walking holiday . . . turns up safe and well.'

Joanna's eyes were calculating quickly. Sales figures, probably. Or shelf space for awards. 'You reckon Ferguson's co-ordinating all these cover-ups?'

Blake didn't answer, reaching for another sheet of printout. He was annoyed to discover that it was blank. 'What's going on?'

Joanna picked up the pile of printouts. Apart from the ones they'd already seen, they were all blank. 'This bloody machine. These ribbons only last about –'

There was a dying electronic noise from behind them. They turned. The monitor on the computer had blinked out.

'What the hell?' asked Joanna.

It was at that moment that the door to her office opened and two security guards entered, looking slightly abashed. 'Sorry, Ms Ball,' one began, as the other marched towards Blake, 'but your guest doesn't have security clearance.'

'Security clearance?' Joanna gave them a look which would have frozen a mammoth. 'What are you talking about?'

'I'm afraid we've been instructed to escort Mr Blake to the nearest exit.'

Joanna looked apologetically at Blake. 'It *is* policy. But it's never actually happened before.'

'Forget it.' Blake waved as he allowed himself to be led away. 'They're only doing somebody else's job.'

Blake went back to the pub, wondering. OK, so he'd flashed an old pass to get in, and maybe somebody had just noticed that and started making enquiries, but at the same time as the network fault, as the printer fault . . . It was enough to make you start thinking the world was against you.

He looked up at the TV in the corner of the bar. Soundless news pictures of civil war in Africa. A reporter walking through a refugee camp.

Maybe it was.

He turned away and concentrated on his pint.

Joanna came in an hour later. They hadn't made any arrangement, just a slope of the shoulders and a certain eye contact as he'd left. The body language of an ex stayed with you like a virus.

'Sorry about that,' she said, sitting down. 'Security's a lot tighter these days.'

'Want a drink?'

'No. You obviously still give off Odour de Newsprint, even if you've turned your back on us.'

Blake shook his head. 'It wasn't who I was that worried them. It was what we were looking at.'

She looked archly at him. A story was one thing, a conspiracy that reached to her doorstep was obviously another. Blake remembered that she'd always tutted when he'd read out stories from *Fortean Times*.

'Steve, I hate to burst your ego, but you should stick to photography. Some crisped corpses and a bent copper do not a vast conspiracy make.'

'How about adding a crashed computer to the scenario?'

She looked a little more uncertain. 'I do know a way around that.'

'How?'

'Come on, I'll show you. Let me buy you lunch.'

They walked through the backstreets, eating bags of chips. 'You're not telling me you don't miss the lifestyle down here?'

Blake waved a chip. 'I miss the glamour, obviously.'

'I didn't believe you'd actually stay away.' She saw his ears prick up. 'Oh, from me maybe. But not from the job.' She threw her empty chip paper into a bin.

Blake's features clouded. 'That was the trouble. It became the same thing in the end, didn't it?'

Her tone remained level. 'One thing our marriage didn't descend into was self-pity. Try and steer clear of it now, will you?'

They'd reached the outside of a corner café. Joanna looked at Blake until he realised that this was where they were going. Hurriedly, he screwed up his paper and licked the vinegar from his fingers.

'Ah,' he said, puzzled. 'Coffee. Good.'

As soon as he stepped through the door, Blake had the same sensation as when he'd caught the top forty on his car radio and didn't recognise any of the bands. At tables all around, people were drinking coffee while tapping away on the keyboards of computers. People that ranged all the way from dreadlocked cyberpunks through nerds in *Red Dwarf* T-shirts to city gents. This was not something Blake had ever heard of, never mind encountered, before.

Joanna went up to a table near the entrance. 'Table thirteen free?' she asked the man who stood there.

'And two cappuccinos, please,' Blake added.

The man raised an eyebrow at Joanna as she passed.

'Techno virgin,' she shouted over her shoulder by way of explanation.

34

The man tapped a key behind the bar to register their presence, and, to Blake's embarrassment, shouted his order on to a barman across the way.

Joanna led him to a table with a terminal, in the shadows at the back of the café.

'What is all this?' he asked as she sat him down and booted up the PC with a familiarity that went into the territory of pet names.

'A cybercafé. Info technology meets the frothy-coffee brigade.' She punched a key and logged in. 'World Wide Web? The Internet? You had heard they discovered the wheel?'

He smiled at her. 'Did you get anything else on Ferguson? Did he oversee all those inquests?'

'Let's find out.'

Blake recognised the address of the web pages she was accessing. The ones on the Zentex network that she'd been denied access to from her building.

'Ah, here we are.'

Two picture files with biographies were scrolling past. Blake kept seeing the word 'Sweethope', but she was finished reading before he could stop her.

'It looks as if there was one other copper involved in each of Ferguson's inquests. Also Central Ops. One Philip Gates.'

Blake looked at the face beside that of Ferguson, and realised that he'd seen the man before. Gates was the policeman he'd spotted at the inquest.

Joanna gasped. 'Hello! It gets tastier. Look how similar these biogs are. Gates and Ferguson seem to go way back.'

'So do a lot of coppers of that rank.'

'But these two are from the same *village*! Or should I say *ex*-village. Sweethope.'

It took a moment for Blake to remember. 'Norfolk coast, four or five years ago. The whole place fell off the edge of a cliff.'

Joanna cross-referenced the word on a search engine and

35

a picture from a newspaper appeared. A group of ragged looking people under the headline 'Miracle Village'.

'Something like that.' Joanna nodded.

'Not bad, eh?' Blake grinned at her. At least his journalist's memory was intact.

'Gates and Ferguson were the two local policemen on duty together on the night of the Sweethope disaster. Both received commendations.'

Blake remembered the full story. An eroded old cliff had suddenly given way. There had been some sort of explosion. And the village had slipped into the sea like a high-speed Dunwich. All the villagers had somehow managed to get out alive. Which was why the story had only persisted for around a week. 'Their village disappearing into the sea didn't seem to do their job prospects any harm.'

'Coppers are like journalists. They need a good disaster to launch their careers.'

She started the printer chuntering away before he could respond to that, skipping through page after page about Sweethope. 'Look at this lot. You ask for details, we give you details. I'll get the whole file printed out.'

Blake chuckled out loud as the cappuccinos arrived, staring at the screen. 'This is fantastic!'

Joanna laughed back. 'You're actually animated. I never thought I'd see that again.' She raised her mug in a toast. 'Here's to you, Rip Van Winkle.'

She seemed to be enjoying seeing him play newshound again, his fellow journoholic. Blake didn't know quite what to say. He was enjoying her company. And he'd had a vision of what life might have been like had he not bought her that cup of tea on a summer Friday to get out of a crowded newsroom. In that life, they had been, and were, friends. She might have seen a bit of that in his eyes, which is why she swigged back her coffee, encouraged him to do the same, and led him out of the café with the printouts under her arm.

* * *

'Do you use that place a lot?' he asked as they walked away.

'Let's just say it's helped me cut a few corners in the past. It's instant access to the web, but it's also anonymous. It's virtually impossible to find out who's searching for what information about who.'

Blake took the printouts from her and scanned through them, fascinated. 'I think I'm going to take a look at Sweethope. It's what this thing's about.'

Joanna was looking at him strangely. Ironic, Blake thought, if she was finally getting intrigued by his personality.

'What's the hurry? You're not in the business any more. Let me at least see if there's anything in all this before you start chasing phantoms.'

He met her gaze seriously. 'I'm not letting this one go.'

They paid attention to the sirens that had been part of the London soundscape only when they squealed to a stop immediately behind them. Two policemen leapt out of the car, its lights still tumbling blue, and ran straight into the café. They started threading their way through the tables towards the darker area at the back.

'Drugs raid?' asked Blake.

'Probably,' replied Joanna, defensively.

'You don't think —?'

'Don't start.'

Blake tried to think of an appropriate way to leave her company, but couldn't quite bring himself to kiss her on the cheek or shake her hand. So he settled on walking briskly away. 'Call me in Sweethope.' He turned back after a few steps. 'Oh, and by the way . . . thank you.'

She grimaced. 'You might at least have paid for the cappuccinos.'

4

TWO MUSEUMS

Blake had come to know Norfolk very well since he'd fled London for Norwich. He loved the emptiness of the county. The flatlands that let you see a clear horizon. The scattered steeples and windmills. He loved the memory of that time he'd stood on the sea wall and watched a full moon over a stormy sea at Sheringham. He loved the myth of Poppylands, the fields and fields of red blooms that the artists of the thirties had splashed over the county in railway posters. He loved the fact that there were still railways, and that they halted against the sea at the top of the county. According to the archaeologists, *Homo sapiens* and the Neanderthals had lived together in the county for thousands of years. Either in separate encampments, or perhaps together, with only slight realisation of the difference. These days, none of the experts could seem to agree on whether the former had exterminated the latter, or intermarried with them to produce modern humans. Blake hoped that it was the latter. The journey back from the city always gave him hope like that and, despite his fears of decaying sunsets, he was sure, as he wound the window of his car down, that the air here smelt and tasted more wholesome.

He drove to Mayston, the coastal town that, a few years ago, had been the neighbour of Sweethope, and wandered about, searching for a bed and breakfast. He finally found a sign in a window offering an artist's cottage to let, and knocked on the door until an old lady came out, blinking in the sunshine. She immediately asked him if he was an artist and made it clear that, if he was, he wasn't getting his hands on her cottage down by the sea.

'Artists!' The woman tutted for the hundredth time as she pulled open the curtains of the little white cottage. 'At least, that's what they called themselves. Looks more like squit to me!'

Blake looked around the interior appreciatively. He had no idea what squit was, but if this was it, he rather liked it. The place was a couple of miles from civilisation, right on the seaside. The artists, whoever they had been, had left enough of their work behind to indicate a swift exit. There were masks above the fireplace, a sculpture in the shape of half a torso in one corner, some half-completed canvases stacked against each other.

He had a sudden desire for a hand-rolled cigarette.

'I've seen worse. You said two weeks with an option for longer?'

She continued, oblivious. 'Could have cleared up before they went. You've missed the good weather.'

'That's all right. I'm not here for the weather.'

She positively leered at him. 'Be just you staying, will there?'

Blake began to lead her towards the door. 'That's the plan.'

'There's four good pubs in Mayston if you get lonely at all.' She cackled like she was in an amateur production of *Macbeth*. 'With you having no company.'

What was it about him, Blake wondered. Did he *look* divorced? 'Actually,' he informed his landlady, taking her hand and shoving six ten pound notes into it, 'I'm more of a library man. There is a library there, I take it?'

Mayston, at closer inspection, brought a little leap of joy to Blake's heart, and he had to forcibly remind himself that he was here on a quest rather than on a much-needed holiday.

The former was going to be healing in the long term, he told himself. After all, one cannot stay in tiny seaside towns and hang out in lovely post offices for ever. There was a baker's that did gingerbread men; one of those vast news-agents that you only find at the seaside – it sold plastic windmills – and a big public library in a red-brick building.

Blake smiled at it before he went inside.

The librarian led him through the children's section to what at first seemed to be a storeroom at the back. It turned out to be some sort of local history area, with a projector set up for school parties, societies and the like. Upon his inquiry about the Sweethope disaster, she'd grabbed a box of slides from under her counter and the key to this room from a ring on the wall.

Blake had been a little concerned that she hadn't needed to look for either.

She was a striking-looking woman in her early thirties, her looks muted by a sober ponytail that confined her blonde hair, and the sort of long floral thing and cardigan that librarians seemed to insist on wearing despite the fact that it played up to their every stereotype. She had such a sigh about her that Blake felt apologetic almost immediately.

'It's good of you to go to all this effort.'

'This is one of the better parts of the job.'

Blake closed the door as she commanded and took a seat. 'Still, you must get sick of nosy types like me asking about Sweethope.'

'There's not much interest in the place these days. Still, it's human nature to be curious about disasters.'

He wanted to cheer her up. To buy her an ice cream. 'Except this wasn't a disaster, was it? Everyone survived. From where I'm sitting, that looks more like a miracle.'

She smiled a 'Dealing with the Public' smile and started to set up the projector. Blake looked around. A collection of local newspapers were laid out for inspection. They all had headlines about Sweethope. 'The Survivors' Own Story'. 'The Village That Disappeared'. 'Swallowed By The Sea'. 'Miracle Village!'

On the walls were more framed front pages, this time from national newspapers. 'The Disappearing Village'. 'How Safe Is Our Coastline?' 'Thanks A Million! *The Sun* Helps Sweethope Survivors!'

There were many, many photos. But one kept recurring, wherever Blake looked. A group of survivors stood on a cliff. Men, women and children. All smiling through. Blake suddenly realised that this wasn't a local-history exhibit. It was a shrine to Sweethope. One that had been here since the disaster. The display had a mournful quality to it that cut right under his new cheerfulness.

The librarian switched off the lights and flicked the power on. The first slide appeared on the screen. A sweet little village on a promontory. A picture postcard.

'Before,' said the librarian.

The picture was replaced by one of a ravaged coastline and an angry sea. The promontory had disappeared.

'After.' She turned to Blake. 'Everyone knew the village's days were numbered because of the gradual subsidence. And that terrible storm. What they hadn't accounted for was the explosives dump.'

'One that the Ministry of Defence had no knowledge of?'

She gave a small, ironic smile. 'No. Or at least, if they did, they're never going to admit it. Apparently, it dated back to World War II. They say there might even be some explosives still down there.'

'Hasn't anybody checked?'

The smile had frozen. 'It seems they've lost any records which might help.'

She clicked the control again. The group shot of about thirty survivors, from the front of so many papers. On this larger version, Blake could see that in the middle of them stood the by now familiar figures of Ferguson and Gates.

41

His attention was also briefly caught by the figure of a little girl, smiling more brightly than any of the adults around her. Her name – he couldn't quite make it out – was emblazoned across her green jumper.

'This photo was taken the morning after,' said the librarian. 'I think they were just glad to be alive.'

Blake studied the screen. He shivered at the thought of the photographer going ahead and posing them. Or maybe they just stood like that for him, daring him to make a record of their tragedy. 'How come they all left the village in time?'

She paused for a long moment before answering. 'Everyone I've spoken to said that somehow they knew. If you believe in that sort of thing.'

'Do you?'

'You'd be better off asking somebody who was there.' Her words had the air of an oft-repeated story. 'I was travelling back to Sweethope that evening. The storm slowed me down. But I was close enough to feel the vibrations of the explosion.'

Blake thought for a moment of the car exploding, the light that had filled the sky. 'Did you see anything?'

'There was a white flash, then a fireball. I stopped the car. When I got out, everything was still. And . . . there was a strange smell.'

Blake felt a constriction in his stomach. 'Something like herbs or lavender burning . . . but not quite either?'

She opened her eyes wide, like she'd been woken from a dream. 'How did you know?'

Blake somehow didn't want to share it with her. It connected to all those old memories. And indicated that some sort of chemical explosive had been the straw that broke Sweethope's back. 'Let's just put it down to experience.'

She looked at him for a moment, unsatisfied, then activated another slide. Ferguson and Gates, as two young policemen, appeared on the screen. They were smiling and holding up medals.

Blake nodded to the image on the wall. 'Superintendent Ferguson when he was just a constable. I take it the other one is a copper called Philip Gates?'

'They took the credit for leading the villagers to safety. The press loved it. That's it, I'm afraid.'

She went to the slide projector and deactivated it.

'Any chance of me talking to any of the Sweethope survivors?' He hadn't given any sort of cover story. With this woman, and her little room of memory, he didn't need one. It was enough that he was interested.

'Not round here, I'm afraid.' She looked at him with those burdened eyes. 'They had nothing to stay for. I'm sorry. Now excuse me, but I have to go back to work.'

The Ministry of Defence sign read: DANGER! DO NOT TRESPASS. EXPLOSIVES. Blake had walked along the seashore to the point where Sweethope had been, thinking about Neanderthals and the chemical foam he saw on some of the beaches and of a librarian and her sad little shrine. And how sad it was that 'sad' was an insult these days.

After a couple of miles' hike along the beaches, shale and clifftops, he'd come to the ragged cliff that marked the edge of Sweethope, three lines of barbed wire that sealed off a section of that cliff, and the sign. There was nothing else to be seen except a rough wooden hut. The wind fluttering the grass. He walked to the edge of the unfenced cliff, and looked down at the sweep of beach far below. White surf breaking, seagulls wheeling, a barbed-wire fence cutting off a slice of the sand and stretching out into the sea.

Blake stood there for a moment, the wind buffeting his ears. Nothing at all. As expected, really. The history of this place had been swept away by a very big tide. But he'd wondered if there might have been some sign, some clue that might direct him in his quest. Maybe he should go back to the artist's cottage and write up what he had so far.

Sod it, he decided, heading for the path that led down from the cliffs. Let's go and have a look at that beach.

The tide was out, exposing the extreme end of the perimeter fence in the sea.

Blake crouched to feel the sand between his fingers, smelt the salt. It was too much to hope for a touch of that terrible scent of unknown explosive. Not after all these years. He examined pebbles in rock pools, and picked up bits of driftwood and that red baler twine you always seemed to find on beaches. Walking at the edge of the brackish surf, he noticed a corner of yellow vinyl sticking up from out of the sand. He reached down and tugged at it. After a great deal of pulling, he managed to free it from the grip of the sand. It was a scrap of a child's sou'wester, faded with age, with a print of a duck on the front.

Surely this couldn't be from . . .? Maybe it could. Maybe the beach was littered with stuff like this. He glanced up from his treasure and saw that he wasn't alone on the sands. A skinny young man was stomping down the steps from the hut on the cliffs, heading for a battered boat that was tethered to a mooring post. Blake folded the sou'wester, pocketed it and headed over to talk to him.

The man had started retrieving lobster pots from the boat. He looked like the genuine article, a driftwood person, his head a bunch of dreads, his clothes a patch-work of rugged utilities. He couldn't have been more than twenty-five, but his skin suggested that he'd spent two decades of that in salty air. He was absorbed in his work, transferring the pots from the boat to the shore.

'Having much luck?' Blake asked him.

The man glanced quickly over his shoulder at Blake, appraising, dismissing and becoming irritated in a moment. 'I was, till you showed up.' His accent was that of a proper Shannock.

'I'm surprised you're allowed to work this area.'

The man turned to confront him. 'Stop playing games,

eh? If you're gonna arrest me then get on with it. If you're not, then piss off.'

Blake raised his hands in peace. 'I'm not from the police or the M.o.D. or anything. I just wanted a chat.'

The man snorted. 'Try the Samaritans.'

'I did, they recommended you. Can I buy you a drink?'

'Where?'

'There must be somewhere.'

'Not thirsty.'

'I'll buy a lobster, then!'

The man's expression became more animated. 'A tenner.'

'A fiver.'

'Done.' He gestured to the pots he'd placed on the sand. 'Give us a hand with these, then.' He picked up several himself and walked off up the beach towards the cliff path.

Blake gingerly picked up one and followed him. 'Aren't you worried about potting out there?'

'All my family fished here down the years. Why should I do any different?'

'Several tons of undetonated explosives.'

'If you believe that.'

'But why else would the M.o.D. cordon the place off? Did they just have a lot of barbed wire they wanted to get rid of?'

They climbed until they reached the hut that Blake had glimpsed earlier.

'Fiver you said?' The man handed Blake a lobster, then went inside.

Blake looked at the crustacean, and gingerly put it back in the basket. Then he followed the man.

The inside of the one-room shack was as ragged and improvised as its owner. A variety of scrap objects had been pressed into domestic use: sea-stained bits of wood; bicycle wheels; a bus-stop sign; and, in pride of place, half a British Rail station sign that was cut off at the SWEETH. The man, who'd identified himself only as David, sat on an orange box, rolling a cigarette as he talked.

'The police have given up trying to turn me off these waters. They might warn me once a month now. Used to be once a day.'

Blake leaned forward. 'When the police were warning you, did you ever come across a copper called Philip Gates? Top brass.'

'Sure. It was him that decided I wasn't worth the bother. Said he remembered me from his days as a bobby on the beat in Sweethope.'

'You're from Sweethope?'

'Wish I was.' He skipped past that before Blake had a chance to question him. 'No, I just used to shoplift there on a Saturday afternoon.'

Blake glanced at the objects that lined the room. 'Still at it, by the looks of things.' He got up from his perch on a barrel and toyed idly with a pile of objects that had been scattered in a corner. A bit of a kettle, a pen, a light bulb, and the remains of a green, hand-knitted jumper with 'Fiona' on the front.

'Be amazed what gets washed up on that beach.' David was looking uneasy. 'I still find something at least once a month.'

On a Jeepy whim, Blake buried his nose in the wool of the jumper and sniffed deeply. He closed his eyes. That smell again. It played with the deepest levels of his memory. It was somewhat like napalm, which was one reason why he'd taken up this quest, because it had taken him back to the places in his mind that needed healing. The floral quality of it was the most obscene thing. That was like all those chemicals one encounters in childhood. Fabric softeners. The artificial whiff of too-frothy soft drinks. Blake wondered whether the froth on those polluted beaches would smell like that. This new explosive had got into everything.

David sounded peevish. 'Put it down. That's my stuff.'

Blake did so. 'All right, all right. I'm sorry. I didn't mean to upset you.' The man must have spent most of his life just about eking out this meagre existence. His possessions were important to him. And like the town librarian, something of him seemed to have vanished with Sweethope, and he was hanging on to the traces of it.

He calmed when Blake moved away from his collection. 'You talked to anyone else from Sweethope?'

'Only a policeman called Ferguson.'

David nodded. 'He's another one. Everybody in Sweethope that night . . .' This seemed to take a major effort of trust. 'Their luck changed.' He kept on nodding, as if to emphasise the seriousness of his words. 'I mean . . . Serious. Midas stuff.'

'And that's what this museum is about?' Blake smiled, touching the wood of the wall. 'You're hoping to catch some luck off it?'

David ignored him, still nodding. 'It had to be something in the village. In the air. Didn't it?' He stared past Blake with a piercing gaze, his thoughts drifting out to sea. 'There's powerful magic still down there.'

Blake took the sou'wester from his pocket and pressed it into David's hands. 'Here's a donation.'

David beamed, turning the garment over and over in his hands.

He was so delighted that he didn't notice Blake leave.

Blake did a little research around the town. When he got back to the cottage, he got straight on the phone, which he found in a corner under a tea cosy, and made some calls. Gates' office was pretty easy to locate, via an old mate at the Police Complaints Authority. Who would not, of course, give up any gossip about Central Ops. His mate's tone had been a bit arch, though. It was also surprisingly easy to set up an interview with the detective chief superintendent. Central Ops was very media-friendly. Finally, he called Joanna, and tried to resist adopting the tone of a little boy who'd tied his shoelaces for the first time. Actually, it was more like Peter Sellers declaring that he'd recovered the ability to walk in one of the *Pink Panther* films. Funny and a bit sad. In both senses of the word.

'Can't you take up a hobby?' she teased. 'What about doing a jigsaw?'

Blake sighed. He'd been pinning up clippings about the case on his mirror, as was his wont. He felt sure that she'd somehow heard that in his tone of voice. 'There are some names I'd like you to check before I see Gates.'

'How many names?'

'Only about two hundred.'

A pause. A deeply tired tone. 'Steve, I am not your assistant –'

'Listen, listen! I'm talking about the two hundred who were saved from Sweethope on the night of the disaster. I just want to know if any of them have done anything significant since.'

'How do you mean?'

'If their careers have taken off, like Gates' and Ferguson's.' He recalled David's words in the shack with an increasing sense of being hot on the trail. 'I think some of them might have been bought off after the accident.'

'And what does this have to do with James Wilson?'

'Nothing. Everything. I'm thinking laterally, OK?'

Another pause and sigh. 'OK. Give me the top twenty names. I'll see what I can do.'

Blake took the photocopy of the Sweethope electoral register from his pocket. 'Great.'

Blake was surprised to discover that the sea smelt of that floral poison. It filled his nostrils with chemical perfume as he walked along the bottom. There were cans down here, shopping bags, batteries, a bicycle wheel. The other half of that railway sign, saying OPE. He had swum to the bottom of the sea in his day clothes, which was perhaps why he was so cold. In his ears rang the muted chimes from Debussy's *Cathedral under the Sea*.

In an underwater valley, a clump of seaweed shifted and blossomed in the lull of the tides. Blake made his way towards it. Blond seaweed. A stalk of something, attached to the sea bed. The oddity of it drew him towards it. Which was always his problem and his curse and these days his quest.

It was a little girl, standing stock-still, her back to him. Her feet were planted in the sand. It was, Blake realised, the girl from the photographs.

She seemed to sense the vibrations in the water, and turned to look at him. A beautiful, trusting, human face. She started to giggle.

And for some reason, Blake suddenly found her presence here terrifying. Her face turned into a skull. He should look at what she was wearing, but he couldn't, because the air rushed out of his nose in a curtain of bubbles, which foamed up through the polluted waters on their way upwards to the grey sun.

He was drowning. He was drowning. He was –

Awake. He was wet with sweat rather than seawater, in the unfamiliar bed of the artist's cottage. He sat up, and tried to shake the images of the nightmare from his mind.

The phone beside the bed rang. He threw back the covers, glad of the air, and answered it.

'Steve.' It was Joanna. 'I've been checking out those names you gave me. You might be right. There is something very strange happening to the Sweethope survivors.'

Blake went to the window and looked out at the moon over the sea. The tips of white waves reflected the moonlight. The sea was disturbed, as if it were troubled by the mystery beneath it.

49

5

THE CHURCH UNDER THE SEA

Detective Chief Superintendent Philip Gates stared at Blake for a moment, then handed back the sheet of statistics that he'd just been presented with. 'Close on two hundred and fifty thousand people went missing in this country last year. You've come up with, what, a dozen instances of so-called "victimless death"?'

Blake studied the man in front of him. Gates had a friendly, very open manner, but there was something false about it, like he'd taken a good PR course. He'd taken care to pop out into his outer office to meet Blake personally, cracking a joke with his secretary as he did so. His office was, similarly, designed with effect in mind. Nothing out of place, personal details arranged to carefully suggest the precise sort of heart that beat beneath the uniform. On the wall was the photo of himself and Ferguson receiving their medals. There were golf trophies. No picture of a proud wife and grinning children, Blake noticed. In the circumstances, that almost counted as an oversight.

He realised that he hadn't replied to the question. He swallowed. Gates' manner was so friendly that he almost felt guilty at throwing his data at the policeman in an attempt to rattle him. 'So far.'

Gates settled back in his chair, the professional chatting with the interested amateur. 'Twelve unidentified accident victims out of an army of the missing. It's not exactly unthinkable, is it?'

'But all these "accidents" –' Blake allowed Gates to hear the scepticism in his voice '– followed identical patterns. A person goes missing, presumed dead, then turns up safe and well. And look at the profiles of these people: energy commissioners; senior civil servants; top military people.'

'The reason that you hear about such cases is that they involve such high-profile people.'

Blake played his trump card. 'And you or Superintendent Ferguson have led every enquiry.'

He shrugged it off. 'Nothing sinister in that, either. It's one of the reasons that the Central Ops unit was formed, to streamline high-profile enquiries.'

'And to provide job opportunities for bobbies from Sweethope.'

Gates smiled, looked aside, chuckled. He was much more assured than his friend Ferguson. 'I was wondering when you were going to get around to that. You chaps usually do.'

'I mention it because you two aren't the only two Sweethope refugees whose careers have rocketed.'

'None of this is news to me, Mr Blake. We've kept in touch since the accident. We follow each others' careers with interest, and no little pride. The modern world doesn't allow many people the gift of strength through adversity. We have that.'

'Out of 122 adults —' Blake glanced at his electoral register '— of working age saved that night, fifteen have risen to the boards of their companies, twelve have become leading traders on the stock exchange —'

'I'm aware —'

'28 run successful businesses from the arms trade to drugs research, ten are now senior officials in government departments and three — *three* of these people — have actually become MPs. It's a record Eton would be proud of.'

'Like I said, we lost everything we had that night. Everything we'd ever worked for.' Gates leaned forward, looking at Blake with eyes that were suddenly cold, as if

51

remembering harsh times. 'You can either go under at the thought of that, or it can drive you on with a force that's . . .' He stopped, as if realising that he was becoming too intense for his friendly image. He cracked a smile. 'Simply awesome.'

Blake smiled back, intrigued at where that had been going. 'So refugees make the best capitalists?'

Gates nodded. 'That's one way of putting it. If you're into politics. Which I'm not. Now, is there anything else you wanted to know?'

When he got back to Norfolk, Blake set about packing up his things at the cottage. He couldn't think what else to do on the coastline, and the trail seemed hotter in London. If it was hot at all. The only thing he had to go on now was Gates' careful defence against his every point. The man was being too precise, too clipped, like a batsman only concerned with not getting out.

He was just taking his photos of all the individuals involved down from the corkboard in the kitchen when there was a knock on the door. He went to answer it.

He was surprised to find the librarian standing there.

'Hello,' she said.

He smiled. 'This isn't about unreturned books, is it? You're not part of the library service flying squad?'

She looked uncomfortable. 'I kept thinking about the other day. You're the first person to ask about Sweethope in a long time. My name is Melissa. Melissa Gates.' She managed a smile at Blake's cartoon-like expression of shock. 'You seem to be as interested in my husband as I am.'

Blake made them coffee, and they took it outside, walking on to the path along the cliffs as the day moved from twilight to dusk. She wasn't Mrs Gates any longer, she explained. There had been a separation, followed by divorce. She seemed to want to tell Blake the story, and did so with a careful precision, as if she wanted to make sure that she was getting the details right as she went. Blake appreciated that. It was as if Melissa was as concerned about the way truth became fiction as he was.

'When I realised that Philip had survived the Sweethope disaster, I was so relieved. So . . . happy, that at first I didn't notice the change in him.'

'Shock does strange things to people.'

'That's how I explained it to myself at first. But the days went by, then the weeks, and I realised that he had changed for good.'

Blake wondered just how emotionally injured she'd been by the incident. In truth, wherever this was leading, it wasn't anywhere he wanted his investigation to go. Whatever alienated condition the former Mrs Gates was suffering from, he didn't see that it had much to do with him. 'I talked to your husband about this. He said he thought the Sweethope survivors became highly motivated because of what they'd been through. Perhaps that's what —'

She cut him off. 'I lost everything too. But I didn't change. Not the way the people who were in the village did that night.'

Blake's mind suddenly made a handbrake turn from feeling compassionate at Melissa's post-divorce paranoia, right back on to the track he'd been following. 'It wasn't just your husband who was different?'

Melissa blinked, as if stunned by his interest. 'People I had known for years were suddenly strangers to me. Their emotions, their ambitions, their personalities . . . everything had changed. And it stayed changed after the evacuation. Philip kept in touch with lots of them, and they never seemed to recover. They never went back to being the people I once knew.' She frowned at the light in Blake's eyes. 'Why do you believe me?'

'Before I came to Sweethope, I saw a man die in a car crash. Or I thought I did.' He leaned closer to her. 'Until I saw the same man alive and well the next day. It's as if something similar has happened here.'

53

Melissa was almost babbling now, her whole face lit up by the unaccustomed pleasure of having somebody listen to her. 'The Ministry of Defence own the land down to the coast. I had thought that might be part of the explanation. Some . . . chemical warfare experiment gone wrong. Maybe even a deliberate "accident"! But –'

'You don't believe that now?'

'I don't know.' She stared out to sea. 'If any army anywhere had a weapon that could cause an explosion like that . . . Would they really be able to keep it secret?'

Blake almost laughed at her innocence. 'There isn't anything that can't be covered up. You've just got to make sure the right people gain by keeping it secret.'

'Who would gain by hiding . . .' She shook her head at the insanity of the possibility. 'A chemical that kills people and then brings them back to life?'

Blake didn't smile back at her. If there was any truth at all to this woman's wild ideas, then he couldn't see many other possibilities that summed up the evidence as well as that one did.

'Thanks,' she said, as he walked her back to her car.

'What for?'

'For making me feel . . . Like I'm not alone in this.'

A sudden thought struck Blake. With the background knowledge he'd collected, he'd been intrigued by Melissa's testimony. There was one other person with that knowledge. 'I think I know somebody who might be able to help us. Would you be willing to talk to them?'

Melissa nodded. 'Yes. Yes, I think so.' She handed Blake her coffee mug and got into her car.

'Oh, and can you get me some copies of those slides?'

She smiled at him like he'd been the first person she'd seen on her first day out of jail. 'Trust me, I'm a librarian.'

After she'd gone, Blake returned to the corkboard, and began to pin the photographs back up again. The truth was unfolding in front of him, and now an important part

54

of it seemed to be right on his doorstep. He stopped as he handled the photo of the group of Sweethope survivors. It was as if he was seeing it for the first time, seeing it through Melissa's eyes. If she'd arrived at the scene a few minutes earlier, she might even have been in it. If the photographer hadn't thought that that would compromise his subject matter.

He stared at the print long and hard, wondering at those unreadable expressions, and that smile on the face of a little girl, a smile that now seemed odd and awkward. There was something he was missing. He couldn't see it yet. But still . . .

He'd been given an entirely new frame for this photograph.

The next morning, Blake visited a local diving club, impressed them with his knowledge of lake diving in Serbia, flashed some rather old certificates and came away with a full set of sub-aqua kit on hire, plus wetsuit.

Then he went to the off-licence.

Then he went to see David who lived on the beach.

The young man was gathering up his pots when Blake reached him, ready for another trip out. He looked up, unimpressed, as Blake approached, a roll-up hanging from the corner of his mouth. The present of the sou'wester seemed to have been forgotten.

Which was why Blake had brought the bottle of whisky, which he brandished before him like a totem. 'Do you do pleasure cruises?' he asked.

David smiled back at him.

After three quick shots of whisky that was rather too expensive to drink like that, David shared his second name with Blake. It was Hallworth. It took two more before they could go back to the boat. Blake had declined to drink with the man, but that hadn't slowed his consumption a jot.

'You're not afraid of the explosives?' he slurred, as he helped Blake load his diving equipment into the back of the little boat.

'You told me you didn't believe in them.'

'I wasn't staking my life on it then, was I?'

'I just need to –'

His sentence was interrupted by the sound of a voice, distorted and projected through a loud-hailer. 'Stay exactly where you are. This is Ministry of Defence property and you are trespassing!'

Blake looked up at the cliffs above. A line of policemen stood there. In amongst them, Blake recognised Ferguson, and the tall figure of Philip Gates, in civvies. Gates was the one with the megaphone.

Hallworth glanced up and kicked his boat, doing a little dance of pain and frustration. 'Thanks a lot!'

Down the beach towards them was running a squad of soldiers. Blake was astonished to see that they were in full combat gear, with their rifles unslung.

All this for little him?

Hallworth argued with the soldiers with a familiar vehemence, like this was an old issue that they all knew inside and out. Maybe, from the smiles on the faces of the squaddies as they pulled his boat up the beach, it was. 'The bloke wanted to see the place!' he was saying. 'All I did was take some of his cash to sail him out there!'

'We've tolerated you long enough, sir,' Ferguson told him. 'If we catch you fishing these waters again, then we'll have no choice but to take legal action.'

Hallworth pointed out to sea. 'What are you saying? That I'm banned from that bit of sea, or that bit? It's always moving, man. Like, which bit do you own?'

While this went on, Gates had taken Blake aside. His manner was a lot more controlled than it had been in his office. It was obviously getting harder to keep up that friendly image. 'You seem to have got your teeth into Sweethope, Mr Blake.'

Blake looked out to sea, regretting that he hadn't been able to get out there and see for himself. 'It's a remarkable story.'

'After our chat yesterday, I thought you understood that it's neither remarkable —' the façade fell away almost entirely, and Blake turned to hear a rasp of anger that was almost exactly like Ferguson's threatening whisper '— or a story.'

He remained calm. 'I might have thought that before I visited the library in Mayston.'

Something flickered beneath the surface of Gates' snarling features. A moment of hesitation. 'You've met Melissa?'

'That's right.'

The policeman took Blake by the arm, a hard, unyielding grip that allowed no argument, and led him even further away from where Hallworth was baiting the soldiers. 'She's a vulnerable, young woman. And if you take advantage of her,' he said in a conversational tone, 'then I will have your arse in a vice sooner than you can say "watch the birdie".'

Blake made himself meet the man's gaze. This was the other part of this journalism business that he disliked. Playing macho power games. He managed to speak fairly normally, without going for the thuggish or girlie squeak options that were springing to mind. 'She doesn't strike me as the type who needs protecting.'

Gates' features softened slightly. It looked deliberate, like he was in control of every muscle under his face and wanted to project exactly the right expression. 'I would have thought that you'd know that first impressions can be very deceptive.' He took a deep breath, as if he was about to admit something. 'The Sweethope disaster took a greater toll on Melissa than any of us.'

'So she said.' What was it going to be now, veiled threats about the reliability of his ex-wife as a witness?

57

More strong-arm moves?

'But I don't expect she told you about her breakdown? About the psychiatric help she needed?'

Blake stared. There was something desperately genuine, suddenly, about the way Gates had said that. As if he'd reached deep inside the public man and pulled it out from some inner reserve of compassion. 'Why are you telling me this?'

'Because I don't want you to expose her to any more pain than she's already suffered.' He looked away, then met Blake's eyes again, this time with a genuine look of shared grief. 'We might be divorced, but I won't see her hurt. That's why I . . . That's why I said what I said earlier. Do we understand each other?'

Blake, to his surprise, found himself nodding.

Gates patted him on the shoulder, and turned away.

That night, Blake had arranged to meet Melissa at the only French restaurant in Mayston. He'd spent the day pondering his encounter with Gates, wondering if he should un-invite his other guest tonight. That anger Gates had felt, that desire to protect the interests of his ex. He understood that. If Gates had pressurised him, then he would have been even more convinced that he was on to something big. But perhaps it all came down to stuff like that. Normal everyday emotions. Defend the realm. Polish the corners. Make everything fit the frame. He wondered if, if he ever got to the bottom of this con- spiracy, he would actually disagree with its aims? What, in the end, was the difference between a conspiracy to protect something-or-other from some scandal and the normal processes of British manners and politics?

Melissa arrived a couple of minutes late, in another floral thing under a different cardigan. Blake, as he stood at her arrival, found that he was searching her face, as if he might see signs of paranoid fantasy there. This was the woman, after all, who had got to the point of thinking that her whole village had been turned into zombies.

'I spoke to your ex-husband today,' he said, after they'd exchanged greetings.

'And?' Did she sound nervous? Worried that Gates might have shared his knowledge about her psychological state?

Blake never got to reply. A familiar voice called his name loudly from the doorway of the restaurant.

'Steve!'

Joanna came over at double flounce, wearing something chic and sultry that she'd probably chosen after a full hour of discarding other options. She cast a quick, appraising glance around the restaurant and let it settle on Melissa. 'How very . . . local.'

Blake made it immediately worse. 'This is Melissa.' He realised what he'd just done and tried to dig himself out. 'I mentioned her on the phone. Melissa . . . Joanna. The editor I told you about.'

Joanna sat down and Melissa shook her hand, casting a worried glance at Blake.

'Pleased to meet you.'

Joanna nodded in return, then turned straight to Blake, cutting Melissa out of the conversation with the angle of her shoulders. 'So, I take it I haven't come all this way just for the seafood?'

Blake sighed. This was going to be harder than he thought.

During the course of the meal, Blake managed to find things in common between the two women, and get them talking. Joanna always tried to make herself as intimidating as possible to new acquaintances, a trait that Blake found . . . Well, he'd once described it to her as 'loathsome'. By mutual, silent, agreement, they didn't mention the business they'd come together to discuss during the meal, Melissa instead having to listen to Joanna's opinions on cinema, music and opera, the last of which Blake knew for a fact that she didn't know a thing about. Melissa looked utterly browbeaten by the end of it, which only added to Blake's worries about how reliable her testimony was going to sound. He picked a moment after Joanna had consumed a suitable quantity of wine and encouraged Melissa to tell her story. Joanna listened, her chin resting on one knuckle, sipping from her glass from time to time, swirling the contents all the while. The coffees arrived just as Melissa finished.

Joanna sighed. 'Melissa, believe me, people wake up every morning and realise that they no longer know the person they married.' A significant glance at Blake. 'It happens, and it doesn't mean a thing.'

Melissa frowned at her, as if she hadn't been listening. 'This isn't about falling out of love. This is about a total change of personality.' She thumped her glass down on the table. 'All I recognise is his . . . outer shell. Everything else . . .' She shook her head.

'I'm sorry about what happened to you. Must hurt like hell. But it is not *news*, dear. And I can't see what it's got to do with the story Steve was pursuing.'

Blake interceded. Melissa was looking ready to throw things at Joanna. He felt as if he'd betrayed her by exposing her to Joanna's scepticism. Or made a fool of himself by introducing Joanna to such a weirdo. Whichever way it went, it didn't feel good. 'Look at the facts, Jo. James Wilson, dead but not dead. Half a dozen others, dead but not dead. Sweethope is the same. Every inhabitant is feared dead, but they turn up safe and well.'

'Did two hundred chargrilled corpses show up in a car park round the corner? No. So it's not the same, then, is it?'

Blake had always felt like grabbing her by the designer lapels at moments like this. 'Let's say the M.o.D. did some tests with chemical weapons at sea. The experiment goes wrong, so they buy off the population of Sweethope with enhanced prospects. Then, they use this chemical on selected members of the establishment –'

Joanna cut him off with a sweep of her hand. 'What does this chemical do, exactly? Do you need to pretend the patient's dead for a couple of hours in order to use it? We are not ready for this stage of argument yet. What's going on still doesn't make sense.' She stopped Blake with a hand to his lips. 'I'm prepared to believe that you've stumbled across some sort of conspiracy, but I wish you'd stop stumbling and get some answers. What's the conspiracy for? Who gains by it? Who loses?'

Blake took the hand away, glanced at Melissa's expression and quickly let go of it. 'In a few years, the Sweethope survivors could form the most powerful network in the country. Then we'll find out who loses, and it'll be too late to do anything about it.'

Joanna mellowed a little at the urgent tone in his voice. She turned back to Melissa. 'OK. So I'm willing to believe that maybe, just maybe, the British intelligence services would be willing to chemically alter the population of a small village –'

Melissa brightened again, looking eager once more. 'Well, not necessarily the *British* intelligence services.'

Joanna looked dubious. 'Not many other suspects these days. The Yanks don't need Sweethope. They've got McDonald's. The Russians can't even control their own backyard.'

Melissa nodded seriously. Her eyes were shining with fervour, as if she were about to announce her most damning piece of evidence. 'So what if you rule out the human race? Where does that take you?'

Joanna's eyebrows rode higher up her brow than Blake had ever seen them go. 'I'm sorry.' She smiled dangerously sweetly. 'But what are you suggesting? Zombies?' A pause with relish. 'Aliens?'

'Why not?' There was a long, uncomfortable silence. 'Look, I've spent the past five years trying to square this circle. You just can't do it using human –'

Joanna cut her off, glancing sadly at Blake then back to

Melissa. 'The only reason I drove out here tonight is that this man used to have an eye for the truth. Where did you two find each other, some sort of self-help group?'

Melissa stared at her, utterly crushed. She got to her feet. 'Excuse me,' she managed to blurt. And she ran off towards the toilets.

Blake was torn between an urge to defend Melissa's crazy theories and an urge to trash them to keep on-side with Joanna. He settled, as always, for something in the middle. 'She might not have an explanation for what she's been through, but you don't have any other answers.'

Joanna got to her feet and threw some large notes on the table. 'Divorce does funny things to people, Steve. That's the only answer I can give.'

He shouted at her as she marched away. 'You've forgotten how to listen!'

'And you've been away too long!' she snapped back. Then she crashed through the doors and was gone into the night.

Steve stared after her, then towards the toilets, wondering which woman he should run after.

Neither, he decided.

He walked Melissa home, restraining an urge to yell at her when she'd come out of the toilets, having obviously been crying, and sat down at the table again.

There had been about a quarter of an hour of silence between them as Blake struggled with his thoughts, wondering how to put what he was feeling nicely. Joanna might have accepted that something out of *The Avengers* was happening in a little Norfolk village, but not something out of *The X-Files*.

'I think,' he began hesitantly, as they marched along a backstreet, 'you might have told me about your . . . line of thinking, before we went in there.'

She was looking at the ground. 'And then you'd have stood up for me in front of your friend, would you?'

'No,' said Blake, feeling brutal. 'Then I wouldn't have arranged the meeting at all.'

'There isn't a rational explanation. You said so yourself.'

'I mean to carry on looking for one. Back on Earth.'

She rounded on him, furious. 'You think I want to believe it? You saw a man killed, then alive again the next day. Do you think that sounds rational?'

'No, but things happen and you have to keep looking.'

'Absolutely. And it always comes back to the same conclusion. That what's going on here goes beyond this planet.'

Sure, and the aliens were listening to this conversation by radar. Blake threw up his hands. 'Melissa, when I spoke to your ex-husband today, he said that after the disaster you'd had some sort of breakdown –'

'I was living in a nightmare.' She sounded like she was trying to stop herself from sobbing or slapping him. 'The person I loved was no longer there for me. He hadn't died. He hadn't left me. He wasn't having an affair. He just wasn't the man I loved any more. I was alone, and nobody could understand. If you want to call that a breakdown, then go ahead. You won't be on your own.'

Blake wanted to shake her. 'If Joanna had decided to go with this, and your history had come out afterwards, they would have crucified you!'

She stared at him, still blazing with anger. 'You really don't see, do you? *They* are going to crucify us anyway.'

She turned and, with as much dignity as she could muster, marched away towards home.

Blake stood watching her go. Somehow he didn't feel able to call her back.

He dreamt of the little girl under the sea again that night. He'd fallen asleep across his bed fully clothed, while leafing through all the papers and photos of the case, trying to find something rational that he could take to Joanna. He hadn't wanted to think about how Melissa had allowed the truth to drift into one of those comforting fictions about flying saucers. About how it was all *their* fault, and not hers. A belief in aliens, to Steve Blake, had always been the biggest example of how humanity distracted itself from the things it really ought to have been worrying about. Rather than fret about people going missing to be tortured and raped, we worry about people going missing to be experimented on. Rather than consider the horrors of Belsen and Bosnia, we consider the imaginary horrors of conspiracies. In the end, he always said, it's always easier to fret about something that is never going to happen. Because he'd liked Melissa and didn't want her to be so deceived by herself, he'd tried to concentrate on his work. But in keeping away from that train of thought, his thoughts had instead drifted to dreaming, and to the sea, and in the sea he found:

'Fiona!' The shout burst from his mouth in bubbles, and he was awake again.

Staring at the colour print of the Sweethope survivors photo. It had stuck to his cheek. He'd pulled it away. And it had fallen right in front of his nose.

There were Gates and Ferguson. But they weren't what his long-neglected instincts were urging him to look at. He found the little girl at the front of the group. Fiona.

That was her name.

That was the name that was emblazoned across her green, hand-knitted jumper.

His eyes opened wide, unable to quite accommodate the truth of what his senses were telling him.

With another shout, he was on his feet and running for the door.

Outside, it was dawn. He sprinted down to the cliffs and along them, his shoes kicking up sand, heading for David Hallworth's shack.

'David!' he shouted, beating on the door, the sharp air catching at his lungs. 'Dave!'

He finally crumpled against the door, frustrated, then launched himself up, and ran around to the other side of the hut to tap urgently on a window. 'David?'

There was still no reply. Blake gave the window an experimental shove and it gave way, swinging upwards. There was just enough room to climb through.

Blake swung one leg up on to the sill and did just that.

He landed somewhere near the sink, with such a thump that he thought he must wake Hallworth, who was lying on a bunk along one side of the hut, snoring messily. But the man didn't move. The empty cans of beer beside his bed explained that.

Blake went straight to the collection of Sweethope memorabilia, and started to sift through it at speed. Finally, he found the green, hand-knitted jumper. His heart leapt when he examined it more closely. Her name was written right across the front of it, just like he'd remembered in the dream.

F for Fiona.

F for Fake.

The out of place object made his mind race. This should have been tucked away at the back of the adolescent Fiona's cupboard, wherever she'd moved to. It was like that old verbal trick. A plane crashes on the border between Switzerland and Germany. Where did they bury the survivors?

Taking the jumper with him, he leapt over to Hallworth and shook him until he woke up. 'David!'

'Shit!' The man stared at Blake like he was something out of a nightmare. 'What you doin' here? What's wrong with you?'

Blake waved the jumper in his face. 'Where did you get this?'

'Piss off and let me sleep.' Hallworth shrugged out of Blake's grasp and rolled over. Blake reached into his pocket and wafted several tenners under the man's nose.

Hungover and irritated, but unwilling to ignore the money, Hallworth opened one eye and just about turned to listen.

'Listen to me! Are you sure you found this on the beach?'

'Of course I did. Everything out there . . . All of it . . . Washed up.'

'When?'

'I've told you. The first morning after the village went under.'

Blake asked his rhetorical question with the zeal of a preacher who'd just experienced a revelation. 'So how could a kid who survived have been wearing it in a photograph taken the same morning?'

Hallworth shrugged, deeply unimpressed. 'Maybe there's more than one?'

Blake shook the jumper, triumphant. 'But it's hand knitted! Not a Marks and Spencers job! Get dressed, I need you to take me out there, right now!'

Hallworth groaned and staggered to his feet. 'You're a bleeding nutter, you know that?'

Blake slapped him on the shoulder. 'Coming from you, that's quite a tribute.'

Hallworth got a few minutes to sober up while Blake ran back to the artist's cottage to collect his diving gear. With Blake's help, he bad-temperedly hauled his boat out, got the little outboard going, and navigated out into the open sea.

Blake spent the journey pulling on his wetsuit, checking his oxygen cylinders, and loading his waterproof camera. He was full of a sense of impending change, like a wave was about to break over him. He was about to discover the truth.

Under that feeling, of course, was a serious fear of just what the nature of this particular truth was. But time enough for that later. He was, on this bright and fresh morning, a journalist again.

Hallworth grunted to Blake, his first words since they'd left the beach. A sly smile. 'If they catch us out here this time, they'll probably just pick us off with a cruise missile.'

Blake sat on the rail of the boat, and strapped on his eyemask. He paused, holding his oxygen mask in his hand. 'You know the trouble with young people these days? No sense of adventure.'

He pulled on the mask, leant backwards, and dived into the water.

It was sharper than his dream. Everything seemed more immediate, more tactile. The water was remarkably clear and unsilted. And of course the only smell was the plastic of the mask and the dry cool of the oxygen mix. Blake swam to the bottom: it was very shallow, he could see the dark shape of the boat overhead. He passed over masses of weed-strewn debris and, eventually, natural rock gave way to the ruins of brick and concrete. He stopped beside a postbox that still stood, marvelling at how it must have slipped down the crumbling slope. Things with solid foundations, like its concrete base, would have made it down into the sea almost intact.

He ignored a sudden whim to try and retrieve the letters. Probably best not to put his fingers in the slot. Some beast of the deep might have taken up residence.

He continued on his way, taking photos as he went, and came to a fallen stone pillar. He scraped away some light encrustation, and found, with a sudden shock, that it was engraved with the words: 'Men of Sweethope who fell'. Then he brushed further and saw the date: 'in the Great War. 1914–1918'.

He swam along what might have been a collapsed street, the slumped shapes of buildings looming to the left and right, and, trying to square it with the photos he'd seen, turned a sudden right past a sprouting mass of seaweed. He was looking for a single, recognisable house, some place he could swim into the lounge of and search for bodies.

Instead, he came to the church. A flint-built belltower looming over the collapsed ruins of the building. It was holding up pretty well. The villagers who lived near Dunwich, the village on this coast that had been taken by the sea several decades ago, alleged that they could still hear the church bells during storms. Blake wondered if that was true of this place, too. If so, it would have been a mournful sound. The wooden doors of the building remained intact against the sea. He pulled on a rusted knocker, but the door wouldn't budge. Which was strange, considering its situation.

One of the stained-glass windows was smashed, and a large dark opening beckoned. Blake swam on past it, intent on finding a house again. But then, spurred by the look of that window and the door that wouldn't open, he turned back.

He'd got that feeling in the pit of his stomach again, the one that you only started to take notice of once you'd had it a few dozen times. He called it Jeepy because he'd had it walking down that side street in a village in Somalia, at that moment when he had wondered where everybody had gone. Why were the usual homeless people and kids with guns and militiamen all absent? So he'd turned like a weathervane, his body a leaf on the wind, and allowed himself to be drawn off along an alley, following the silence until he heard noise. That noise had been the sound of all those people, all together, taking their anger out on a Jeep that belonged to one of the local armed gangs. It had stuck in a rut in a road, one wheel off, and the gangsters had foolishly left their weapons on the kerb. They'd suddenly found themselves ambushed, not by a rival gang, but by the streetfolk, who thought they were rich, or belonged to a gang that owned a different bit of town, or had sided with the hated Americans, or were just arms-bearers in the wrong place at the wrong time. They turned the Jeep over on top of them, and slowly killed them with blows and rocks and curses and finally with their own grenades.

They'd allowed Blake to watch, and take photographs, but not to leave.

Not that he'd wanted to.

And all that, he thought with a moment of nausea, he'd boiled down into one harmless word: Jeepy. But, like the Ancient Mariner, his unconscious often made him relive the story when he used it. The word actually meant 'this way to the mass grave', and these days he regretted inventing it.

But not having the instincts that caused it.

He paused on the edge of the window, then swam inside.

Blake emerged into a new, surreal, world. The bizarre collapsed angles of gothic masonry criss-crossed to form a tunnel that resembled nothing less under the glare of Blake's torch beam than the entrance to heaven.

He came to a chamber, formed from the protection of the fallen roof. The altar was still just about intact. Rain-bowing shafts of light, shifting in the currents of the sea outside, illuminated the entire area through the remaining stained-glass windows.

The scene was so beautiful that Blake reached straight for his camera.

But as he raised his arm to frame the shot, his elbow brushed against something. He glanced to look at it. And then spun round, his breath roaring in his ears as his body absorbed the shock.

A skull was looming towards him through the water, a skeleton intact beneath it. Rags still clung to the swaying scarecrow of bones. Controlling his breath, Blake raised his torch and let the beam play down the pews of the church. He'd entered halfway to the altar, and hadn't thought to look behind him.

The pews were filled with skeletons. Maybe two

hundred of them, all in ribbons of clothing, their limbs swaying in the water where once they would have held each other or prayed to God.

The door had been sealed, Blake realised. This wasn't just the mass grave, this was the killing ground too. They had been herded in here and then . . . Thrown into the sea with their whole village.

Their whole village.

Oh shit. It was all true.

He snapped photo after photo, exulting in his ability, just for once, to pull hard evidence back out of the jaws of fiction. Swimming between the bodies to get new angles, he found a sense of communion with them. Yes, you were the victims of a terrible thing. But I am a journalist, and I will tell the world your story.

It was then he saw the ring.

It was gold, obviously personal, obviously evidence. He pulled it from the knucklebone of a skeleton in floral rags, and put it on his own finger.

The skeleton seemed to snap back into place after he'd let go of it. It was as if something had been holding it in place.

The way they were sitting, it was as if something were holding them all in place. It all looked very artificial. Surely, by now predators would have –

He noticed a ripple in the water. A sudden rush, as if some sort of lever had been pulled, and something big had moved nearby. He looked round in alarm. The skeletons all around him were moving, stirred into a silent, dead, panic by the swirling currents that were rushing through the chamber.

Blake's instincts screamed minefield. And he'd stepped right on the mine.

He pointed his body at the broken window through which he'd entered, and kicked up out of the skeletons towards it.

* * *

70

Blake clawed his way straight up towards the surface, arm over arm, panting like this was a scene out of a nightmare. He could sense the drowned village below shifting, crumbling, clouds of silt billowing up at his feet as the ground prepared for a bigger convulsion which –

Broke beneath him with a thump that nearly burst his eardrums. The shockwave travelled up through the water, sending Blake spiralling upwards like a helpless leaf in a twister, as shards of stone and bone and rag shot past him, sent flying by the vast explosion.

As his head broke the surface, and he ripped the stifling mask from his face, the water around him erupted in a concussive white sheet. The billowing white continued for several minutes as everything that had lain below was destroyed in a fire that Blake dipped his head under several times to see. A flickering, fusing light that went on far longer than anything of that kind should.

Finally, Blake lay back on the water, horrified and lost.

Horrified, because it was all true. The inhabitants of Sweethope were both dead and alive.

And lost because he knew that, thanks to the booby trap he'd set off, he would never be able to prove it.

It was probably during that thought that he lost consciousness.

6

THE SWEETHOPE DIASPORA

The black, starlike shape was hovering right in front of his eyes.

Something had just happened. He was at the dentist's. No, he was recovering from an operation. Invasive. Somebody had said something about relaxing, about letting go.

No, there had been the water. The explosion. The ocean hadn't been a dream this time.

The hand moved back from his face, and Blake realised that his eyes were already open. He was looking up at Gates and Ferguson. Gates had just straightened up from leaning over him, his hand having been the looming thing that Blake had seen.

They were almost smirking at him.

He managed to stop himself from scuttling back from them in dread. He wanted to shout that they were dead. Replaced. Not real.

He coughed up a little water. 'What's going on?'

Gates glanced merrily at Ferguson before he replied, slipping his leather glove back on to his hand. 'You're under arrest.'

Mayston police station was entirely like every other police station Blake had been in. Its only nod towards Ealing Comedy was the rather sweet local copper who brought two cups of tea to the door of the interview room.

Gates took one, but didn't offer Blake the other. He just closed the door in the copper's face and moved to sit behind the desk. This wasn't a formal interview, Blake noted. There was no tape recorder or witness.

He was left alone with the zombie or the foreign agent or whatever Gates was. He tried not to let the unease of it show on his face. Especially when Gates plucked the phone from its cradle.

'You seem to have a nasty habit of recruiting the vulnerable to help your cause,' the thing that looked like a policeman said. 'Your friend Mr Hallworth has lost his home and his livelihood. Because of you.'

Blake couldn't keep it in. 'I've seen the bodies, Gates. Whose are they?' Go on, say they belong to you and your friends.

Gates ignored him contemptuously. 'What do you think you're doing this *for*? A relatively small sum of money? Fifteen minutes of fame?'

Blake leaned forward and looked Gates in the eye. It no longer felt as if he were convincing himself. 'I saw Wilson die in his car, then he was alive and well. And it's happened before. And all the investigations are managed by you and Ferguson. Then my underwater "accident" happens and here you are again.'

'I'm here because some irrelevant half-wit with a death wish has gone swimming around a site full of live explosives.'

Blake shook his head. He would *not* believe that version of events any more. 'So irrelevant that you just tried to get me killed!'

'Nobody tried anything of the sort.' Gates remained impassive. 'You're paranoid. Your delusions flatter you.'

'Is that what you told Melissa? That she was imagining things?' He dared everything now. 'I'm on to you!'

Gates looked at him like he was an insect seen down the bore of a powerful microscope. He seemed amused at being talked to like that. 'You're "on to me", but you don't know what I've done. You can "see through me", but you don't know who I am.' Blake looked around at that terrifying admission, hoping that there was somebody

73

to hear. There was not. Gates was playing his brinkmanship right back at him, and Blake was suddenly fearful about surviving the next twenty-four hours. 'Tell me.' Gates smiled. 'What exactly is it I should be scared of?'

Blake made himself look back up the microscope and confronted that inhuman stare. 'The truth.'

They sized each other up for a moment, the true nature of their conflict finally before them.

Then Gates glanced towards the door and shouted offhandedly to the unknowing pawns he had surrounded himself with. 'Get him out of here!'

The friendly-looking, all-too-human local copper returned, and, being as brusque as he could manage, led Blake towards the door. Blake wanted to say something to him about being manipulated, about not helping the enemy. But he was aware that his world view had now entered the land of the deluded, the paranoid and the mad. His words would count for very little now, even if he had the truth on his side.

He looked back to see Gates watching him go. The policeman was looking almost sorry. Sorry at what would soon happen to the photographer.

When Blake had left, the thing that knew a small, particular portion of itself as 'Philip Gates' put its hand to its face, relaxed the expression which it was sure had induced exactly the right emotions in Steve Blake, and said, to somebody a long way away, 'He's on-line.'

Blake stepped into the sunshine outside the village police station wondering that the world could be so different from what he'd always imagined it was. He really didn't know where to go next. His paranoia had come true, and he now really was an insignificant speck fighting a vast conspiracy. And nobody was going to believe his side of the story.

He realised he'd been fingering his ring nervously. A

habit he'd picked up from Joanna.

Then he realised that it wasn't his wedding ring. It was the ring he'd plucked off the skeleton's finger, down below. Some evidence had survived, after all.

Blake found David Hallworth on the beach below his clifftop shack, making a bonfire of his property. As the photographer approached, he flung the sou'wester on to the flames. Bits of charred green wool were drifting into the smoke overhead.

Blake could have yelled at the man if he hadn't felt so responsible. 'What are you doing?'

'What does it look like?' Hallworth said bitterly. 'I'm getting out. Nothing here for me now. Thanks to you.'

'Have they scared you off?' Blake tried to gee the man up, despite his feeling that Hallworth was lucky to still be alive.

'No. You scared me off. Them and you. You nearly got us both killed.' He held out his hand towards Blake. 'The least you can do is give me my train fare.'

Blake smiled sadly. There was something dependable in Hallworth's concern for the basics. He pulled out a twenty pound note.

Hallworth looked at it. 'I was thinking of going a bit further than that.'

Blake sighed. 'How far did you have in mind?'

Hallworth reached down into the pile of junk he'd assembled beside the bonfire, and dangled Blake's underwater camera over the flames, a canny smile playing upon his weatherbeaten features. 'This far.'

Blake had created darkrooms in many odd circumstances all over the world. Now he taped heavy sheets across the windows of the artist's cottage, and bought a red bulb for a bedside lamp. The sink became his developing bath.

Hallworth, in return for the camera, had demanded enough train fare to make it to Scotland or France. Blake thought that, wherever he went, he'd make some sort of existence for himself. If *they* let him.

He developed the negatives from the underwater camera carefully, not rushing it, though he wanted to. He wanted to see that these images were real, and not just things he'd imagined. He watched as the key image of that skeletal congregation became clearer and clearer on the photographic paper, as it moved from being fiction back to being fact again.

He looked at it directly and unblinkingly. It was all true. Unfortunately.

It was early evening by the time Blake got to Melissa's house. He'd found it via the local phone book. He carried an envelope with one set of the precious prints in it.

He rang her doorbell, saw a curtain twitch, waited and then rang again. He kept on ringing until she opened the door.

She didn't say anything, just looked at him angrily.

'I need to talk to you,' he said.

'Fine, as long as I don't need to listen.'

She went to shut the door, but Blake stepped forward and put his body in the way.

'Look, Melissa, I don't know who that man is walking around calling himself Gates but he isn't your husband!'

She stared at him, wondering if he was just humouring her.

'I've got proof of that now.'

After a moment, she let him inside.

Melissa's living room was bright and airy, with stripped, polished floorboards and rugs. The shelves sagged with books and there were tasteful framed prints on the wall. Blake had expected the impressionists, but he got Escher and Miro.

She didn't offer him anything to drink. He just handed her the photographs, and watched as she gazed at them,

76

smoothing the surface of one with her hand, as if she wanted to touch the contents. Then she leafed through until she came to the skeletons. She stared for a while, and Blake thought she was going to cry.

But she visibly pulled herself together and asked: 'How many, would you say?'

'Difficult to know. Enough to be the entire population of Sweethope.'

She put the photos down. Shook her head. 'No. This isn't them, this can't be them.'

'These are the Sweethope villagers, Melissa. They all died on the night of the original explosion.' He lowered his voice, realising that he was making concrete the nightmare that had haunted this woman all these years. 'Including your husband.'

'No! That woman was right. I was talking rubbish! They can't be *dead*. They've been changed. Some drug, something . . .' She was almost panicking, searching Blake's face for evidence that bringing all her terrors to life was just some sort of sick joke on his part.

'You felt you no longer knew people you had known for years. You were right. It wasn't them any more.'

'Maybe I was wrong.' She was babbling now. 'Maybe it was something in me. Maybe the doctors were right!'

'Melissa, it happened five years ago in Sweethope. It could be happening again. Wilson's resurrection proves that. I saw the man die!'

'I wanted my life back! Not this. I didn't want this!'

Blake didn't know if he should reach out to comfort her. He hadn't realised what demands this late obituary for her husband would make on her.

She subsided to a whisper. 'I want my life back.'

Blake made her look at him, and spoke with a new resolve. She couldn't stay like this. They needed the whole truth now. Both of them. Whatever the risks. 'Find out who the people pretending to be the villagers are. And you'll get your life back!' He took the golden ring from his finger and put it down on the table. 'I took this from the church. It's got initials engraved on the inside of the band. Does "EM" mean anything to you?'

Melissa picked up the ring, and stared at it for a long moment, but Blake knew from her expression that she hadn't engaged with what he'd been saying. She put it down again. Suddenly. Like it was hot. 'I'm sorry, Steve. I've found out all I want to know. My husband's dead. That's enough for me.'

Blake could hardly believe it. He grabbed the photo and held it up, holding on to the reality he'd found down there. She flinched at the image, already denying it.

'Melissa, I need your help!'

She looked at him for a long time. Then she pushed the photos and the ring back to him. 'I'm finished with all this stuff, Steve. I'm sorry.'

Blake closed his mouth, finding no words to reply to her.

He left without the ring. By the time he'd realised that, he found that he had no words with which to call her, either.

Blake spent the evening in the company of the *Directory of British Companies* and the 1997 edition of *Who's Who*. As well as a bottle of whisky and, to counter the whisky, a frightening number of cups of coffee. None of these things stopped him from feeling very alone. He was cross-referencing his reference books with the list of Sweethope survivors that Joanna had supplied. The list was now covered with Blake's own notes. 'Mary Madigan, M.o.D. lawyer' had, scrawled beside it, 'MP for Norfolk East'. That had been due to a by-election last year, the sitting MP having died suddenly. Madigan had increased her majority at the General Election. Other names down the list had things written beside them like 'Spokesman for the D.T.I.' and 'Also on the Board of B.P.', 'Council member', 'lobbyist for Marconi', 'Treasury'. The list swam before Blake's eyes. Every one of these people, if he could still call them that, was either in a high-ranking job or on the way to one.

He went to the fridge for a can of alcohol-free lager. On the way, with the phone in the crook of his shoulder, he called Joanna. 'Tell me this. Why would an ex-manager of a garage now be an under-secretary at Trade and Industry?'

She paused for just long enough to let him know that his story was now a long way down her list. He could hear the chink of a bottle and glass.

'Perhaps he did an oil change for Margaret Beckett and it went on from there.'

Blake headed back to his chair, keeping his tone conversational. 'The Sweethope survivors have got someone in every major government department and on the boards of oil companies, the stock exchange, drugs research. Three of them are MPs. If it's not a conspiracy I'm looking at, what is it?'

'Insomnia?' she asked sweetly.

'I'm right. You know I'm right. They're taking over the country. I've got photographic evidence that they're not who they say they are.'

'Oh, yeah? Taken by you or your sidekick, Mystic Meg?' There was a long silence. 'You're doing that thing you used to do, aren't you?'

'What thing?'

'Counting to ten under your breath when I start to annoy you.'

Blake stopped counting. 'No.'

'You really have photographs?'

'Yes. Really.'

'OK.' Joanna's long-suffering voice. 'Bring them to me, let me see what I can do.'

'You don't get off that easily. Some of this info you sent me is already out of date. Have another dig around, eh? See what they've been up to recently.'

'Anything else? The moon on a stick perhaps?'

'No thanks.' He was just grateful that she was still taking him seriously after that eventful dinner with Melissa. 'I seem to remember you promised me that once before and it never arrived.'

Blake lay on the beach. Somebody had said something about an operation, and he'd agreed. Which had been a mistake, because he didn't want it inside him. The hand moved back from his face, and Blake realised that his eyes were already open. He was looking up at Gates and Ferguson. Gates had just straightened up from leaning over him, his hand having been the looming thing that Blake had seen.

His hand had touched him tenderly on the forehead.

Blake reared up, his muscles protesting, and opened his eyes.

He was sitting up in bed or, rather, on the covers, still fully dressed.

Ouch. He felt the top of his nose, the site of a sudden, splitting headache. Were dreams like that a natural con-sequence of *them* being out to get you? Or a natural consequence of whisky and coffee before bed?

The clock radio came on behind him, making him jump and wince again. He reached into his dresser, and started trying to figure out where he'd hidden the aspirin, ignoring the *Today* programme.

'Farmers throughout Europe,' the newsreader was saying, 'are seeking a compensation package for massive crop failure due to the freak heat wave this autumn. Combined with the effects of the infestation of the so-called "super beetle", a very low crop yield, and possible food shortages across the continent, are predicted by the European Agricultural Committee . . .'

The doorbell interrupted Blake before he'd found the pills.

* * *

Blake signed for a package feeling almost unable to talk, such was the pain in his head.

Inside was a notelet indicating that the contents were 'From the Office of Joanna Ball', with the masthead of her paper beside her name. He pulled the rest of the papers out of the package, and started leafing through newspaper cuttings and advertising material, all centred around the company who made Joanna's office computers, Zentex Software. Certain items had been highlighted in felt-tip pen. A picture of a husband and wife under the headline 'Couple That Sparked An Economic Miracle'. They looked vaguely familiar. They were in the next article too: 'Sweethope Survivors Make Good'. Blake smiled to himself. They could keep that headline and just keep reprinting it. This time the couple were standing in a busy factory, which, judging by their proprietorial air, belonged to them.

It was Zentex Software itself. Their company.

He went to his own collection of photos, and compared *Pride in Our Computer Business One* to *Smile, You're Supposed to have Survived the Sweethope Disaster One*.

These two were standing behind Fiona, the little girl in the green jumper. So they were her parents, which made them – he glanced down his list – Patrick and Pauline Leonard. He confirmed their names from the articles and ringed their heads in biro.

'Got you,' he whispered. That was two more accounted for.

Amongst the Zentex material that was now scattered over his table, Blake found a recruitment flyer, advertising the 'Zentex 2000 Recruitment Day'. He pinned it to his corkboard and stared at it for a while.

At exactly the moment when he decided what his next move was going to be, his headache stopped.

7

HELLO, SPACEBOY

After Melissa Gates had shown Steve to the door the previous night she'd made a decision.

She had to do it. She couldn't draw a line under this until she did. She didn't want to believe the evidence that was sitting in front of her. But she couldn't see how any logical person, and through these hard years she had taken pride in being a logical person, could fail to believe it.

So, tomorrow, she would find her own kind of proof. The proof of emotions and people, rather than Blake's proof of hard evidence. She slept well on her decision.

The next morning, she showered and dressed without even considering the question.

Because today she would know. After waiting for some answer all these years, she would finally know.

The Central Ops building in Norwich was different from how it had been in Melissa's imagination. She'd never been there, and when she thought of Philip going to work, following his promotion, she'd always thought of somewhere more imposing. A tower. A castle. A fortress full of people who she was never told about, who she would never see.

The plaque outside reception listed several departments, including Special Operations, East. She selected that as the most likely department within which to enquire, and headed inside.

The interior was very swish, all discreet lighting and potted plants. It was more like a publishers' building than a police station. She couldn't imagine being intimidated even if she'd been hauled in here in irons. That was, in normal circumstances. Right now, she was feeling intimidated by everything from the air conditioning to the talking lifts.

She talked to a smiling policewoman behind the front desk, who told her which floor she had to go to, and passed her on to another policewoman by an electronic barrier, who searched her bag like it was an unfortunate necessity. Considering how much she was shaking, and that she'd told them she wanted a quick word with her ex-husband, it was a wonder they hadn't stripped her and run metal detectors over her.

She got out of the polite lift on the fourth floor, and explained her mission to that receptionist. He tried to reach Philip, but found on his PC terminal that he'd requested not to take any calls.

So, still feeling guilty of something, a potential assassin, she sat on the sofa that still smelt of the shop, and waited until he would.

Five minutes into her vigil, she was surprised to see him emerge from one of the internal doors, chatting to a serious, distinguished-looking man who vanished through the exit before she could get a good look at him. She thought that maybe she'd seen him in an advert –

But then Philip saw her, looked stunned to see her. And she was suddenly quite frightened. Mainly at the difference between a face and a posture that she was still deeply in love with, and her scary theory about just what it was that she now loved.

He spoke first, thank God. 'Melissa?'

'I wondered if you had time to talk?' It had come out as a squeak.

Philip looked at his watch. 'Sure,' he said.

He took her into his office, and she was shocked by how it looked. Philip was . . . Had been . . . Messy. Disorganised. A good copper, of course, she'd never thought otherwise, but she was always chiding him for leaving piles of balled-up socks in the corner.

This was definitely somebody else's office. Yet it had his name on the desk. He motioned to her to sit down, and she did so.

'What is it? Are you OK?'

She swallowed. 'I'm fine. I just want . . . I just want you to explain what happened in Sweethope yesterday morning.'

'Quite simple. Steve Blake, whom I believe you know –' A hint of bitterness? No. Just the facts. '– Went diving in the village ruins. His little jaunt must have triggered off old explosives. We saved him.'

'And, as far as you knew, that was all that was down there? Rubble and explosives?'

He rubbed a hand across his brow. 'Melissa, what else could be down there?'

She didn't want to answer him. Didn't want to bring her whole extreme world view into the light. 'The night Sweethope was destroyed. The first explosion, you're certain everyone was saved?'

'You know they were.'

She thought about the last time they had had sex. She was used to him being passionate, rough. She had wanted him inside her on the night after the disaster, in their hotel room in Mayston. He had grudgingly agreed, as if she was asking him to watch one of her classic serials that he had so detested. He had been like a virgin. Clumsy, all passion deflected by inexperience. He had come almost instantly, and then looked at her distantly, as if wanting to hear that he'd done it right. In an awkward kitchen scene afterwards, he had put it down to stress, to the horror of the disaster. She had nodded and smiled, feeling scared, though then she didn't know why. Stress would have been inability, or crudity, or something which would have broken him, at least, allowed out the emotions she thought he'd been holding in. They could at least

84

have cuddled up. What she'd felt had, instead, spoken of adolescence. And an awkward coldness that went through and through. Nothing to release. No feelings to speak of.

They'd never made love again, after that. Never spoken of it after a couple of weeks. Gradually, that night had become a subject of recurring nightmares for Melissa. Where he looked down at her while his fellow crew-members, with their long spindly fingers, drew a little white child out of her, its big black eyes gleaming.

She'd read too many UFO books as her suspicions had taken hold of her, that was true. A lot of what she'd read was rubbish. But a lot of it was too credible for comfort. She'd filled the Occult section at the library with her research material, and hid the books under the sofa when Philip walked through the door.

She had sworn, as she became more certain and started to sleep on the sofa, that he'd started to smell different, that his skin had acquired the odour of cardboard and floral chemicals.

Now she wanted to know for certain. To give him enough rope to hang himself. 'There were no strangers in the village that night? No soldiers? No M.o.D. men? Anybody who might not have been so easily accounted for?'

'Why are we going over this again?'

'Because I want to find out the secret that destroyed our marriage.' She wanted to hear him come out with a big cover story. Something about government experiments that would convince her and let her walk away.

What he said instead surprised her. 'If I knew why you stopped loving me, why you started to doubt me . . . I've asked myself those questions a thousand times.'

There was a moment when they looked at each other, when she was certain that this was her husband looking at her, if from far away.

'This is to do with Steve Blake, isn't it?'

She shook her head vehemently. Yelled at him, for

some reason she didn't understand. 'It's to do with us!'

'It's to do with you!' Still his old snarl. It would be so wonderfully normal to have a row. A jealous row.

She gave him another chance. A better chance to tell her any sort of convincing lie. 'Just tell me what you're hiding.'

He didn't give her that. He just looked at her and, in that look, she saw Philip Gates shrink away into the depths of his big black eyes, filed in some distant place for this thing's own personal use. Its own eyes were dull, and non-reflective and nothing to do with anything human.

In that moment, she got what she came for.

After all these years of fear, she finally knew. 'Thank you,' she said.

Blake had got talking to one of Melissa's friends behind the desk at the library when he returned the reference books that morning. He was surprised to find that the woman regarded him as Prince Charming, come to put light in Melissa's life again. It was entertaining to be suddenly aware of the smalltown gossip, until he realised that Melissa's colleague thought that he'd spirited her away last night, because she hadn't reported for work that morning. Suddenly, all he could think of was the ring, how valuable it was, and what *they* might do to get it back.

'You're sure Melissa didn't phone in? Leave a message of any sort?' he asked.

'Sorry, not a word.' She looked disappointed that her fantasies hadn't turned out to be true. 'I'm sure she will call.'

'If she does, could you tell her that Steve Blake came in and that I need to talk to her urgently.'

That brightened her up a little.

Mrs Melissa Gates stood on the jetty beside the ocean that had once been Sweethope. She'd driven back from the city far too fast. She'd managed to hold back the tears until now. Until she could look at the place where once she'd lived.

The place where her husband had been murdered.

She looked down at her clenched fist, and revealed the object that she'd kept in her bag like a talisman during her visit with the thing that wore her husband's body. The ring Steve had found on the skeleton's finger. The most solid of solid evidence. If only he knew how solid. It was the sight of this that had scared her: it wasn't nice to be told that your nightmares were all true.

She examined the initials she'd seen on the ring once again. 'EM'. It was real.

She thrust the ring deep into her pocket and turned to walk back to her car.

Ms Melissa Prentice, the widow, had a job to do.

Blake had made a quick search of the village, checked out Melissa's cottage. No sign of her. But no sign of violence, either.

Finally, he went back to the cottage. It was still only early afternoon. He switched on the radio and listened to the news for a while, not really paying attention.

'The Pacific coast has been hit by severe gales and storms for the fourth night running,' the newsreader was saying. 'Police fear that over sixty people may have perished with thousands more injured . . .'

He would give it until tea time, then . . . he'd panic.

He picked up the Zentex Recruitment Day flyer. 'Are you part of our future?' it read. One of the dates mentioned was that very day.

'OK,' he muttered, sticking it in his bag pocket and going to switch off the radio. 'Let's pretend that I am.'

The Zentex factory complex was located in the flatlands, just off a motorway exit, an industrial estate devoted to just one company. Blake drove right round it in the rain, observing the high security of the perimeter fence. Cameras, motion sensors, what looked like the junction boxes for some pretty serious electric fencing. It was hard to tell whether or not that was normal for such a high-powered business. Finding something as big as Microsoft in the wilds of Norfolk was a surprise. This factory was seriously out of place. And what was a serious success story for the British economy was, and Blake was getting a feel for this stuff, another example of the sort of framing error that the Sweethope diaspora specialised in.

At the end of his circuit, he stopped his car at the gates. He'd seen people in overalls coming and going inside the fence, making their way between buildings, occasionally driving little golf carts or forklifts. They all wore overalls, and these came in three different colours: red, blue and black. Like this was the bloody Starship *Enterprise*, or the place was being run by Blofeld, who was ready to escape in his private submersible.

A security guard approached the car window. Blake wound it down.

'Recruitment?'

'Through the gates, park close to reception, follow the signs.' And then the burly man opened his mouth wide and gave Blake the sweetest of grins. 'And welcome to Zentex, friend.'

'Thanks,' Blake muttered, a little unnerved.

As the barrier was raised, the guard added, 'And have a nice day.'

He parked in a pleasant, tree-lined car park and headed towards reception, passing workers of all three colours, who were marching purposefully to and fro. Their bright colours looked particularly incongruous under the stormy sky. Zentex lorries stood in rows, ready for loading. A sign stood in front of the reception building: ZENTEX 2000 – RECRUITMENT DAY. According to the flyer, Zentex held them three times a month, with the stated aim of achieving their 'perfect staff' by the year 2000. Until he could find Melissa, this seemed to be a perfect opportunity to get under the skin of the Sweethope Survivors Self-Preservation Society.

Blake followed the signs into the building. Behind him entered a businessman in a serious suit, and, to Blake's shock, a sombre-looking crusty, trying to look as respectable as possible in his rags and patches. What sort of job could these two both be applying for?

They all joined a queue of applicants, who had to fill in a form. Blake lied with the sort of freedom that he normally reserved for calls from double-glazing salespeople. Then they were led, in a large group, into a room full of computer consoles. Each of them was directed to a specific seat. Then a man walked between them, handing out headphones, which he instructed them to put on, and, rather more worryingly, strapping an instrument of some kind to their wrists.

Blake put his headphones on and examined the device. It was a bit like one of those bands that they attached to your wrist at a pop festival, but there was definitely some sort of instrumentation pressed close to the artery in his wrist.

He looked up as a voice entered his headphones. At the front of the room, under a framed photograph of Mr and Mrs Leonard, their little Fiona and a small boy, sat a woman with a severely cropped haircut. She was smiling with the same sort of corporate joy that that security guard had exhibited. At least she was wearing an ordinary suit.

'Welcome to Zentex. Welcome to the future,' she said. 'It isn't just the product that is revolutionary here at Zentex Software, but the whole manufacturing process. That is why we rigorously assess your suitability to become part of the Zentex family, even as day-workers.'

Blake glanced at the crusty, sitting two rows behind him.

'We want you,' the woman continued. 'But only if you want us.' She gazed happily around the group, then gestured to the computers. 'If you'd care to begin, you have precisely –' she glanced at her watch '– sixty minutes to complete the Zentex Entry Challenge.'

The first question flashed up on the screen in front of Blake. 'If you saw a beggar on the street in front of you, would you cross over the road?'

Blake stared at it, surprised, and got the feeling that several of those sitting around him were surprised as well. The woman in front of him, however, was already tapping away. Maybe she was used to stuff like this in whatever industry she came from. This stuff reminded Blake of nothing more than the 'free personality test' a shop-front cult had once offered him. He'd tried it, but the happy assistants had been rather worried by his answers. They'd found, as he'd joked to his mates afterwards, that he'd got one.

He typed his answer: 'No'. Then he added 'never' and tapped the ENTER key. Ethics weren't going to be a problem, but if it asked him who his favourite Spice Girl was, he was really going to be in trouble.

The monitor showed the image from the camera inside Steve Blake's monitor. He was working at his computer terminal, smiling at his Aptitude Test. Moving his mouse.

Two people stood watching the monitor, in an office which belonged to one of them.

'Is this wise?' said Patrick Leonard. He was grey-haired and looked affable, rumpled. Or had done, a long time ago.

'You worry too much,' said James Wilson. 'He's under control.'

'And the risk?'

Wilson stood, and walked to the door. 'What risk? He's tagged. He's like a rat in a maze. No, he'll do his job very nicely.'

Wilson took a green inhaler from his pocket and sprayed a shot of it into his body's lungs.

* * *

There had been more than a hundred questions. Blake had lied freely about everything personal, including his sexuality, politics and health history, opting for the most radical approach possible every time. He'd told the truth about his reaction to every ethical dilemma.

He looked around his intake group as they had the amulets taken off their wrists. None of them were looking outraged by the questions they'd been asked.

The woman at the front of the room looked down at a monitor of her own and brightly looked up once more to address the room. 'Thank you, everybody. Peter Timmins and Joyce Sangster?'

Blake saw a man and a woman almost leap in the air with delight. The rest of them, himself included, looked at each other and at their feet, and started to shuffle towards the door. None of them seemed to want to annoy the various smiling Zentex functionaries as they passed. Blake didn't know if that was because they might get a chance to try again, or if that was just one of those things about the British and big organisations. The crusty flicked a V sign behind his back, which made Blake feel a bit better.

'You both did well enough to progress on to our next stage,' the woman was saying to the two lucky winners. 'We'd like you to come back tomorrow after completing these.' She handed them pamphlets.

Blake, at the back of the group, was just about out of the door when he heard her call his name. 'Not you, Mr Blake.'

Blake turned back, wondering at what he'd done right. She ushered him back into the room. He caught envious glances from his fellow contestants as the door closed between them.

'My name is Rose,' the woman said, leading him to join Mr Timmins and Ms Sangster, who grinned at him like he'd just admitted he was an alcoholic. 'You were wonderful. Congratulations. Your test results are

91

excellent. You have won the opportunity to train as a day-worker.'

He didn't say he'd like to come back next week and try for the holiday. Just. He just smiled and shook Rose's hand.

'I trust you have no other plans for today?' she asked. It took a moment for Blake to realise that that was actually a rhetorical question. 'Welcome to Zentex.'

Rose led her three new charges through the maze of air-conditioned corridors and gleaming office areas. Sangster and Timmins were handed over to the grinning heads of different departments as they went. Blake tried to think of a conversation he could strike up with Rose as they marched along yet another corridor together, but failed at the sight of the purposeful gleam in her eye. There was something about efficiency that just made the British uncomfortable, he reflected.

He was shown through a big pair of doors labelled DESPATCH, and discovered that this was to be his destiny. Conveyor belts whirred in several lines, Zentex packages being created out of component disks, booklets, bubble-wrap and styrofoam blocks.

'This is just one of twenty despatch units,' Rose told him. 'Working twenty-four hours a day, seven days a week.'

'Pretty big operation, then?'

'The biggest. Fifty thousand units a day go out from here alone. That still gets nowhere near meeting the demands of the global market. You'll have heard of the Zentex Odyssey range?'

Blake nodded knowledgeably. 'Of course.'

'We're very proud of it. Can you work nights, Steve?'

'Not a problem. I think sleep's overrated.'

'And you have no problem starting at basic rate? We call it Grade Red.'

'Sorry?'

'You haven't read the brochure.' She tutted like a schoolteacher. 'I really think you should. Grade Red refers to your code level. It tells us you're new. So everybody will know you need extra help.'

Blake smiled against the grain of what he was thinking. 'I'll wear a pink tutu if it gets me the job.'

The tempo of her smile didn't actually change. 'That won't be necessary. This is where you'll be working.'

They walked through the door where the conveyor belts went.

Rows of boxed-up software were packed on shelves which stretched to the ceiling. Forklifts were moving back and forth along the aisles. People in blue or black overalls were bringing in more boxes all the time.

Rose took Blake over to meet a cheerful-looking man in a black overall, who was moving along the stacks with a clipboard, nodding approvingly as he ticked items off. He looked more like an ex-con than a foreman. When he noticed Rose approaching, he smiled a survivor's smile, and reached out to shake Blake warmly by the hand.

'This is Steve Blake,' Rose said to him. Then she turned to Blake. 'Mr Beck will be your section supervisor.'

'Pleased to meet you. Welcome to Zentex.' He had a pleasant Somerset accent. Very *Animal Magic*. With an edge that suggested something nasty in the haystack.

As Blake shook Beck's hand, he noticed that one of the blue-overalled workers nearby was paying particular attention to their meeting. He was an edgy, thin chap in his early thirties, with a care-lined face. And he seemed to have that Sid James sparkle in his eye that Blake had so far been missing in these happy, committed individuals.

He looked quickly back to his task when Beck glanced in his direction.

Rose patted Blake on the back and left. 'Mr Beck will look after you.'

'So.' Blake rubbed his hands together. 'What's my job?'

'Job?' Beck laughed. 'Oh, you've landed more than a job here. You've landed the chance of a lifetime. You might only be a day-worker right now, but who knows? If you keep your nose clean, try and fit in, take some pride in what you're doing –' Blake felt a sudden twinge, listening to that rough voice deliver such homilies, that he was indeed in a prison '– then Mr Leonard might even ask you to join our community on the five-year plan.'

'That'd be nice. But I'm not sure I'm ready for a long-term commitment.'

'Not even one that pays a three-hundred-per-cent bonus at the end of it?'

Beck handed Blake a plastic tag, and Blake realised that that was another rhetorical question.

'Go and get your work suit. And welcome to the future!'

Melissa sat in the waiting area, feeling lost amongst the understated marble and the leather sofas, playing with the ring in her pocket. She was certain that the receptionist was glancing at her questioningly from time to time, as if asking herself if this dowdy woman could really have a genuine appointment here. She felt very alienated, very uninvited.

Ten minutes past the appointed time, an interior door opened, and Mary Madigan MP came out of it. She was a heavy-set, matronly woman, with the savagely caring expression of an old-fashioned nanny. She wore the uniform of the female politician, with a shawl that set off her expensive hairdo. Melissa had known Mary since she first moved to Sweethope. They'd been to local Labour Party meetings together. But after the disaster, Mary's politics had changed completely. Against the direction that virtually the whole country was moving in, she joined the Tories, moved swiftly up their ranks, and, against all electoral logic, won the seat for them and kept it. Melissa had long lost sight of her by then, of course. She remembered an ironic photo from the local paper, printed a couple of days after the election. Mary and herself on the platform at the Labour Party conference a few years before, singing 'The Red Flag'.

These days, Mary was every inch the Conservative businesswoman, a tall, intimidating woman in her late forties with a brusque, unashamed confidence. She offered Melissa her hand. 'Melissa! What a lovely surprise to hear from you! How long has it been?'

'Four years.'

Mary shook her head in wonder. 'Four years. And you're looking so well.'

She took Melissa's arm, a gesture which almost made Melissa flinch with its alien PR precision.

'Now, it'll have to be a quick coffee, I'm afraid. I have to head off fairly promptly. Never have a minute these days.'

The strong arm lead Melissa towards Mary's office.

There was a framed photo on the wall of Mary shaking hands with John Major. A space was open on the wall beside it, ready, Melissa didn't doubt, for a similar scene featuring William Hague. Mary's secretary brought in coffee as her boss listened to Melissa's simple request, getting more uncomfortable all the time.

'I'd love to be able to say yes, Melissa. But I'm afraid mother has been very confused for some time now.'

Melissa felt genuinely troubled for a moment, until she remembered, as she had to remind herself continuously while talking to this Torified version of her old friend, where this quest had already led her. 'I'm sorry, I didn't know. Was it the accident at Sweethope that affected her?'

Mary paused. Adopted her sincere voice. 'It didn't help. But she was already rather mixed up when it happened.' She sighed. 'I finally admitted to myself that I couldn't cope any more. The nursing home she's in is really terribly good.'

Melissa grinned, tried to gee up the alien woman in front of her. 'I expect she enjoys having visitors, doesn't she? And it takes the strain off you.'

Mary sipped quickly at her coffee and glanced at the top sheet of papers on her desk, as if wanting to get on, but unwilling to throw Melissa out. 'I really don't think it's a good idea.'

'Mary . . .' Melissa, against all logic, found herself trying to appeal to the humanity of someone she, logically if not instinctively, knew wasn't human. 'You know I had a lot of problems after Sweethope . . .'

'Milk?' the MP asked, as a junior arrived with the tea tray.

'Thank you,' Melissa muttered, distracted from her mission for a second. 'No sugar.'

Mary leapt right back on track as the tea-maker left. 'I did hear you'd been . . . troubled.'

'I remember your mother from when I first moved to the village. She was very kind to me.'

'As I said, Melissa, I'd love to be able to say yes. But I have to think of mother first. You do see that, don't you?' She stood up. That was her last word on the matter.

Melissa stood too, frustrated. 'Yes,' she said. 'Of course.'

Without having received any kind of signal that Melissa had seen, Mary's secretary arrived to show her out.

'She's the best MP we've ever had,' the secretary declared as they headed for the door of the building. 'She's a wonderful woman, isn't she?'

'And success hasn't changed her one bit,' Melissa purred.

The secretary stopped, searching her face as if interested in every scrap of information about her boss. This was definitely *human* nature she was looking at, Melissa decided. 'So you've known Mary for quite a while?'

'Yes. Her mother was a neighbour of mine. I was *so*

looking forward to seeing her again.'

'I'm sure she'd be delighted to see you.'

The secretary hadn't been informed, Melissa realised, and was too excited to pick up on the negative tone. Her PR training and urge to better her position had triumphed over actually listening to what Melissa had said.

A slow smile spread over Melissa's face. 'I can never remember how to get to the nursing home. I always get lost. I'll just pop back and ask Mary –'

The secretary stopped her, with a little jump of nerves. 'Oh no! She's got a very full afternoon. If I remember correctly, I should take the A140, on to the B1149, then once you're on the Cromer road look out for signs for Thornfield Hall.'

Melissa thanked God for human nature. 'The A140! Excellent. Thank you!'

She left the building with a smile on her face. Mary Madigan had confirmed what she'd always suspected. That if one wanted to infiltrate the highest echelons of the establishment, there was no point in subverting New Labour.

So William Hague had one more thing to worry about. Unless *he* was one of them. That thought made Melissa smile even more as she headed for her car.

Melissa was led through the gardens of the nursing home by a pleasant old matron. There were gently swaying trees, immaculately tended grass, and a pond with lilies and fish. That was where they found Elizabeth Madigan, in her wheelchair. She was staring at her reflection in the water.

Melissa gulped down a sudden fear at the sight of the white-haired woman in her eighties. She hadn't thought about how hard this would be. She had loved, been close to, Elizabeth Madigan before the accident. Remembered her as sweet and considerate, with a wicked sense of humour, even if there had been moments when she couldn't quite remember Melissa's name, and called her Mary instead.

Melissa made herself remember the photograph of the skeletons, and, steeled for what was to come, stepped forward.

'Hello, Mrs Madigan.'

Elizabeth lifted her head from the pond and stared at Melissa. There was no hint of recognition in her eyes. Melissa hadn't known quite what to expect from this confrontation. Perhaps a hyper-alert and scheming Elizabeth clone. Which was why this nursing-home business had surprised her in the first place. But the woman in front of her didn't look like she knew what day it was.

'This lady has something for you,' the matron explained gently.

Elizabeth pointed at Melissa. 'Is this your daughter or my daughter?' Her voice was plummy and questioning, like a professor enquiring into a matter of great importance.

The matron smiled wryly at Melissa and patted the old lady on the arm. 'Neither. I'll leave you to talk, shall I?' And she left.

Melissa squatted down beside the wheelchair and started her experiment. She reached into her pocket and produced the ring that Steven had found underwater. 'I think it's yours,' she said, placing it in Elizabeth's gnarled palm. 'I've seen you wear it. And look at the initials.'

Elizabeth opened her mouth in a wrinkled 'oh'.

Then she grabbed Melissa's face and kissed her.

Melissa swayed back on her ankles, a little flustered. This was not what she had expected from a duplicate Elizabeth. Absolute confirmation, perhaps, even some clue she might have gained from the most frail of these duplicates. But this sudden human love was enough to make her wonder if she'd been wrong all along.

'I am with strangers,' Elizabeth told her seriously, staring into her eyes.

Melissa was flustered enough to try and placate her. 'You must have made friends with somebody here, Elizabeth. You really don't know anybody?'

The old woman's grip didn't soften. It was as if this message were the most urgent thing in the world. 'Do you know the strangers I am with? The people who say they know me and look like people I used to know? Can you tell me, dear, who they really are?'

Melissa took Elizabeth's hands in her own. This must be her, the real Elizabeth! She'd escaped the culling of the village, she must have left her ring behind! That was why Mary had exiled her here! 'Elizabeth! Are you saying that your daughter isn't who she says she is?'

Elizabeth seemed to lose the plot for a moment. She looked puzzled, searching her memories, and then said, in the tone of somebody who was reassuring themselves of an established truth: 'We have come here to be among strangers.'

'No, Elizabeth. What you said before . . . I want you to tell me again. Can you do that?'

Elizabeth only gave her a beautiful smile.

'Can you explain? Elizabeth?'

There was only emptiness.

'Elizabeth? Is this you? Tell me it's you!'

There was a long pause.

Elizabeth sighed. 'Who are you?' she asked sadly.

The voice of the returning matron surprised Melissa. 'I've spent hours like this. It won't get you anywhere. I think she's probably a little bit tired.'

Melissa got to her feet, confused. 'I didn't think.' In truth, she didn't know what *to* think. 'It was insensitive of me. I'm sorry.' She smiled and waved to Elizabeth, and followed the matron back to the main building.

She turned back only once, to see Elizabeth half-saying something after her. It was like a question. But Melissa had no idea what it might have meant.

* * *

99

The Elizabeth Madigan and the driver battled for control of the head. Its muscles twitched as the Elizabeth Madigan memories managed to take control. The driver ached at how it was lost and confused, hearing always the commands and concerns of the others, but unable to take the actions it wanted to take . . . Whatever they had been. This system's construction was faulty. The Elizabeth Madigan memories took up all the room, and the driver had no space to remember what it had been, and forgot when the others told it. Every time it tried to form connections, they decayed. The Elizabeth Madigan seemed to thrive on those decaying connections, changing with them, free to wash through the system like liquid light.

So the driver and the Elizabeth Madigan watched as Melissa, whoever she was, went back into the home.

Then they looked down and saw the ring that remained in the right palm of their body. Wedding ring, the Elizabeth Madigan memories noted. Jack. He had it engraved after her: 'EM'.

Then they opened the left palm of their body. And the same wedding ring was in that one.

Which left them both very confused.

8

THE BRITISH INVASION

Blake was knocking at Melissa's door when she called up to him from the beach. 'Hey!'

He turned, relieved. He had been about to resume his search for her. It was tea time, the end of his first working day with Zentex. He'd spent the hours moving software packages from one place to another, wondering why he needed to be so carefully selected to do that.

It had been good to get out of those overalls and back into his jeans. He'd never been comfortable with uniforms.

Now he ran down to Melissa's side, oblivious of the fact that they'd parted on such bad terms. He didn't care whether or not she felt able to help him, he realised. Just whether or not she was OK.

'Hi!' he said. 'I've been trying to get hold of you.'

Melissa smiled. 'I heard. I popped into the library.'

'You OK?'

She shook her head at the question, impatient with it. 'I've got some news. I traced the owner of the ring.'

Blake found that he was smiling all over his face. 'But I thought –'

'So I'm a complicated librarian.' She indicated the shoreline with a wave of her cardiganed arm. 'Are you coming for a walk or what?'

They walked along the beach and back again, until the sun was going down. Melissa explained about her visit to the party offices and then to the nursing home. Blake watched her mouth as she carefully explained, emphasising exactly the right words, careful of every detail. He couldn't help but wonder what had caused this complete reversal in her attitude, what had convinced her?

'Elizabeth Madigan,' she was saying, 'has got Alzheimer's. But when I gave her the ring she was very clear that she wanted to tell me something. It was as though she knew what I'd been through. About the villagers changing.'

Blake managed not to be churlish about Melissa leaving his prize bit of evidence with an old woman. He, after all, had left it with Melissa. 'What about the daughter, Mary?'

'Another success story. Before the Sweethope incident she was a solicitor in family law. Now she's MP for Norfolk East.'

'And her office uses Zentex Software.'

Melissa thought for a moment and then nodded. 'How did you know that?'

'Zentex is run by Patrick Leonard. One of the Sweethope survivors. I guarantee you, Zentex is at the heart of whatever's going on.'

Mélissa frowned, concentrating. 'So what do they want with their own computer system?'

'What would anyone want? Control.'

'They've already got a pretty effective way of getting control. That husk who used to be my husband . . .' He wondered at the certainty behind her words now. 'He's testimony to that. Why can't they do that to everybody?'

'Whatever's going on, it goes beyond mere personality changes.'

Melissa sagged a little, pulling the cardigan closer around her shoulders. The breeze from over the water was becoming colder. 'Personality changes? Is that what you're calling it now? I thought you'd accepted that —'

'I'm just taking it slowly. I accept that your fellow villagers were all killed, and that the people who look like them now aren't really them —'

'They aren't people either! I know this sounds crazy, but, believe me —'

'Oh, not the alien theory again?' Blake wanted to shake her. There was certainly something extreme going on. Something beyond the technology that he was used to. But he knew what human beings were capable of. The minds who'd come up with napalm and concentration camps were certainly capable of creating these clones, or whatever they were. 'Melissa, if aliens came here to invade, why wouldn't they just do it like *Independence Day*? Zap us all with their blasters?'

She was biting her lip, her eyes glowing with anger, and suddenly Blake realised that he'd been almost deliberately provoking her, wanting to shake something out of her. He was still deeply divorced, and, unfortunately, still deeply divorceable.

'Look!' she snapped, grabbing his arm to stop him from marching off along the sand. 'There may be no bombs, no guns, no hurry. But it's still an invasion. How else do you explain it? I can't!'

He softened his tone, feeling guilty. 'I know some very weird stuff is happening. I know the world seems to have slipped out of focus, but that doesn't mean there isn't a reasonable explanation.' He slipped from her grasp to head for the house.

'That isn't "reason".' She danced into his way, her feet doing a little shuffle with the breaking waves, and grabbed his shoulder. 'It's denial. And it's because you're scared of the truth and what it might mean that you're trying so hard to avoid it!'

Blake looked away, out to the bland modern sunset, disturbed by her words.

And by the terrible feeling that they might be true.

After work the next day, Blake picked Melissa up in his car, and they drove out in the direction of the nursing home. He didn't tell her, as they whizzed along the country roads, that he'd dreamt about her last night. She'd been burning a vast bonfire of his photos. For some

103

reason, it had been a really good dream.

Even if she was a UFO nutter, he thought, as he glanced at her sitting beside him, her too-serious eyes watching the bushes by the road like something might leap out of them, she was a very sweet UFO nutter. He was certain that she'd done something different with her hair today. But, being a bloke, he had no idea what and didn't want to reveal his ignorance by asking.

At Melissa's request, he parked the car a long way from the entrance to the nursing home. They got out, and scampered across to where some scrub woodland ran alongside the road. Blake felt like they were sneaking off school, or running away from his parents' house to go and snog in the woods. Which wouldn't actually be –

He fell against the trunk of one of the trees, stumbling blindly as waves of pain rushed up his brow into his forehead. It was so intense that he had to literally grit his teeth to avoid screaming. It was as if something had shifted position inside his head, grinding against the inside of his skull as it went. It was still shifting, and with every twitch his nervous system reacted with this immense pain.

'Steve!' Melissa was shouting. 'Are you OK? What is it?'

He managed to open his eyes, to beg her to get him to a hospital.

And then the pain stopped again. He blinked, and quickly licked his lips. He took a quick breath, and managed a nervous smile for Melissa. 'Must be lack of sleep.'

He avoided all her questions and concern as they picked their way through the woodlands.

'It could be some sort of weapon,' she said. 'They fire it at you when they think you're getting close.'

'So why don't they just zap . . .' He noticed that dangerous look in her eyes. 'I mean, why don't they just kill me?'

They reached a low fence that divided the woodlands from the grounds of the nursing home. Blake took a long look at the lost souls being helped around the flower beds, and hoped that if his brain did get frazzled they'd put him somewhere that looked as nice as this.

Melissa tapped him on the shoulder, and pointed to where an old lady was sitting by the pond, staring into it. She seemed to be weighing her clenched fists against each other in endless debate, like some surreal garden ornament.

'Elizabeth,' said Melissa.

Blake put his foot on the lowest bar of the fence. 'What's the penalty for breaking into a nursing home?'

'You have to stay there.'

Blake hopped over and helped her climb after him.

They made their way across the lawns, Blake feeling very exposed by the open greenery of it all, and along a gravel path through a rose garden. Finally, they reached Elizabeth, sitting in her wheelchair by the pond. She didn't look up to greet them, absorbed as she was in her own reflection.

'Hello, Elizabeth,' said Melissa. 'This is my friend Steve. We thought we'd come back for another chat. When I came to see you the other day you said you were "with strangers". Do you remember? The last time I visited . . .'

There was no response.

'The wedding ring?'

The old woman looked up at them suddenly. 'That's right. You brought the other ring.'

Melissa glanced at Blake worriedly. 'How do you mean? The other ring?'

'I am two, not one.' Elizabeth giggled. 'Now we both have a ring!' Her tone suddenly became urgent. 'But you must not tell that woman!'

'Which woman's that?' asked Blake, bemused.

'The one that is dressed in my daughter's skin, of course!'

Blake and Melissa shared a long, disturbed look. Blake took the old woman's hands in his. He was certain now that Mary Madigan had hidden this old lady here because of her unfortunate capacity for blurting out secret plans. Good to know, in a way, that the enemy didn't descend to killing off pensioners. But whose skeleton had he plucked the wedding ring from? Melissa had told him that Elizabeth's husband had died many years before the Sweethope disaster.

'Elizabeth, do you know why you are here?'

To Blake's shock, the voice that came from the old woman was now entirely different. It sounded old, yes, but clear and somewhat petulant. Like it had fought its way to the front of a crowd. 'Because we are many, but we are one! We must breathe our own, not share your air.'

'Who must?'

Now the voice sounded very peeved indeed. 'You go too slowly. We need to help you on your way.'

'On our way?' asked Melissa. 'To where?'

'On your way to your destiny.' Elizabeth, still talking in the officious, uptight voice, gave them one of her lovely smiles. 'You go too slow.'

'Our destiny?' If it wasn't for the vocal shift, Blake wasn't sure if he'd have regarded this stuff as anything more than ramblings.

'Your end. Your full stop.' Elizabeth nodded, happy at the grim words. 'Your destiny.' Like flowers opening, her fists uncurled. Each of her hands contained a wedding ring. She gazed at Blake and Melissa, one eye sparkling with life, the other dully reflecting the noonday sun. 'I am two, not one.'

Blake got slowly to his feet from where he'd been kneeling by the old woman. Melissa was looking horrified. Suddenly, he had many more questions. He glanced towards the house, wondering if they could wheel Elizabeth into some quiet lounge, or even escape with her to the car.

And saw Mary Madigan MP, a harried-looking nurse

trailing in her wake, marching across the lawns towards them.

'We've got company,' he said.

Melissa registered the imminent arrival, took her note-pad from her pocket, scrawled a note and urgently passed it to Elizabeth. The old woman grasped it in her palms, along with both rings, and began to weigh them against each other again, staring once more into the pond.

Blake decided that it wouldn't be decorous to be caught wrestling an MP's mother for her wedding ring. So he clasped his hands behind his back and chatted with Melissa about the weather until Mary Madigan was upon them.

'I knew you'd had problems in the past.'

Mary led them, with an honour guard of thunderous-looking nurses, to the front doors of the nursing home, addressing Melissa like she was a naughty schoolgirl. Blake was watching the MP's movements with the interest of an ornithologist.

'But I'd heard you'd recovered. I see I was mistaken. You're still deluded.'

Blake shrugged. 'Blame me. I've been tracing Sweet-hope survivors and I thought it would be good to meet your mother.'

'Good?' she shrieked at him. 'Pummel a confused old lady with questions she can't answer? That's your idea of "good", is it, Mr Blake?'

Blake paused for a long moment, and then smiled. 'Well, that's the interesting thing. She doesn't actually seem all that confused.'

The two of them locked stares. Blake felt the weight of the woman's will, but wasn't about to back down. Not now he was so close.

Mary Madigan was the first to break the silence. 'I shall be taking out an injunction forbidding either of you from setting foot in here ever again.' She spun on her heel and stalked out of the home.

107

As soon as she was out of earshot, Blake whispered triumphantly into Melissa's ear. 'How did she know my name?'

Philip Gates was working in his office, signing letters that would send police officers to or away from things that needed, or most certainly didn't need, their presence. In the background, he had the television on, listening to what the newsreader was saying. There was a map of Antarctica on the graphic behind him.

'There is certainly deep division amongst the member states as to the effect of oil exploration on this natural wasteland . . .'

Philip Gates nodded at that. Then he felt the connection forming, and put his pen down to concentrate.

Patrick and Pauline Leonard, and their children, Fiona and David, were watching the same item on the ITV early evening news.

The Leonards were sitting absolutely still.

They had concentrated in order to connect. The chemical change had swept through their bodies, and turned their eyes completely white.

Their eyelids were flickering wildly. The bodies, they had found to their amusement, thought their minds were dreaming when they were connecting.

Mary Madigan MP sat at her desk, leaning slightly forward in a position of utmost concentration, her eyes blank as she connected.

Gates was connected now, his arms rigid by his sides. The news report continued to play in the background, its graphics reflecting off the blank white ovals of his eyes.

'Professor Gerald Ryle, chief mineralogist of the Nuclear Research Institute, is leading the scientific community's argument against these new plans . . .'

Gates ended the connection and tapped his chin as he watched the screen, his pupils growing back into his eyes. He smiled at a picture of the bearded Professor Ryle. 'Hello,' he said.

The next morning, Blake was walking across the Zentex complex, on his way to work, having got his overall from the overall building, when he ran across two familiar figures. He'd seen them in the pictures that were everywhere in the factory complex. They were the children in that family group shot of the Leonards. The blonde little girl and her brother were amongst a group of children playing on a climbing frame at the edge of the housing area.

This must be Fiona, Blake realised, stopping at the shock of it. He almost wanted to go over and ask if she still had a green, hand-knitted woollen jumper with her name on it. Or rather, an exact copy. That might have been why they locked the villagers in the church, Blake thought, shivering suddenly. To record every detail of their looks, clothes, body language. Had that taken an evening, or had eyes been looking down at the village for weeks or years, watching Fiona skip and play by satellite? Perhaps *they*, whoever they were, had had agents among the villagers for long before the disaster, making notes.

He was going to walk on at that thought, but suddenly he realised. The Sweethope disaster had been several years ago. And yet these were still children. They were playing listlessly, uninterestedly, as if it was something they were obliged to do, but they were still visibly the same age they'd been when the disaster occurred.

One little girl fell from the climbing frame and started to cry. Blake watched as the others stopped what they were doing and gathered around her, staring down at her wordlessly, as if fascinated by her tears. Some of them put their hands over their ears. Not as a nasty gesture, but simply, it seemed, because they didn't like the noise. She cried even more loudly, and they started to walk away, to head back to their homes. All except Fiona, who stayed watching her.

Blake took this as his opportunity to intervene. He walked over to the crying girl, helped her up, and gave her his hankie to wipe her face. 'Come on, there's nothing to be frightened of. Are you OK? Your mates are a bit silly, aren't they?'

She smiled at him, happier now. 'Ta.'

Blake turned to the little girl who was still watching them. 'It's Fiona, isn't it? Fiona Leonard?'

She looked unsurprised. 'Who are you?'

'I saw a photograph of you, in a newspaper, the morning after your village, Sweethope, disappeared.'

'I was just a child then!' It sounded like something that she'd been taught to repeat whenever anybody said anything about the disaster.

'And you're just a child now, aren't you?' Blake whispered.

She hadn't changed in the slightest since that photo was taken. Puberty was never going to catch up with Fiona Leonard. She smirked secretly back at him.

'Do you remember anything about that night?'

She just turned and walked away. The girl Blake had helped gave him another sweet smile and scampered after her.

Blake stared after them, feeling angry suddenly. The people who had been murdered in Sweethope had had everything stolen from them, including, in at least one case, the dignity of adulthood.

As he was thinking that, the man in the blue overalls who'd been watching him the other day walked past. And winked at him.

Joanna Ball was not at all surprised when Mystic Meg from Norfolk showed up at her building. It was the way with people who had a formula for fuel from water or the plans or a perpetual-motion machine. They didn't go away. The fact that this one had attached herself to an ex-husband that he was still rather fond of was doubly galling.

Nevertheless, the receptionist had been assured that this mad woman was delivering something from Steve Blake, so Joanna had allowed her up.

The photographs that Melissa – Joanna vowed not to call her Meg out loud – spread on her desk were thus doubly amazing. Very Steve to pull them out of the hat like that. She held up one of the mass grave underwater, a slow smile spreading across her face.

Sitting opposite her, Melissa was looking vindicated.

'Did Steve say how soon we could send our own divers down?' Joanna asked her.

The smug look on Melissa's face faded. 'You, erm, can't . . . The whole lot went up just after Steve took these.'

'So these are all the proof you've got?'

'Well, it's a pretty big "all"!'

She'd gone into banshee mode again. Joanna toyed with a photo, reluctant to meet her gaze. These were pretty damn impressive, and from someone who used to be a trusted correspondent. Steve, despite his abiding interest in fakes, would never fake a photo himself. He was too interested in the truth. Tiresomely so. Even if he was bonking a woman like . . . She glanced suspiciously at Melissa. 'Why didn't Steve bring these to me?'

'I think after the last meeting he feels uncomfortable.'

Joanna nodded slowly, understanding. They were back in Enid Blyton territory again. 'He doesn't know you're here, does he?'

'No. But I know we need your help to get the photos placed.'

Joanna smiled tersely. 'Melissa, if Steve wanted to place them he could ring any editor in the country.'

'He feels . . . he's been away too long.'

He feels? 'This is Steve Blake we're talking about.'

'I know.'

111

'You don't really know him at all, do you?'

'What?'

Joanna got to her feet, feeling halfway between malice and compassion for this poor, deluded woman in a cardigan. 'I think introductions are in order . . .'

Joanna led Melissa through the cuttings library, to the section labelled STEVE BLAKE. She took a couple of files at random, and spread the prints from them out on one of the illuminated tables. Images of death, torture and suffering. Steve's three specialities. She watched Melissa's face as she leafed through them.

'What made him want to leave this behind?' she asked, interested in exactly the worried and potentially terminal way that Joanna expected.

'If he hasn't told you I'm not going to.'

'You don't like me much, do you?' She looked up from the prints.

Joanna didn't want a row with a mad person. 'I don't know enough about you to like or dislike you.' She paused for just the right length of time to make her point. 'I just care about Steve.'

'I think he's capable of looking after himself.'

Joanna spoke more sharply than she intended. 'No he isn't! Not yet. He doesn't know what he wants.' Time to find out the answer to the big question. 'Did you know about his ex-wife?'

'I didn't, no.' She looked all innocent. 'But I don't see why that should concern me, do you?'

'No . . .' Joanna found, to her surprise, that she was quite pleased by that answer. 'But I think you should know it was me he was married to.' The impact was quite gratifying. Melissa glanced quickly back to the photos, unable to look Joanna in the eye.

Nice to know that Steven was still picking up the waifs and strays.

* * *

That afternoon, Blake was assigned to a higher level of responsibility: placing software boxes on to a pallet, assembling orders, item by item, from a list.

Just when he was starting to wonder how many days of this he could take in the name of investigative journalism, a chime sounded over the PA system. The workers round him all stopped what they were doing and happily headed for refreshment trolleys that were wheeled in at every exit. He went to get the last item on his current list off the shelf before joining his colleagues, but one of them, a 'Blue', noticed that he was still working, came back over and tapped him on the shoulder.

'Come on, friend, we like to share our tea break,' he said.

'I won't be a minute.'

The man sighed mockingly, as if sharing the common feeling that this was just one of those jobs you couldn't help but be swept up in. He patted Blake on the shoulder and went back to get his tea.

Blake found his last item, and saw the note on the front of the box, indicating its destination. There he saw a familiar name. 'Ordered by: J. Wilson. British Nuclear Power. Quantity required: 79 units.'

Blake glanced about him, pulled out his notebook and noted the items ordered.

He jumped when a figure appeared at his shoulder. It was the sharp-faced chancer he'd noticed the day before.

The man winked again. 'I shouldn't go showing anybody you can write, man. Education's the new leprosy here. Know what I mean?' Then, with an enigmatic smile, he went on his way.

After a moment of bewilderment about what on earth the man had been on about, Blake went back to his task. He moved along to the next package and the next, spotting a number of familiar names. He was getting to be able to spot a Sweethope survivor's name without having to really think about it. After a moment, he crossed to the order board and started to search down that list as well.

He went back to the first package as he saw that Beck had re-entered the workspace and was heading straight for him, that cheerful smile on his features again.

'If you're that keen to work, Steve, drop these off at P.D.U. for me,' he said, holding out a package.

Blake dropped the book into his pocket and took the package. 'P.D.U.?'

'Program Development Unit. It's in Block C. Just across the lawn.'

So Blake walked across the lawn and took his package to Block C. The interior of this part of the complex turned out to be staffed by an entirely new sort of drone: the 'Whites'. They looked like computer programmers to Blake. He was sure they were resisting the temptation to cover their white overalls in badges. Several of them sported those trendy little hobo beards that made him feel happy to be old. Blake stood inside the doorway, unnoticed, and watched as they marched excitedly to and fro, between long tables of linked PCs. The programmers had obviously not decorated the walls of their abode themselves. There was not a poster of that impossibly buxom woman from that computer game in sight. Instead, there were mottoes like: 'Think laterally, friend!' and 'Say something Nice about a Fellow Worker!' There were several whiteboards set up as well, on which were scrawled in felt tip sprawling diagrams of lines connected to boxes.

After a while, one of the programmers looked up from his work station and noticed Blake and his package. 'Just put it in there,' he said, gesturing to a room. 'And toddle off, would you?'

The door was marked NO UNAUTHORISED PERSONNEL. It was locked by an electronic card lock on the wall beside it.

'Sure.' Blake nodded solemnly. 'Yeah.'

The programmer had returned to his work. Then he realised something was wrong. He looked up again with a theatrical sigh, pulled a card with a magnetic strip from his pocket, and, using the minimum of effort, swiped it down the channel in the lock. 'In there. Through *this* door. Under code B.' He shook his head as the door swung open and Blake stepped merrily inside. 'Day-workers!'

When the door closed behind him, Blake found himself in a storeroom, metal shelves filled with colour-coded disks in rows, like the CD section in a public library. He found the row marked CODE B and placed the disks from his package in that row.

Then he found CODE A, took a disk from it, and slipped it into his pocket.

'Not yet!'

Patrick Leonard put a restraining hand on the arm of the security guard who'd been about to leave his office. They were watching a monitor. On it was the image of Steve Blake in the storeroom, about to leave with his prize.

'It's under control,' Leonard assured the security man.

At the end of the working day, after they'd changed back into their everyday clothes, Blake and his software-packing colleagues joined the rest of the day-workers in the long trudge across the estate, through the underground tunnel, to the front gates of the main building.

Blake was shocked to see that Beck, the blue-overalled, edgy man who had spoken to him earlier, and several others were searching everybody on their way out. The disk in his jacket suddenly felt very heavy. This hadn't happened before.

'Random search,' muttered the chap beside him. 'They can't be too careful, can they?'

Blake wondered if he could make an excuse and drop the disk somewhere. No, just moving back from the mass of moving people would be an admission of guilt.

'It's only a search. Please understand,' Beck was saying to the employees as they passed. 'It's not that we suspect you personally, it's that we don't want anybody taking advantage of Mr Leonard's trust.'

Blake tried to look calm as the edgy man with the weather-beaten face frisked him, slapping down the outside of his legs and then the insides like a professional.

'Nothing to be worried about, my friend, nothing at all,' he murmured. He had a gentle Lancastrian accent. 'Open the jacket.'

Blake stiffened as the man slapped his hand right over the secret pouch in the lining of his leather jacket. Their eyes met for a moment, the man looking surprised. It was all over. He was going to be thrown out on his ear, possibly charged with theft, and there wasn't necessarily going to be a newspaper to back him up.

The man reached inside the lining of Blake's jacket.

Found the disk.

Palmed it into his own pocket like a magician and whispered conspiratorially to Blake. 'Where did you get it?'

'Program Development.'

The man nodded, sizing Blake up. 'Not bad for a first timer. Hopelessly off target, but pretty damned audacious I have to say.'

Beck looked up from where he'd searched three workers in the time the long-haired man had been searching Blake. 'Problem, Gary?'

'No, no.' Gary waved aside the query. 'We were just chatting. Steve here's taken, er, quite a shine to the place. Wants to see what sort of roof Mr Leonard puts over our heads. He's thinking of moving in.'

Beck smiled his boxer's smile again. 'Good lad, Steve! I had a feeling about you from the start!'

'OK if I show him now?' The man called Gary made to lead Steve off.

Beck waved them out of the door. 'Be our guest.'

* * *

116

Gary Cartwright was his name, and Blake was startled to find that he and his father actually lived on the Zentex estate. He led Blake across the complex, past a play area and a cluster of small units that included a newsagent's, a grocery shop and, to Blake's surprise, a pub, the British Lion.

'Wouldn't go in there,' Cartwright advised him. 'You can't get a proper pint. All that bottled rubbish. Good quiz machine, mind you.'

He showed Blake into his square house with its little square garden, one of a row of square houses. The living room was covered in piles of magazines and computer junk, but otherwise had a kind of style to it. Amongst the mess, a frail-looking old man was asleep on the sofa.

'Don't worry about Dad,' said Cartwright, leading Blake to his PC on a corner desk. 'He'll be dead to the world until supper time.' He pulled out another chair for Blake and booted up the computer. 'It's mainly because of his health care that we're here at all.'

'They look after the workers' dependants as well?'

'From the cradle to the grave.' Cartwright slipped the disk from his sleeve and inserted it in the machine. 'Pull up a pew.'

Blake did so. Cartwright punched a few keys and a Zentex logo came up. Then a list of enclosed files.

'See what you were trying to nick? That's a sub-branch of something they were working on last week. What makes you want to steal that?'

'I'm working for one of Zentex's rivals.'

To Blake's consternation, Cartwright laughed at him grimly. 'A bad answer for two reasons. One, Zentex doesn't have any rivals, on account of they make the best operating software in the world. And two, any industrial spies know that once it's already on disk, it's old news.'

'So why didn't you turn me in?'

'Because I've been watching you. And I think you think this place is as unhealthy as I do.'

Blake blinked. 'But they've given you a job, they've

117

given you security –'

'Yeah, yeah, yeah. But I'm not one of your Americans or your Japanese workers. I'm British. *Ipso facto*, I bite the hand that feeds me. Sure the Leonards saved my skin, sure they saved his.' He jerked a thumb in the direction of the sofa. 'Sure they put a roof over our heads. But –' he tapped his nose furtively '– what's in it for them?'

Blake was warming to this man. 'Why don't you ask them?'

'And lose my five-year bonus on disciplinary grounds? No way. I didn't say I wanted to leave. I just want some of their power. In their programs there's stuff buried I've never even dreamed of. And I've hacked into every major software house in the world. So I want to know what's going on.'

'How do you mean?' Blake saw his sudden interest startle Cartwright. 'What sort of stuff? Like . . . What are they called? Computer viruses?'

Cartwright looked at him as though he were a foolish child. 'This is beyond viruses. This is . . .' He smiled edgily. 'Pity I can't show you, eh? If we could just get into that Development Suite . . .'

'I take it you haven't been issued with a key?'

'Not exactly. They know I worked in computers, but they don't know that I could tell their Head of Development a thing or two. I lied all over my entrance examination. Guessed what they were after. Ah!' He'd been rummaging in his desk drawer. Now he produced the sort of device that Blake had seen used in shops to swipe credit cards. 'Give me your banker's card.'

Blake did so. Cartwright swiped it through the machine and handed it back to him.

'I made a master of all the doors on my first night here. Should do the trick.' He leant back in his chair and chuckled. 'They call it security. I call it a push-button obstacle race.'

* * *

They walked back across the complex, heading towards the P.D.U. in the twilight, as Cartwright explained his philosophy.

'Don't get me wrong. The system here works very well. Very neat and tidy. Everybody's on basic pay, but if you make it to Grade Black in five years you make it to the three-hundred-per-cent bonus. And there are similar bonus packages past that level. All the way up.'

'So paradise is always round the corner?'

'But not that close if you mess up. They can pull the rug from under you the day before your five years is up, given sufficient reason of course.' Cartwright's jolly tone indicated that he was never going to give them that, because he was never going to get caught.

Beck emerged from a door in the building they were passing, and called happily to Blake. 'You still here?'

'This one —' Cartwright indicated Blake '— he's got so many questions, John! I think he's going to make the team in record time!'

Cartwright slapped Blake's shoulder as Beck moved on. 'We are definitely in a fish barrel gunfire situation here.'

The mutant credit card worked admirably, and the door to the P.D.U. suite swung open. Cartwright refused to switch on any of the lights in the darkened room, so the only illumination as he tapped away at a keyboard was the gothic glow of the monitor itself. He glanced up at the clock in the corner as he sat down in front of a monitor.

'Keep an eye on the second hand, Steve. I can only time-lapse the cameras for a six-minute sequence. And it's taken me six months to do that.'

'You do this every night?' Blake boggled at the thought of this human rodent burrowing into Zentex's systems from the inside. It was comforting that all their careful selection processes and high security couldn't stop a creative individual like Cartwright from buggering everything up.

'And I'm still no further on. I can get into most of their

119

programs OK, but I can't crack the encoding.' He glanced up at a security camera in the corner of the room. 'And it's no fun working in six-minute bursts. Us programmers, we can't work unless we get to play "Doom" every sixty seconds, you know?'

A thought came to Blake as he watched Cartwright's slim fingers scuttling over the keys. On the screen, a maze of linked programs was developing in graphic form, looking like an atomic diagram of conspiracy. Security barriers kept flashing up as Cartwright tried approach after approach.

'If you did manage to break in, could you alter a program in development?'

'I'm not interested in sabotage, Steve!' Cartwright sounded horrified. 'I just want to know! I'm a control freak.'

'But if you were interested, you . . . could?'

Cartwright sighed with mock conceit. 'Since you ask, I could make software so faulty that the whole system would collapse. Banks, companies, government departments would all be at my command.'

'And Zentex Software could do that too?'

'Sure. If they wanted to.' Cartwright flicked a bemused glance at Blake.

He stared levelly back. 'What makes you think that they don't?'

Cartwright frowned for a moment, his fingers leaving the keyboard. Then he glanced at the clock again. 'We've got to go.'

With scavenger speed, he shut down the computer and hustled Blake out of the room.

For some reason, Cartwright wouldn't let them try again that same night. Blake got the feeling that, for the first time in ages, the young man was actually afraid.

Patrick Leonard sat on his sofa in his living room, his arms rigid by his side, talking to himself. 'We're certain he's made contact with another dissident.'

Detective Chief Superintendent Philip Gates sat on his chair in his office, his arms rigid by his side, talking to himself. 'And he's still connected?'

'Yes,' said Leonard. 'Now's the time to reel him in. Before he does any damage.'

'You're not telling me that one man can bring the castle down,' muttered Gates. 'What harm can he do when he's trailing a thread? All we have to do is follow it.' And with that, Gates suddenly shut his eyes.

Leonard blinked with surprise and got to his feet, looking rather angry. He headed for his front door. He was going to his office.

John Beck stood outside Mr Leonard's office door, waiting for him. He didn't like having to do this, but rules were rules, just like they'd been in the army. Beck had had an unfortunate incident in his regiment, one that he'd regret for the rest of his life. He'd been drunk, because everybody that night was drunk, and he'd got into a fight with this young lad about a girl behind the bar. Stupid. She didn't care for either of them. Beck had swung first. None of this kicking stuff. Good solid punch. And had broken his knuckle and the boy's nose. Splinters of bone entered the boy's brain, they'd told him later.

One of his own regiment.

Beck had taken everything after on the chin. He'd accepted his dismissal. Never touched alcohol again. Even gone to explain to the boy's dad and listened to the man scream at him for an hour until the wife kicked him out.

The army had been everything to him. So he went looking for something else. He got offers from old mates. Security firms, one in East Timor, even. He didn't fancy being in an army again. He might have joined a church of some kind, because he had found a solid nut of something spiritual inside. But how was he going to live?

The first wave of Zentex recruiting had sorted that.

He'd understood the questions they'd asked him completely. They came down to what sort of man you were. He'd told the truth and got in. Kept his nose clean. Had a laugh with the boys with his pint of orangeade. Lived on-site. After a year, he realised he was whole and settled, and planted a tree in his little garden.

Having got all that, he knew there were things he had to give.

Mr Leonard rounded the corner by his office, popping in for a spot of late-night work as he usually did. He raised a merry eyebrow to see Beck there.

'Sorry to bother you, sir, I thought we'd better have a word.' He stepped out of the way to allow Mr Leonard to unlock his door. 'It's about Cartwright. I think he's been spying for the opposition.'

'Cartwright? That's an interesting idea, John.'

Beck had always liked the clipped, precise tone in Mr Leonard's voice.

'What makes you think that?' Leonard asked, as he entered his office, poured himself a whisky and went to sit on his sofa.

'I've seen him and a Grade Red fraternising, sir.' Beck remained standing. He'd taken his cap off before coming into the office. Now he was twisting it awkwardly in his hands.

'Fraternising? Has it been getting in the way of their work?'

'Not exactly, no, sir.' Beck found that he was having trouble with what he had to say. It was like ratting on one of your own lads. 'I really don't like doing this, sir. Last night I saw them coming out of Program Development! That's off limits for Reds and Blues . . .' His voice died away as he met that powerful, infinitely compassionate gaze. 'As you know.'

'I see. What's he called, this casual that Cartwright has fallen in with?'

'Blake, sir. Steve Blake.'

Mr Leonard seemed almost amused. 'And you think he's a threat?'

'Not to the whole section, sir.' Nothing could be a threat to that. 'I'm not sure what he's up to. But I'd rather not have him in with my lads. If that's all right with you, sir.' That was a good compromise. A bit of a gentle hint. Just don't let this bloke bugger up my little corner.

Unfortunately, Mr Leonard frowned disapprovingly. 'I've spent a long time trying to create harmony here, John. A balance between the company's requirements and yours. Security, guidance, opportunity . . . my five-year plan.'

Beck found that he was suddenly babbling. 'Of course, sir. We're all very grateful.'

'I may have to be cruel to be kind.'

'You mean . . . get rid of Cartwright, sir?' Beck hoped that was what he meant.

'You are the section leader. You have to be responsible for your own men.'

Christ. Beck's mouth went dry. He'd said just the wrong thing. He was teetering on the edge of messing up again. 'I've only got four months, sir,' he pleaded. 'Before —'

Mr Leonard reached out and patted him on the arm. 'I'll be monitoring your section very closely,' he said.

Beck stared at him, and felt his whole world in the pit of his stomach. Again.

'That'll be all, John,' said Mr Leonard.

9

LATE CAPITALISM

Blake was lying with his head on the floor, his feet in Melissa's window seat. She was lying along it, and their feet were mingling, sort of, by accident. He was trying to concentrate on his theory.

'No, listen. Mary Madigan said her mother already had Alzheimer's before Sweethope, right?'

'Right.' She sounded dubious. As if he was about to have a go at her alien invasion theory again. He decided to steer clear of that.

'Let's just say she has been the victim of, I don't know, some sort of psycho-spiritual takeover –'

'Oh. Not as far-fetched as an alien invasion, then?'

Blake ignored that. Granted, he had been struggling to construct something even slightly rational from his encounter with Elizabeth Madigan, not to mention that weird meeting with little Fiona, but he wasn't going to buy into anything as ragingly camp as a full-blooded alien invasion. 'A lot of her memories have already gone. Her true self is only half there. So her mind wanders and she talks from both sides. Her real self, and the self they've . . . I don't know, programmed her with. Perhaps she was some sort of experiment where they . . . kept the original bodies.'

It sounded lame, and Melissa responded appropriately, playfully. 'And why do they let her?'

He sat up and faced her. 'I suppose she hasn't been a threat, has she? Just a confused old lady who nobody listened to until we came along. Maybe they don't want to harm one of their own?'

124

'Maybe Joanna needs to hear this?' Melissa said, hopefully.

Blake knew full well what Joanna would say if she heard it. 'I, erm, think she needs a bit more than our old lady to go for it.'

'She's already going for it.'

Blake saw Melissa react to his puzzled expression. She looked half proud, half guilty at her actions, like the loyal member of the Famous Five she was.

'She's seen the photos.'

'What?'

'I went to see her. I took them.'

Blake failed to control the anger that rose in his stomach. 'So what inspired you to go behind my back?' He leapt up, grabbed the phone and started to dial. Who knew what havoc Melissa had created at the newspaper offices? What wild stories she'd told Joanna?

Or, said a small voice from inside Blake's paranoid unconscious, what wild stories Joanna had told her?

'Oh, I see!' said Melissa, flexing her stockinged feet. 'You think I should have been more open? The way you've been with me?'

Blake put one hand over the receiver as the phone at the other end rang. 'Yes, I —'

'Why didn't you tell me she was your ex-wife?'

Blake lowered the phone slightly, his worst fears already coming true. 'Does it matter?'

'It matters that I've told you everything, but you hide your past from me. We're supposed to *trust* each other!'

Blake was about to bellow something about trust being a two-way street when Joanna answered her phone.

'Joanna?' It wasn't quite a shout. He took a deep breath and levelled his tone. 'It's me. I *just heard* about the photographs.'

Melissa wrinkled her nose at him.

He wanted to say, Listen, I'm a professional, just because my assistant has some weird ideas . . . And once upon a time he would have said just that, but now he found he couldn't. Which was just as well, because, to his surprise, Joanna started to congratulate them both on the photos and their work in general.

'Well, I'm glad you liked them.'

She told him the bad news then.

'No one will go with them?'

She protested that she really needed more to help him.

'Well, I'm glad for your help so far, you know I am. The Zentex stuff has been brilliant —'

Her shout of 'What Zentex stuff?' stopped him in his tracks.

He found all the relationship angst had drained from him, replaced by that now-familiar sense of being manipulated. 'What?' He glanced at Melissa. He needed someone to trust, somebody to be on his side. 'Are you sure? Maybe someone from your office?'

Joanna told him that people in her office did exactly what they were told.

'Right. OK. Yeah. I'll call you back.'

He hung up, turned to Melissa, and tried to defuse that 'I told you so' anger in her eyes with the seriousness of his words. He grabbed his jacket from the peg, suddenly aware of what he had to do next.

'Joanna said she didn't send me the Zentex cuttings. She had no idea there was a Sweethope connection.'

It had the desired effect. Melissa opened her mouth, astonished. 'So who did?'

Blake drew his car up in front of the Zentex complex. He'd driven like a maniac, but he'd enjoyed the drive none the less. With the moon over the ocean and the empty roads of the early hours, he could almost make himself believe that all was right with the world. Not that it was. He was on a serious mission, one that, if he thought about it too much, made this night feel like a calm interlude before the end. He just hoped that he'd

126

turn from what he had to do to see Melissa again.

The lights of the estate blotched the sky with their flare. Blazed out the stars. Blake showed his pass to a tired security guard and used his sudden hatred of the lights and the concrete buildings to look equally put out.

'Grade Red day shift. You're twelve hours too early, friend,' said the guard, after checking Blake's shift code.

'Yeah, tell me about it. They just called me in to do lights.'

The guard shrugged, and went back to his post to raise the barrier and let Blake's car through.

Blake waited outside the P.D.U. building, glancing at his watch from time to time. Where the hell was Cartwright? There was nobody else who was on their side, nobody who would have sent Blake into Zentex out of compassion. That meant that this was some sort of trap. And while Blake could walk away from it, Cartwright couldn't.

A security guard trudged along his route nearby. Blake ducked into the shadows. A few minutes later, he heard another set of footsteps approaching from another direction. He poked his head out from the shadow of the building.

It was Cartwright.

Blake stepped out in front of him.

The man leapt back at the sight of Blake, and stopped a cry with the back of his hand. 'Steve!' he whispered. 'Lousy entrance, but great timing. Listen —'

Blake wasn't in the mood. He wanted to deliver his warning and go. 'You've got to stop this, Gary. It's too dangerous. I'm telling you, you don't know what you're getting into!'

'Can't stop now, mate. I'm on a roll. I've got inside the program! The seagull has landed!' He took a credit card from his pocket and swiped it down the lock. The door of

127

the P.D.U. swung open, and he scampered inside, still energised by his own cleverness.

Blake, with a wave of rising apprehension in his stomach, had no choice but to follow.

Beck walked uncertainly to the corner by the toilet block where his four senior foremen waited. He had spent the day brooding about Leonard's veiled threat. He knew how he looked. His usually cheerful face crushed into a severe frown.

McKay, a greying, forty-something man from Aberdeen, broke the silence. 'So how did Leonard take it?'

'Worse than I thought.' He paused, then broke the news. 'He's only talking about getting rid of the section leaders.'

'What?' McKay exploded, looking between Beck and the fear on the faces of the other three. 'He can't! He's bluffing. Isn't he?'

'I'm not going to risk it.' Beck felt a fountain of anger suddenly rise into his chest. 'From the look on his face, Mr Leonard seems to know all about Cartwright. He's testing me. Making sure I don't mess up again.' Beck looked at his shoes, uneasy with the rage that was building inside him. 'I'm not letting Cartwright lose me my money just because he's suddenly decided to take a stroll on the wild side!'

'Time for a quiet word,' McKay muttered.

'Too right.' Beck nodded. 'Too right.' He led the others off towards the housing area.

Inside the P.D.U., Cartwright was clicking away at his usual keyboard just as before. Blake watched him fearfully glancing up at the clock overhead every minute.

'Look, Gary. I can walk away from this, you can't. You're the one in danger.'

Cartwright wasn't listening. He was concentrating on the hierarchy of images flashing up in front of him. This

128

time, Blake noted, there weren't so many prohibitions appearing in his way.

'You know who gave me the idea for a suicide virus? You did!'

Blake nearly shook him. 'Somebody wanted me to come here. I've been set up! Probably set up to catch you!'

The programmer's face was alight with the joy of his occupation. 'Think about it, right? All the time I've been working on how the main program protects itself, its anti-viral devices. And all along I should have been looking at how it self-destructs! It's designed to do that, right? To fall apart! That leaves gaps, places you can lever it.'

'Gary, listen to me –'

'Don't you see it? I reckon the security system is mutable, mind you. If it suspects it's being penetrated, it changes. I have to sneak up on it!'

Blake looked between the monitor, the clock and the security camera. Maybe Cartwright was infested with a suicide virus too.

Melissa had made herself a late dinner, and was picking at it worrying about what had taken Steven away so urgently. He'd muttered something about protecting his sources. In the background, she had the television tuned to a late-night news show. Round a table sat a genial, fine-featured man who'd just been introduced as some sort of government scientific advisor. A name plaque in front of him identified him as Gerald Ryle. The camera panned to introduce two more experts.

Melissa put down her fork when she realised that she recognised one of them. It was that man from the advert. James . . . James Wilson! The interviewer had just said his name. The man who Philip had been talking to . . . was the man who Steven had seen killed.

She turned the sound up.

'Global warming is already occurring faster in the Antarctic than anywhere else on Earth,' Ryle was saying.

129

'The moment oil exploitation begins, we can multiply the rate of meltdown by ten.'

'You're chief executive of British Nuclear Power,' the interviewer said to Wilson. 'Yes or no? Are you helping us to self-destruct?'

'Of course not,' replied Wilson, curtly. 'We're on our way to better use of our potential.'

'On our way to our destiny,' Melissa whispered to herself, hearing that schoolmasterly tone in Wilson's voice. The tone of the dark side of Elizabeth. 'Your end. Your full stop.'

The phone rang, making her jump.

She killed the sound on the TV and went to answer it. 'Hello?'

There was silence. The images of the debate flickered over her face. 'Hello?'

A familiar, confused voice at the other end. 'I . . . I . . .'

'Mrs Madigan? Elizabeth? Is that you?'

'You have to help . . .' Her voice sounded like it was coming from very far away. 'We're invisible because we're everywhere. Don't you see? You must warn people, you must warn me . . .' Melissa heard the desperation in her voice, the humanity trying to heave its head up out of the alien ocean within. 'Who wins? The army with one big weapon? Or the army with thousands of small ones?' It sounded like a serious question for Elizabeth Madigan.

'Can I come and talk to you again? Can you ask to see me?' asked Melissa.

Silence.

'Elizabeth? Hello? Hello?'

Elizabeth had been quite scared to find herself awake and in control of her body that night, just before she was due to go to sleep. She had read the phone number on the piece of paper that girl had given her, and had known exactly what she wanted to say to her.

And now she had done. Probably. Things got confused. But the words had all been there. If the human had listened!

She was angry at herself, as she heard the sound of Matron approaching her room. Divided, her mind raged, her hand dropped the receiver of the phone, and she couldn't quite claw it back on to its . . . phone thing.

Matron, when she arrived, helped the trembling vehicle back into bed, and tucked her in, the sweet child full of oxygen. 'Now then, Mrs Madigan, have you been trying to call Mary? You know we can arrange that. You only have to ask.'

Elizabeth nodded happily, but the eyes let her down. They stared at the piece of paper, which the right hand had failed to crumple enough. Matron followed her gaze, and went to pick up the paper, which she studied in puzzlement.

Elizabeth made herself shut up by holding her lips together.

Beck and the others had made their way to Cartwright's little square house. They'd gone by way of the stores, where Beck had used his authority to take, without signature, sacking, rope and sledgehammers. He was not under orders, he knew. But he was under silent orders. The sort that meant either the end or the beginning of everything.

'Cartwright!' he bellowed at the door. 'Cartwright! You better come out, or we're coming in!'

A neighbour opened the door adjacent.

McKay dealt with him with a hard look. 'Get back inside. Keep out of it,' he advised.

The neighbour did so.

There was still no response from the darkened flat. Beck, his fingers feeling too large, scrabbled in his pocket for his master key. He was the police on the estate. The judge too. And he was going to put an end to this cuckoo in the nest. 'You better be home, Cartwright!' he called. 'Cos we're coming in!'

Cartwright was tapping away faster and faster. They'd fled to hide in a corner for two minutes when the camera swept this way, but Blake hadn't been able to convince the programmer to leave well alone. The man was obsessed, his goal nearly in sight.

'A suicide chip, a chameleon code,' Cartwright was muttering now. 'These guys are nearly as brilliant as me!'

Blake couldn't leave him. Much as he wanted to.

Beck advanced into the Cartwright home, looking around for his quarry. He was relying on the others to restrain him when he found the offending Blue Grade.

Cartwright's aged father stumbled into view, holding his hands up in front of his body like the men were burglars or something.

'Just tell us where your son is, Mr Cartwright,' Beck said, fairly. 'And you won't get hurt.'

But the old man still backed away, mumbling something incoherent.

Beck ran forward and grabbed the old bugger by the shoulders. 'Tell me!'

Another six minutes had gone by. Cartwright leapt up from his keyboard and flipped off the power switch on the monitor in frustration.

They leapt out of the room just in time, Cartwright swinging the door closed behind them with a well-practised movement. Blake saw the red light come on atop the security camera inside the room.

Cartwright turned away, and Blake thought for a second that he was going to call it a night.

But then he heard the catch of breath in the man's throat, and turned to see what he saw.

132

At the end of the corridor stood a gang of men.

'Steve,' the leader said, his voice full of restrained fury. He stepped into the light, and Blake recognised him as Beck. 'I trusted you. And this is the way you repay me.'

There was another door behind them. Blake and Cartwright turned for it, but just as they did so, it burst open. Three men lunged at them.

The shock of physical contact stunned Blake. He hadn't been in a fight for a decade. He strained against the arm that slid around his thrashing neck, and then held it tight. He could smell the man's aftershave.

Beck and his men stepped forward. Blake felt his heartbeat speed up at the sight of what they were carrying. Mob weapons. Rope and sacking and hammers.

'Come on, John!' Cartwright's mateyness had taken on a frantic edge as he yelled from under another man's arm. His legs were twisting beneath him as his captor swung him off-balance. 'You know me! What are you doing? I thought we were mates?'

'So did I, Gary.'

Blake heard Beck breathing heavily, and fought down a quantity of vomit in his throat.

'And that's what really hurts.' Beck thrust a sacking hood over Cartwright's head.

Cartwright started to scream inside it.

Blake tensed as Beck approached him, holding out a hood for him. He was terrified beyond speech, because he knew this scenario. He knew where they were going. He was going to be submitted to the will of a yelling mob. He was going to be taken to the mass grave.

The darkness closed over his head.

He just managed not to scream himself.

Melissa ran out into the night, and threw her cassette recorder on to the front seat of her car, then buckled her seatbelt and roared off.

She was going to take Elizabeth Madigan's testimony. Before she was silenced.

The charge nurse led Mary Madigan MP along the corridor of the nursing home. 'I'm sorry to have called you out at this hour. It's just that you did say . . . If those people tried to get in touch . . .'

'Don't worry,' the MP purred. 'I wasn't doing anything special. You're certain they haven't been back?'

'Yes, we're certain. We've tightened up security. I really don't know how she got hold of their number.'

The nurse opened the door of Elizabeth Madigan's room. The old woman was lying in bed, but her eyes were open. They met Mary's instantly.

'Elizabeth,' said the charge nurse, uselessly. 'Mary's here to see you.'

'They know,' said the body of the old woman. 'I've told them everything.'

The charge nurse was saying something, trying to make the old woman aware that this was her daughter. But the two in the room with her were together now, and knew what they were talking about. They talked past her while the Elizabeth Madigan called out to them.

'I haven't got a daughter,' she said proudly, meeting the gaze of both her non-daughter and, inside, herself. 'We have no need of sons and daughters,' she read from what her other self had told her.

And yes, she knew that not-Mary knew that.

The charge nurse seemed to feel the atmosphere that had pervaded the room. She nodded to the Mary Madigan MP body and left.

'Mother,' said Mary, for the benefit of the deception and the disguise.

'Why do you keep telling them you're my daughter?' exploded the Elizabeth Madigan. 'I want to talk to the other two! They understood. Let me talk to the other two!'

But even as she said it, she knew the two in the room were talking through her, and that they would never let her talk to the other two.

The Mary Madigan MP took the hand of the Elizabeth Madigan and pretended to smile at her.

Blake heard his own breathing rasping inside the hood as the men jostled and shoved him down the corridors. Every now and then they kicked the feet from under him, just for the hell of it. They slammed his head against door brackets and bruised his elbows on hinges.

To make him not a person, but a sack of meat. Against that, he could hear Cartwright yelling, asserting his speech. Good idea, but Blake couldn't think of anything to say. He didn't want to be taken to the pit silent, but all he could think of was Melissa, alone, and how he'd hated his bullies in the playground, and how he'd stopped his job because he thought he'd gazed at them and become one of them.

They dragged the sacrifices through a familiar sound space, the packing area. Blake could hear the conveyor belts humming. And the friendly chatter of the night shift. Becoming quickly silent.

'Please!' Cartwright shouted. He'd heard them too. 'Lads! I promise, no more! Please let me go! I can't breathe! Let me go!'

There was, to Blake's rage, silence from the workers who must be on all sides now. Beck and the other men dragging them hadn't even had to say anything.

That was the price, then, of a human life, he tried to say as they dragged him through the door to the stairwell. A three-hundred-per-cent bonus.

But the breath was knocked out of him and he couldn't say it.

Mr Leonard was watching in his office, with four security men with batons and shields beside him. He watched the stair door close behind Blake and Cartwright. Then he dropped his hand, as if he were starting a race. 'Get over to D block double fast! Roof area! Quickly!'

The guards rushed from the office.

Leonard checked his watch and nodded, as if to himself.

There was a cold, sharp wind and the echoing sound of a high place around Blake when they pulled the hood off.

The first thing he saw was the hole. The round hole in the architectural miracle of the roof beneath his feet. Harsh floodlights allowed him to see with absolute clarity the pattern of the paving stones far below. The entrance area to the packing department. Plants, gravel, and a very hard-looking fountain that could pierce him.

He'd looked up and wondered about this hole, he realised. A nice solar feature. The sun made a brilliant display across the concourse at lunch time.

But it had a function. Christ, was this a regular thing? Was this the pit he was going to be thrown down as a matter of routine?

Cartwright's hood was pulled off, too. He yelled at the fall in front of him.

Beck stepped around to the other side of the hole and addressed them. He still sounded like a disappointed football coach, excusing himself for the imminent execution of his team. 'Five years I've got at stake here! You've got my five years in your greasy little hands!'

'John,' Cartwright was shrieking. 'I promise you, no more. I promise you, you've got to believe me!'

'I want more than promises.' Beck came to stand behind them, where the other men were holding their shoulders, their feet on the edge of the pit. 'I want to see you so clean you squeak. Understand?'

Blake sagged at the words. This was a punishment ritual, not an execution. They were only being threatened! That was why the workers beneath had been so silent.

'Anything. Anything!' Cartwright muttered. 'Please, stop! Stop!'

136

Blake saw Beck's face relax into an ugly grin and nearly emptied his bowels down the hole.

Then the shout rang out across the roof. 'Stop!'

Four security men, in helmets, with shields, were sprinting towards them.

Beck and the others spun round, surprised. The look on Beck's face was one of utter betrayal.

Blake lost the hands holding his shoulders and grabbed the arm of one of the men.

He didn't see just what happened to Cartwright. Maybe he tottered too far. Maybe his feet slipped. Maybe somebody just pushed.

He twisted and cried out as he fell through the gap.

'No!' Blake screamed, looking Gary Cartwright in the face as his every limb missed the edge of the circle and he sprawled in mid-air.

Fell screaming.

And quite quickly hit the paving stones with a thump like meat landing on a slab.

His limbs had passed through him at awkward angles, and his head was lost somewhere beneath him.

Blake staggered back from the hole as the security guards closed around them, holding on to Beck for support, looking at the sky, the startled men, anything but the flesh on the ground.

Beck clung to him right back. But unlike Blake, he didn't seem able to look away.

The driver was talking through the Elizabeth Madigan's mouth. 'When are we going to move? When are we going to be able to breathe again?'

The Mary Madigan was mixing a milky drink for the Elizabeth. Elizabeth saw, through her other half, that she was gently dropping a little puff of powder on to its surface and mixing it in.

'Why do you keep saying these things?' Mary muttered, staying within her disguise.

137

They both struggled for the body. Neither of them wanted to die. The driver shared its knowledge in a rush with Elizabeth, and stepped away to let her to the mouth. 'Why are you pretending you don't know, when you've got the taste of salt in your mouth?'

'I don't know what you mean.'

'You can't taste the salt? I can. Me and you and the rest of Sweethope buried at sea. They only have to look hard enough to find us. They've been to see me.' The driver chipped in, desperate. Elizabeth started to feel friendly towards the other side of herself. 'They know who we are.'

'Now you have to rest.' The Mary Madigan MP turned towards the bed, carrying the drink. She sat down, sniffed the brew, wiped the edge of the mug, and put one hand on the back of the Elizabeth Madigan's neck. 'Come along, Mother. Drink up.'

The driver and the Elizabeth Madigan both wanted to yell out that there was no need for the disguise, that the Mary Madigan MP was breaking the law by killing her own kind. They were unified and friends in this, but the driver was loyal to the cause, and couldn't disobey an order, and gulped down the milk with the tart poison that would kill both of them.

The driver and the one that was killing her had been friends, above the friendship they all shared.

The Elizabeth and Mary memories had been linked too, in the way that many of the memories they'd found in the cellular matter were.

And the driver and the Elizabeth Madigan were friends as they felt the poison enter the stomach and spread through the body. The driver offered the Elizabeth Madigan pain-free places to hide.

The Mary Madigan MP looked at her stolen memory's mother, laid its head back on the pillow and stood. Now she had to run for the door.

We know you have to run. So go, and take your cause with you to a dark place.

'Good girl,' she said.

She put down the cup and sprinted out.

Blake was no longer surprised to see that the leader of the policemen who arrived at the scene of Cartwright's death was Philip Gates. He went straight to Blake, as his scene-of-the-crime officers gathered around the body like vultures. Blake recognised the man with him as Patrick Leonard.

'You're becoming a regular bad-luck charm, aren't you, Steve?' Gates began.

'He was killed!' Blake shouted. 'You can't paint over this one!'

Gates, with all the time in the world, took an inhaler from his pocket and fired a puff into his mouth. Blake wondered that the man was tense enough for his asthma to be acting up.

'I've got a feeling about all this, Steve. Call it a copper's instinct, but this looks like a suicide to me.'

'Poor Cartwright,' Leonard chimed in. 'He wasn't the most balanced of men.' He glanced at where Beck was explaining desperately to a young policeman. 'Even you must have noticed that.'

'He was murdered!'

Gates shrugged. 'But who by? All those men over there have alibis. Or will have. You're the only one who admits to being up on the roof at the time. You can see how it looks.'

'You can't tell me what I saw!' Blake was still coming down from the procession with the sack, never mind the murder of Cartwright. 'You won't get inside my head!'

'Steve.' Gates must have inherited this practical, copper's malice from the original Philip Gates. Blake had heard it so many times before, from so many different law-enforcement agencies. 'If you were on the roof it could be murder. If you weren't, then I think it was suicide. Now. I'll ask you again. Were you up on the roof with him?'

139

Blake could only glower at him. He turned away, and watched Cartwright being put into a bag. The policemen were walking away from Beck, but he was trotting after them, as if wanting to offer more and more information. As if wanting to be punished.

Poor human bastards. All of them.

Melissa drew her car up in front of the nursing home with a swish of gravel. She'd narrowly missed another car that had rushed out of the gates, only at that moment switching its headlights on.

She quickly got out and ran in, taking her cassette recorder with her.

Mary Madigan drove fast through the twisting roads, missing several cars, making their drivers blare their horns.

She drove until she reached a lay-by, swung the wheel, and pulled up in it. These awkward things they'd learnt from the cell memories. These mysterious skills that made them feel like vermin, crawling through every narrow opening available.

How had she come to be a murderer? They'd decided, after Blake and the woman had come to the home, that the Elizabeth Madigan had to die. But why did it have to be her who did it?

She switched off the engine and leant back in the seat, grasping the wheel hard. She should have warned them all, but the Elizabeth Madigan's telephone call had stolen time from them. She'd had to do her murder straight away.

She waited for the moment to come upon her.

Gates and Leonard were walking away, and Blake was running after them, still shouting and pointing his finger. He knew he was out of control, but he couldn't help himself.

'You don't think I can touch you, do you?'

140

'The words come out of your mouth but they never make sense.' Gates' voice had adopted a sing-song quality, like he was toying with Blake, goading him into something rash.

'This one was a bit blatant for you, wasn't it? A bit clumsy. Maybe you're getting desperate.'

Gates swung to address him, smiling. 'Maybe you —'

Then his hands flew to his face, and he stumbled back, his back spasming as it connected with a wall. He sunk to his knees, shouting unintelligible things.

Blake heard a cry from behind him, and saw that Patrick Leonard had also fallen against the wall. Blood was bursting from his nose and mouth.

Blake looked between them, horrified.

The blood flowed from Mary Madigan's nose, mouth, ears and eyes. It covered her suit. It filled her vision. She cried out at the pain. Her own fault. Because —

The body of Elizabeth Madigan convulsed on its bed, blood bursting from every orifice. It thrashed as hard as its muscles could thrash, and the blood flew in all directions.

Melissa was yelling at the night receptionist at the nursing home. 'I have to talk to her. She *asked* to see me. This isn't a prison, is it?'

The receptionist had consulted some sort of list when Melissa arrived. A list of unwanted visitors, probably. 'I'm afraid you're going to have to leave, or I'll call security.'

If there was one thing Melissa hated, it was being treated like she was mad. 'I need to see her! She's been trying to tell me something very important!'

With an 'I told you so' look, the receptionist picked up her phone and hit a single number. 'Hello, Jack? Could you come over? I've got a problem on the front desk.'

Just as Melissa had decided to run up the stairs, she

141

saw somebody was running down them. A nurse, who was calling briskly as she came, 'Call an ambulance! Mrs Madigan's having some sort of attack!'

She turned and ran back up again, as did several others who emerged from a side room where they'd been having tea. Melissa, ignoring the yell of the receptionist, turned and sprinted up the stairs with them.

Gates made a choking sound. Blake was close by him now, looking down at the man, wondering what he could do to help. He didn't have much in the way of first aid. He would have guessed at a cerebral haemorrhage, the way that the blood had splattered down his shirt and tie.

The policeman opened his eyes suddenly, and Blake stepped back. They were blank white, the pupils had vanished. He glanced at Leonard. Exactly the same thing had happened to him. For a moment, Blake wondered if some sort of weapon, one of Melissa's zap beams, had caught these two. But he'd been standing between them when they'd had their seizures. He'd felt something, perhaps, a vague headache, but why it should have affected these two so much?

Astonished at his own audacity, Blake reached for the blood. He wanted to touch it, smell it. Maybe take it away and analyse it.

Before he could do so, Gates' pupils grew back into his eyes. He looked at Blake with a stare that was arrogant, detached, and totally alien. As if the blood on his shirt were a fashion detail.

He came from a different frame. And in that moment, Blake knew that what Melissa had said was true. 'Who are you?' he whispered. 'What are you?'

The thing that looked like Patrick Leonard slid up the wall to its feet. 'I think it's fair to say that I am not Patrick Leonard.'

Blake spun to shout at it. 'What are you? What do you

142

want? Why didn't you let them kill me when they had the chance?'

Gates also slid to his feet. He didn't bother to address his clothes, but just stood there. 'Because you're no threat. Simple as that.'

'If I was no threat you'd ignore me!' Blake wondered dizzily why he was insisting that these . . . whatever they were . . . should pay attention to him. 'And now I know more than ever!'

'And if you knew how little that was,' Leonard said, laughing, 'you wouldn't be standing there bragging about it.'

'But you saved me. Why did you save me?'

Gates smiled his knifey smile. 'Don't worry, you'll find out soon enough.'

And the two aliens looked at each other, adjusted their bloody suits with exactly the same awkward little tug, and walked off into the night like a musical-comedy duo.

Blake stared after them, wondering what would be more difficult: telling the world that it was being invaded, or telling Melissa that she was right.

The charge nurse was giving Elizabeth the kiss of life when Melissa and the matron and the other nurses ran into the room. Melissa put a hand to her mouth, shocked at the blood everywhere. Somebody had killed her, she knew in that second. Somebody had actually had this old lady put to death.

'Come on, Elizabeth, come on!' the charge nurse was saying, as she took a breath and began to pump Elizabeth's heart.

The matron took her pulse. 'How long have you been trying?'

'Two minutes.'

The matron shook her head curtly. 'Leave her.'

It was probably just the callousness of the professional, but Melissa reacted all the same. 'No!' she shouted.

143

But the charge nurse stopped all the same. She moved away from the body and touched Melissa on the arm compassionately. Melissa sank down and took Elizabeth's cold hand. 'I'm sorry, Elizabeth. I'm so sorry.'

She let go of the hand, and it fell limply by the side of the blood-spattered bed.

And Melissa suddenly found that she couldn't be in the same room as the silent, distantly professional nurses, because she felt responsible for bringing about the attention that had caused the old woman's death.

So she turned and fled out to her car, and drove off as fast as she could make the thing go.

Blake drove slowly back towards Mayston, feeling as if he hadn't slept for a hundred years. The police had kept him for his statement for another two hours, and now the signs of dawn were playing with the clouds on the eastern horizon. The world had taken another twist on its axis, and once more it was as if he was looking at his surroundings through a new frame.

Aliens. Bloody aliens. It was all true.

As he took a bend, he was surprised to see the flickering lights of emergency ahead. The blue of ambulances and police cars, the red and yellow of the fire service and the fire itself.

He would have driven past, but for a sudden horror at what he glimpsed in his rear-view mirror.

He stopped the car quickly on a verge, and jogged back to the scene of the accident, his teeth chattering with the cold of the night and the lack of sleep and the fear that was becoming his life.

There were trees scorched with a terrible heat, and that alien scent of floral death in the air and, at the centre of it all, its nose ploughed up against a fence, a terrible, familiar car.

A copper stopped him. 'There's nothing to see, mate. On your way.'

'I thought I recognised the car.'

'We've already got an ID for the owner.'

Blake wanted to say it for him. 'The owner's registered as Melissa Gates, isn't she?'

The policeman stared at him for a moment, and then gave a curt nod.

Blake felt the horror bite into him.

10

THE SECOND WAVE

Blake drove home, beginning to grieve. He hadn't realised what a space inside him Melissa had opened up. A place where fond things were stored. He hadn't started to feel the anger, but he was sure it would come. They had killed her, in one of the ways they always used to kill human beings, but they were letting him live, as if they needed a witness to their colonisation of the planet.

His mind stabbed back to the car crumpled against the tree. He was still in shock from Cartwright. He hadn't stayed to see Melissa tangled, her legs broken, her clothes and flesh fried into a foetal ball.

That thought made him start to cry before he knew he was doing it.

He drove into his parking space behind the artist's cottage wiping the moisture from his eyes, wanting to hit something. He was out of the car and on the way to the door before he realised that the lights of the house were on.

Melissa came to the window. Smiled and waved to him. Vanished again.

He started to rush forward, a smile lighting up his face.

And then he realised. The punch of it made him lean on the car to support himself.

It wasn't her. The bastards had replaced her. The shock of having his hope pumped up and then drained away, plus the lack of sleep and the shock, nearly made him faint.

He pulled the house keys from his pocket, and stumbled towards the front door, numb.

* * *

She was on the phone, obscenely, when he got inside, establishing her alibi with the police. Telling them that her car had been stolen from outside her house. She might even be talking to her ex, Philip Gates, now they were joined once more as the undead. Blake slumped into a corner, beneath his lists of the Sweethope diaspora, the photos and clippings. He stared at Melissa, watching the way she pushed back her hair, the shift of her hips under her skirt. There was no way to tell. Unless she suddenly started spasming, and blood flowed from her nose.

So, with a nightmarish sense of inevitability, he told her that he'd seen her car after it had been written off. She feigned indignation, called the garage responsible for the recovery, and then stared at him in mock horror.

'You were right. It's been written off!'

'No sign of the driver?' Blake played along.

'None. They think he got away. Bloody joyriders.'

Blake fell silent, stung by the familiarity of her words.

After a moment, Melissa came and sat beside him. She looked as tired as he did. 'What is it, Steve?'

He leant his head on his hands. 'What time did you get here this morning?'

'About an hour ago. Why?'

OK. He was going to risk it all. He had to ask, despite, or because of, his physical certainty that this was Melissa. Her movements, her thigh against his now, all spoke of her, but . . . 'Because I want to know I'm wrong to worry about who was driving that car!'

'You suspect me?' She looked like she'd been slapped in the face. 'I'm on trial?'

'Nobody said anything about a trial.' He got to his feet. Suddenly he felt like a jealous lover, questioning the comings and goings of his faithful partner.

Melissa leapt up, furious. 'Well, what would you call it?' She put a hand to her chest. 'You look at me and you don't know?! Suddenly *I'm* answerable to *you*? I've lived with this, Steve! I know what somebody who's been

147

replaced is like!' Her voice had that paranoid edge to it that made him wince.

'Every part of me tells me that you're still you.' Blake found himself yelling, the tightening screw of the night's tension being released. 'But I saw the car! It was a burning wreck! Your car. What am I expected to do? Shrug my shoulders and laugh at the coincidence?'

'Of course it isn't a coincidence! It's obviously a set up. Philip probably arranged it!'

'What for?'

'For this!' She held her arms out wide, looking at Blake imploringly. 'We don't trust each other any more, and he knows that's our only strength!'

Blake wanted to hold her. 'I want to trust you. I really do.'

'But?'

Blake remained silent. He'd been through too much. Both after encountering James Wilson and . . . before. This was as much about divorce as it was about invasion. Are you the person I first met? Or are you not the woman I thought you were?

Melissa shook her head at his lost expression, looking a little lost herself. 'I'm sorry. That's not good enough.' And she walked out of the artist's cottage.

Blake ran to the door after she went, wondering if he should run after her. Finally, he settled on locking and bolting the door. Then he staggered to bed, fell on it, and fell asleep fully clothed.

When Blake finally woke, around noon, and shambled into the front room of the cottage, contemplating taking his clothes off, he found a note from Melissa. It had been posted through the door. Roughly, if the condition of the paper was anything to go by.

'Elizabeth Madigan's inquest. They're holding it in Mayston today. (She died, you know. Suspicious haste.) Come along, if you want.' The letter went on to give curt

148

details of Melissa's call from, and meeting with the corpse of, Elizabeth Madigan. It was signed 'the Alien'.

Blake checked his watch, winced, and wandered towards the bathroom.

Pat and Graham had been on their way back from an emergency call to a motorway pile-up when it happened. Arlene, the driver of their ambulance, had yelled over their conversation in the back and suddenly accelerated. A moment later, they'd heard the roar of something mechanical passing straight over their heads. A light plane.

Arlene had brought the vehicle to a halt with her usual kung fu sense of immediacy, and they'd all tumbled out the back. The light aircraft, a Cessna, Graham had informed them, was definitely in trouble. A trail of grey smoke was sputtering from its engine. It was circling a ploughed field.

'Too small, mate,' Arlene had said.

The pilot went for it anyway, cutting the engine and gliding down towards the mud at far too steep an angle. Even as he did so, the paramedics hustled a stretcher from the back of the vehicle. They didn't like to watch accidents happen.

But he made it, angling down, and then bringing the nose of the little plane up at the last second so that it stalled just above the ground, and dropped on to its wheels, a little ungainly, but whole and safe.

'That,' Arlene said, admiringly, 'is the best emergency landing that I have ever seen.'

They waited for a moment.

Nobody got out of the aircraft.

'Come on,' said Graham grimly. He started to climb the gate into the field.

The patient was a smartly dressed man in his mid-forties, sitting upright in the cockpit.

149

'Banged my head,' he said, when they opened the cockpit door. 'Feel a bit groggy.'

Then he closed his eyes and was still.

They examined him swiftly. The credit card in his pocket named him as Philip Boyd. He was certainly unconscious, but there were no apparent injuries. They fixed a neck brace and stretchered him back to the ambulance.

They called the police about the aircraft.

Boyd's breathing was so shallow and ragged that, en route, they added an oxygen mask and a saline drip as well. The heart monitor indicated a sporadic and wilfully bizarre pulse. As the ambulance bounced round the corners of the country roads, the siren blaring, Pat leaned forward to try and wake the unconscious man. 'Mr Boyd? Philip! Philip! Can you hear me? Squeeze my hand if you can hear me!'

'His B.P.'s dropping, it's really low.' Graham consulted the monitor.

Pat looked puzzled. 'Internal haemorrhage?' She eased herself back to the patient. 'Philip! Philip!'

Graham shouted, to the front, 'How long to the hospital, Arlene?'

'About ten minutes,' she called back.

He looked back at the monitor. 'B.P.'s getting really low.'

'OK.' Pat nodded. 'Let's put a line up.'

Graham did so.

They heard the monitor alarm going a moment later: the squalling single note of flatline. She ripped open the patient's shirt and started a cardiac massage. This was so insane. This man was just dying, for no apparent reason.

Graham, his face now empty of its usual humour, had the paddles ready to fibrillate him. 'Charge, stand clear, shocking,' he said.

Pat moved back as Graham slapped the paddles against the man's chest. He triggered the pulse –

And the man stayed absolutely still.

'No pulse,' she said, astonished.

Not even corpses did that.

Blake was becoming familiar with the interior of coroners' courts. This one was tiny. He'd nodded to Melissa as he entered, feeling rather better for his shower. But she just gave him the tiniest of cold glances back. The seating arrangements meant that Blake had to sit next to her.

He perked up when the first witness took the stand. Mary Madigan, MP. She gave him a meaningful look when she stepped up to speak, looking at her smartest. The coroner, a thin, grey-looking man with ratty spectacles, treated her with vast deference, establishing the circumstances of the death. Finally, as Blake was shifting in his seat, he came to the point.

'Nothing in your mother's behaviour that night indicated she was likely to have taken her own life?'

'If there had been anything, any reason at all . . . I wouldn't have left her side for a moment.'

Mary certainly looked to be in a bad way. Blake had seen the physical effects when one of their number died. Now he wondered if the aliens felt grief for their fellows too, because, if this was an act, it was a very good one. She was shivering, white with shock, looking increasingly nauseous. Blake tried to catch Melissa's eye, but she was staring too.

'You mentioned a phone call which you feel may have disturbed her?' the coroner continued.

'Yes. She'd had visitors. Two people.'

She managed to look up at Blake and Melissa, and Blake suddenly felt like he'd walked into a trap, but then Madigan stopped, held on to the table in front of her with both hands.

'I'm . . . sorry.'

She reached up, touched the corner of her nose. There was a small drop of blood there. Blake was entranced. He

151

knew what was going to happen next.

It did. Sort of. Madigan's eyes closed, and she collapsed into her chair. Court officials rushed forward, and the MP became the centre of a murmuring group of concerned individuals. The nosebleed had become a flood, and Mary Madigan was breathing in vast gulps, screeching for air. She pressed an inhaler to her lips and sucked in its contents.

Blake quickly looked at Melissa. The aliens did this together, whatever it was.

And Melissa wasn't doing it. She glanced back at him with hard eyes, visibly wondering why he was so interested.

'We'll adjourn for thirty minutes,' said the coroner.

The ambulance roared through central Norwich, causing cars to move up on to the pavement.

Inside, Graham was continuing his attempts to make the body of Philip Boyd respond like any other human body would. Pat wondered if this was some sort of nightmare or test, if they were transporting a lifelike dummy to casualty. Graham had upped the charge on the pads and smeared Boyd's chest with conductive gel. Now he tried again.

'Charge, stand clear, shocking!'

He triggered the charge. Pat checked the monitor. Nothing. And nothing from the body, either. A real, animal, thing, even a corpse, would react to the electricity, its nerves and muscles making it leap. This one just took it and lay there. Graham mumbled something urgent and unintelligible and tried again. Still nothing. He glanced back at Pat, resigned.

'OK.' Pat nodded. 'Leave it. We've lost him.'

Graham put down the paddles and shrugged. 'How?'

The Philip Gates slowly came round, blinking the blood back from its eyes. The Philip Boyd had gone. He'd vanished from the whole. He sat up and started to wipe the blood from his uniform. The phone rang. This would be someone telling him what he already knew. But, above all else, he wanted to know why. Two in two days. Too many. Too quickly. He picked up the phone.

Melissa had avoided Blake in the intermission. He'd wandered about the precincts of the court, hoping to find Mary Madigan. But where her aides had spirited her away to, Blake couldn't tell. He was feeling a little better about Melissa, though. He'd felt his head start to throb slightly as Mary Madigan started to bleed, but Melissa seemed to have got through it all without a frown. Whatever this effect was, it seemed to affect humans slightly, and aliens utterly. The difference was vast. Unless Melissa was protected in some way. But no. They'd have protected Mary Madigan too.

Unless, of course, this display was for his benefit.

That was the trouble with paranoia. It was like megalomania. It made you into the centre of the world.

He returned to the court after the appointed half-hour. Mary Madigan managed to finish her evidence. There was a report from the matron of the nursing home, who stated that the poison involved was one that the institution used on a regular basis to control pests. She seemed very upset, and the coroner was comforting. Nobody else was implicated in the death, to Blake's relief. Perhaps Mary Madigan had taken some advice concerning slander. Melissa and he could both prove they weren't there when Elizabeth had been given the poison, and the implication that their influence had been responsible for her suicide . . . He smiled at the thought of taking on the aliens in the courts.

The coroner began his summing up. 'Elizabeth Madigan was elderly and infirm and undoubtedly was no longer capable of indicating her basic needs. The only clue that she may have been in some distress on the day of her death was her increasingly bizarre and disturbed behaviour. However, there is no way that the dedicated staff of the nursing home could be expected to watch her every move. My verdict is suicide while being of unsound mind.'

And that was that. Everybody got to their feet. Mary Madigan was led away, still very upset.

Blake and Melissa were left looking uneasily at each other.

Until Melissa turned and left.

Dr Sarah Armstrong always felt a little nervous when dealing with Philip Gates. He conducted his inquiries with the kind of arrogance one normally associated with juntas, as if he could have her dragged out into the street and shot her at any moment. He'd always been like that, ever since she'd first encountered him. He'd barged into her office at three o'clock that afternoon, and asked to see everything she had regarding the body that had been brought in the previous day, the Philip Boyd case.

So she'd taken a deep breath, ordered coffee, and found the files for him.

Now he sat on the other side of her desk, his nose cocked towards the ceiling like it was his office, imperiously reading the notes, page by excruciating page.

Sarah decided to speed things up for him. 'According to the paramedics, Mr Boyd showed no sign of any serious external injuries. He was an experienced light-aircraft pilot and it was a routine crash landing. He'd banged his head, felt groggy, then fell unconscious. In the ambulance he suffered a sudden deterioration.'

'And they have no idea why?'

'That's my job, not theirs.' Sarah was doing her best to indicate via her body language that Gates was taking up too much of her precious time. 'I'll send you a full post-mortem report.'

'It won't be necessary for you to do the post-mortem.'

Gates looked at her with that sneering smile of his. 'That's why I'm here.'

Sarah smiled back, hearing the crunch of jackboots. 'I don't understand.'

'The air crash involved a Ministry of Defence plane. That makes the post–mortem a Central Ops matter. We should be in charge of any such investigation.'

'And do you have the necessary authorisation to remove Philip Boyd's remains?' I mean, what is this, a fascist state?

Evidently not. Gates suddenly switched on his charm. Like it was an approach he'd learnt on a training course somewhere. 'I can't quite believe that we're sitting here arguing about a corpse like two butchers at a meat market.'

'Philip Boyd died in the ambulance on his way to hospital. And unless you get a specific order from the Home Office then, I'm sorry, but he stays here.'

He spread his arms like a haggling market trader. 'I'm doing you a favour!'

'Thank you, but I can do without your favours, Chief Superintendent.'

Next came the threats, like night following day. She'd never pressed him this far before. But she'd never hated the way this always went so much, before. She'd become a pathologist to impose order on the messy uncertainties of death. To make sure the dead got their due process, their witness. This man, and she was sure that he was the tip of a bureaucratic iceberg that one day she'd go to the *Guardian* about, wanted to banish order and run things through mates and favours and nudges. He always seemed to want to rush things through and brush significant details aside.

'I don't think you appreciate what you're getting into. Philip Boyd was an important person,' he said.

'You can be sure I'll treat him with the respect he deserves.' She stood up, willing him to go.

He stood as well. 'And when the news gets out that a chief executive of the Nuclear Research Institute died because of negligence, and that there was an attempted cover-up by the pathologist . . .'

She stared at him. You little bastard. You are everything I hate. She felt like grabbing his lapels and bullying him back, like the emotional toddler he undoubtedly was. She contented herself with a very hard look. 'My findings will be a matter of public record.' And then a smile that matched his, will for will. 'Keeping secrets isn't something that corpses are good at.'

To her great relief, he turned to go. Looked at her sideways, like she was something he was filing away, and left without another word.

She clenched her fist triumphantly. 'Yes!'

This Boyd bloke was going to get the most thorough post-mortem she had ever carried out.

Blake followed Melissa as she walked off down the steps of the coroner's court. 'You saw the bleeding?'

'Yes.' She didn't respond to his smile. 'Quite a show.'

'So one of them must have come to grief.' He quickly explained what he hadn't told her last night. About the seizures Gates and Leonard had suffered. He left out the bit about Cartwright. 'If we find out which one died this time, I think it gives us another way in.'

She was still not really listening to him. Blake shut up for a moment, and looked into her eyes. She was deeply hurt.

'What are you so excited about, Steve? The fact that Mary Madigan bled, or that I didn't?'

She marched off. Blake looked after her, and cursed himself for underestimating, yet again, what that woman had been through.

It was early evening by the time Sarah began the post-mortem. She'd had a word with her two most trusted lab

The stars of the TV series
From left to right: Leslie Grantham as
Chief Superintendent Gates, Douglas Hodge as
Steve Blake and Lia Williams as Melissa Gates.

Turning Points
When Steve Blake witnesses the explosive death of James Wilson, and Melissa Gates talks to a woman who claims that she is already dead (Jean Anderson as Elizabeth Madigan), their lives are changed forever.

The Face of the Enemy
Chief Superintendent Gates sits at the heart
of a web of intrigue.

Allies
Hard-bitten journalist Joanna (Sylvestra le Touzel) and inquisitive pathologist Sarah Armstrong (Caroline Lee Jackson).

Secrets
No matter how hard Blake tries to uncover the
truth, Gates is always there to keep it hidden.

Setbacks
The underwater evidence of the conspiracy
is obliterated, as Gates and Ferguson
(Ian Brimble) keep a watchful eye on Blake.

Together
Blake and Melissa stand united – but
will it be enough?

THEY ARE ALREADY AMONG US

assistants, got them to stay after hours. And she'd locked all the doors.

The body of Philip Boyd, naked but full of secrets, lay on the slab before them now. They were suited up in their green disposable smocks, ready to explore. In the movies, she'd be tucking into a sandwich right now. As if anybody could have managed that. You learnt to treat the human body as a building, sure. A normal place to be. But the smell always got you at a much more basic level. Supper was out of the question.

She activated the tape recorder beside the slab and spoke into the microphone that hung above the corpse. 'The accident victim is a male of forty-two years, Philip Boyd. Since death, rigor has set in and the victim is unusually discoloured. His skin is purple, indicating internal bleeding. Other than that there are no indications on his head or body of the cause of death. No lesions, no puncture wounds, no sign of any swelling at the front or back of the cranium. Simon?'

One of her assistants made the first incision, down the side of the head, and then the long one from sternum to stomach.

The smell was different to, worse than, anything she'd ever encountered before. The incision gave way, at the end, under the weight of the blade, as if –

As if the body was hollow.

'My God!' she said.

The two assistants turned away, trying to control their nausea. They weren't having much success.

The inside of the body cavity was hollow, fired like the interior of a blackened pot, fresh out of the kiln. Sarah stared into the empty shell in front of her, and clicked on the recorder once more. 'An unusual and . . . extreme internal deterioration has occurred since death.'

'You can say that again!' muttered Simon. 'Are you sure this is the right guy?'

* * *

Blake lay in the bath, digesting his Chinese takeaway. A photo of Gates was looking at him from the wall of the hallway. Blake had put such reminders up everywhere. Upon reflection, he'd decided that the leftovers of a number eight, a number twenty-five and two number seventies were not only more attractive than the ex-copper, but possibly now made of much the same stuff.

Just thinking about it seemed insane. He really wished he didn't have to. What were they? Had they changed their physical shape into that of human beings, or did they sit inside the heads of these human forms, either physically or mentally? And where did they come from? None of the planets of this solar system, surely. Which meant interstellar travel. Which meant vast technology. So why did they have to fart around with all this disguise business? Especially since they'd, rather sportingly, decided to work their way up through the British establishment.

Beside him, the radio news was on. 'In New York today, fears were raised of a mystery illness when the new Japanese representative to the United Nations collapsed at a charity breakfast. A severe nosebleed and dizziness cut short his inaugural speech. Three other members of the Security Council, including one top aide to the Russian President, suffered the same symptoms. An investigation is under way into the probable cause . . .'

Blake had got out of the bath, pulled on his jeans, and thundered downstairs to pick up the phone before he realised just how ridiculous what he had been going to say was going to sound. He put the phone down again.

There was a knock at the door.

It was Melissa. She stood on the doorstep in another floral thing under a different cardigan. She had her hair in a ponytail.

Blake grinned from ear to ear. 'Melissa.' He tried to sound less delighted than he was.

'Hello,' she said. She looked desperately sorry. Thank God.

'I was just going to call you. Did you hear the news?'

'Yes, on the car radio.'

'I'll bet the nosebleeds would work out to be at about the same time as –'

'Mary Madigan, in the coroner's court. I know.'

'So what triggered it? Another death?'

'Probably.' She outlined her new theory carefully. 'That's what I came over to say to you. Listen, we know that Elizabeth Madigan's death weakened Gates and Leonard for a few moments even though she was bottom of their pile. If we can get closer to the top then it might have a more devastating effect.'

Blake found that he was smiling again. 'Or they might be better equipped to resist it.'

She smiled back. 'Perhaps I'd better come in.'

'Yes. Perhaps you had.'

He stepped aside to allow her access. If he was paranoid, at least he still had somebody to share that hobby with.

Sarah circled the body, opened now to display the blackened husks of its internal organs. She spoke into her tape recorder, wonderingly, as one of her assistants inserted a thermometer into the body cavity. 'Pancreas, liver, kidneys, remain recognisable, but are all . . . severely burnt. I must emphasise that this is not the sort of damage associated with fire victims. The internal organs appear to have . . . slowly cooked from the inside.'

She saw that Doug, the man with the thermometer, was shaking his head, slowly, astonished by what the device was telling him. He shook it, and checked again.

'The internal body temperature is?' Sarah prompted.

'Must be something wrong with this thermometer.'

Sarah snapped off the recorder. 'What's the reading?'

He hesitated to tell her. He came over with the thermometer and showed her. 'Forty-nine degrees,' he said.

Sarah leant heavily on the table, smiling in incredulity.

She clicked the recorder on again, and spoke with deliberate precision. 'The deceased's internal body temperature has risen twelve degrees Celsius since death.'

She and the lab assistants looked at each other in utter puzzlement. How could you do a post-mortem on an impossibility?

Blake had made a cup of coffee for them both, and they sat watching the fire in the grate, talking about the distances between the stars, and the possibility of life on Europa, and that episode of *The Outer Limits* where a whole town gets abducted by aliens.

And she told him about the scary stuff in those books she'd read. About abductions from cars and beds, about people's memories not being their own. Blake started to shake his head violently at that point. That was mythology, stuff that spoke to him about human needs and fears. This invasion was something that was happening in reality, a manipulation of events by real people, albeit alien people. The only way they got into one's thoughts and dreams was because they looked like friends and other humans. And the alienation of that was an effect that you could get with ordinary humans. Every now and then.

And suddenly he'd said, before his thoughts could quite keep up with his words, that he wanted her to know what it was about him, the thing that had made him the way he was. His twenty-five words or less.

'You don't have to tell me,' she said. She looked very interested, and a little scared. Like he was going to confess to murder.

'I want to. It's important.' A long pause. 'I was in Zaire. It was maybe my twentieth assignment in ten years. I'd taken a picture of a mother cradling her dead baby in her arms. When she saw my camera she just flew at me in a rage of grief and anger. I stood there trying to reason with her, argued with her . . .' He stopped, shaking his head at all the unthought things that had defined him then. It

160

seemed like he'd been a character in a book, somebody who just moved and acted, without caring what happened because of those moves and actions. 'And in the end she gave up, exhausted. When I got back, I didn't want to use the picture. I felt it was wrong.'

'Why then?' She sounded like that had been the end of the story, and she was disappointed somehow. 'You must have intruded on grief before.'

'An hour after she'd spoken to me, the mother . . . with her dead child . . . deliberately stepped on a land-mine. She was looking at me.' Blake had provided the punchline.

It was Melissa's turn for a long pause. 'Joanna was your editor then, wasn't she? Did you explain that to her?'

'I'd already filed it, but she promised me she wouldn't use it. And then she went ahead and published it anyway.'

'Did you ask her why?'

'She said that I had no conscience when I took the photo. It wasn't her job to add one on my behalf.'

Melissa looked into her coffee cup. 'Maybe she had a point.'

Blake shook his head. 'I can't explain it. At the time I found it a real betrayal. And now I find it difficult . . . almost impossible . . . to trust anyone.'

He brought his gaze up to look at her, and she met his eyes. It was so appropriate that the aliens had come across him, he realised. Because he was the best possible judge of what was in the picture, how much a human was a human inside. And of whether or not he himself could be trusted. He looked deep into Melissa's eyes, and realised that she had had exactly the same experience, over all these years.

'I'm sorry I didn't trust you. I'm really sorry.'

She touched his face, wonderingly. 'It's all right. It's all right.'

Her hand trailed to his mouth and then left his face, as if she didn't know whether it should stay there beyond a gesture of comfort.

So he grabbed her and kissed her. And to his great relief he found that her mouth was as eager for him as he was for her.

They stood, at once, and tottered around the room, kissing like teenagers, excited by the feel of it, and the extraordinary sensation of skin on skin. It had been a long time, Blake assumed, for both of them. The surrender into the ordinary human kissing stuff was a huge release for them both.

Blake broke away, wondering at how soft Melissa's hair felt in his hands. 'You know, you always frown before you smile.'

She frowned and then smiled. Then she nuzzled her brow against his, rolled her face to meet his in one sensual movement, took the back of his head solidly in her palm, wanted him.

He swept his papers from the big old table and rolled her on to it, and then himself on top of her. He was just thinking that they were probably going to end up doing it right there and then on the table, apart from a moment's consideration about lack of condoms and having to pop down to a chemist's and if one was going to be open and maybe they'd just make do, and wasn't it great to be having to worry about that sort of stuff again when –

The telephone rang. They both looked at it, waiting for it to stop. But it wasn't going to.

'I'm sorry,' he said.

Melissa looked wonderfully ruffled and frustrated back.

Blake finally reached over and picked it up.

Sarah looked across the lab at her two baffled lab assistants. She was just returning their shrug when Steve Blake finally answered his phone. He sounded a little breathless.

'Mr Blake? Sarah Armstrong here. Yes, the pathologist in the Wilson case. I've got something here that I really think you ought to see. Well, right now would be good.'

* * *

Blake drove Melissa to the Pathology Labs in Norwich. He caught her smirking at him quite a few times during the journey. They talked about lifestyle stuff: favourite films – she laughed at how shallow his taste was; books; things like that. They were, Blake realised as he drew up outside the smart, modern building in the twilight, going on a date to a pathology lab.

Sarah Armstrong was waiting for them in reception. She looked like she was all too willing to play gooseberry.

'Come into my office,' she said, after Blake had made introductions. 'Let's do this without the smell.'

She hadn't switched the lights on in her office, letting the light from the television screen be the only illumination. Blake couldn't help but be reminded of Cartwright, and shivered reflexively. What was on the screen didn't help: Sarah and her assistants looking astonished and disturbed by the burnt contents of a body. Blake glanced from the screen to where Melissa was crossing her legs, and felt a little disquieted himself.

'Normal on the outside, burnt on the inside,' Sarah was saying. 'The lab assistants have nicknamed him Microwave Man. You're interested in mysterious explosive chemicals. I just thought this was your sort of thing.'

'Who is he?' asked Blake.

'Philip Boyd, bigwig in the Nuclear Research Institute. But he's got police connections too.'

'Chief Superintendent Gates?' Melissa said it with absolute confidence that she was right.

Sarah raised an eyebrow. 'That's the one. He turned up here, said Philip Boyd was a police matter and the police pathologist should conduct the post-mortem.'

'I take it you didn't agree?' Blake was pleased at how to the point Melissa was becoming. Once you'd taken her world view on board, she was suddenly a serious investigator.

Sarah smiled. 'Never come between a pathologist and a corpse.'

Blake glanced at Melissa. 'I can see why he might want to keep this one quiet.' Then he added, for Sarah's benefit, 'It's quite a mess.'

Melissa interrupted Sarah's questioning look. 'How would you explain it?'

'I can't. Not yet. If it's some sort of shock, I've never come across it before. None of his internal reactions match his externals.'

'How do you mean?' Melissa was studying the internal details of the corpse analytically.

Blake wondered if she was thinking about what might be inside her ex-husband these days.

'His skin wasn't punctured, he hadn't broken anything, he wasn't injured.'

They all stared at the images for a moment.

Blake broke the silence. 'Can we take a look at him?'

Blake and Melissa walked downstairs with Sarah into the basement, where they kept the dead. Blake wanted to ask the obvious question: was this bloke basically . . . human? The coincidence of timing was too much for this weird death not to be the alien fatality. Gates' interest confirmed it. It sounded to him like this body had sustained some sort of damage which would have threatened or exposed the alien, so some sort of suicide capsule had been activated, dissolving anything weird that would give any clues about the way the body was made.

Sarah went straight to a metal drawer labelled A and pulled it open. It was empty. Sarah opened her mouth, then slammed the door closed again.

Blake glanced at Melissa. They were both sharing that rush of paranoia again.

Sarah yelled across the room to where a man in a lab coat was sitting at a desk. 'Greg, what's going on?'

'I thought you knew.' Greg sounded apologetic. 'The body was released to the police.'

'You mean you just handed it over?'

The man nodded. 'About half an hour ago. I didn't ave any choice.'

'I never authorised this.' Sarah looked like she simply ouldn't believe this had happened.

'The paperwork was in order,' Greg protested. 'It was igned by the coroner.' He stepped away quickly.

'Greg!' Sarah pursued him, looking stormy.

'So what do we do now?' asked Melissa.

'We go public,' Blake said.

3lake drove Melissa back to her doorstep. There was an twkward little moment just after he stopped the car.

'Well, I am tired,' she said, carefully. 'And since we're going to London on the first train tomorrow . . .'

So Blake kissed her quickly and bid her goodnight.

He went back to the artist's cottage feeling paranoid and excited and vulnerable. Altogether, he thought, it was exactly like being a teenager again.

Despite the aliens and their invasion, he slept very well that night.

Sarah Armstrong went to visit the coroner the next morning, wearing her biggest suit with the most dangerous possible shoulderpads. She'd always liked Robert. He looked and sounded like he should have been one of those shooting and fishing types, the kind of man who proudly declares that he gets on very well with the blacks. But as she'd discovered over her first cup of tea with him, he was actually extraordinarily sweet, and wanted nothing more than to tell her about his daughter and proudly show off his photos of her graduation. It was unthinkable that somebody as deeply ethical as he was would have given in in the face of pressure from Gates.

But something had made him do it. She didn't stop outside his door today. She shouldered straight through it without knocking.

Robert even smiled at her from behind his desk when

she entered. But she still felt betrayed, and she found herself blurting out her issue with him straight away.

'Do you mind telling me who gave permission to move Philip Boyd's remains?'

'I did.' The voice came from over her shoulder.

She turned to see a thin, cunning-looking man in his late-forties sitting in a chair in the corner. It was James Wilson. The man who hadn't died. What the hell was he doing here?

'I'm sorry,' she breathed, taken off guard. 'I don't think we've been introduced, have we?'

Robert got to his feet and gestured to the chair in front of his desk. 'I think you'd better sit down, Sarah.'

Joanna entered her lounge carrying a bulging file and threw the contents all over her desk. Then she went to fill her kettle. She didn't look at Melissa. She hadn't looked at Melissa, Blake noted, since they'd entered twenty minutes ago.

The train journey to London had been full of meaningful glances and brushes of hands and *double entendres*. They hadn't spoken about the events of the sofa the night before, probably because it was more fun that way. Instead, they'd concentrated on their private world of conspiracies and duplication. Thank God they'd caught the early train. An hour later and they'd have had to have spoken in paraphrases beside a couple of businessmen.

Blake picked up one of the photos in the file, and realised that this must be the library's entire collection of entries on Philip Boyd.

'Philip Boyd was a government scientist and policy adviser,' Joanna told him, preparing tea.

Her flat was an insane monument to her tastes. Lots of light, plants, and hideous purple furniture, including a sofa upon which Blake was trying desperately to sit at a reasonable distance from Melissa.

'Special interest: the effects of mineral mining in the

Antarctic and the breakdown of the treaty.'

'Was he for or against?' Blake asked. Melissa wasn't about to take the lead in this company.

'He was against any mineral mining until six months ago. In fact he and another top researcher pretty much had the argument sewn up.'

'So what happened to change his mind?'

Joanna glanced at where Melissa was leafing through some of the other photos. With a little twitch of the eyebrows that indicated that she thought they were now entering the Twilight Zone, she said, 'It might have been one of those accidents you're so fond of. The victimless deaths?'

She pulled out a secondary file of cuttings. 'Fuel Man Killed in Chopper Crash'. 'Helicopter Accident Claims Top Scientist'. 'Miracle Escape for Prof!'

Melissa looked at the photos over Blake's shoulder. 'We were right,' she whispered. 'He's been renewed. That'd explain the autopsy results.'

Joanna brought the tea, smiling the smile of an indulgent schoolmistress. She would never miss a whisper. 'He's been what?'

Melissa sighed deeply. 'He seems to die then turns up alive and renewed. Changed. It just seems an apt way to describe it.'

Joanna sat down and set the tea in front of them. Her grin grew slightly too wide for her face. 'Well, he's certainly changed. His about-turn allowed the British government to get in bed with the Yanks and screw the treaty all ends up. The Tories, that was, but the other lot don't seem to want to do anything about it.'

'Can you get any more information?' Blake said.

'Not today I can't. The computer's caught a cold. Whole system's down.'

Blake glanced at Melissa again. 'You use Zentex, don't you?' he asked.

'Of course. Who doesn't?'

167

'You said there were two scientists resisting the break up of the Antarctic treaty?' Melissa asked. Blake thought there was something cute in how Melissa kept trying to gain Joanna's attention, and/or eye-line.

'Yes.' She once more addressed her answer to Blake. 'The other man's name is Gerald Ryle. He's senior at the Nuclear Research Institute. Still calling for a re instatement of the treaty and a ban on oil exploration. He's even threatening to take it to the UN.'

'Will he get anywhere?' Blake asked, noticing the look of resentment building in Melissa's expression.

'He can make quite a nuisance of himself, slow down any expansion in the programme, that sort of thing.'

'I think we may have found their next target,' Blake told Melissa. And, before Joanna could ask what their current theory was on who they were, he added in her direction, 'Can you get us an in with this Gerald Ryle character?'

Joanna nodded gaily. 'Oh, yeah! Like I'm going to use my name and contacts so you can go and ask this guy if he's seen any suspicious footsteps at the bottom of his garden?' She got up as if she'd remembered something more important that she had to do.

Blake started mentally counting to ten. He failed at five and stood up to yell at her. 'Look at it this way: if we get anything juicy, we give you the exclusive.'

'At last, an argument I can understand.' She reached for the telephone, sharing a complex old-days smile with Blake which was designer-fashioned to exclude Melissa. 'You always did know the way to my heart.'

Blake glanced at Melissa uncomfortably as Joanna made the call. He took a deep breath at her fiery gaze and straightened up. Joanna might be flirting with him, but he wasn't going to flirt back. Absolutely not.

James Wilson had formally introduced himself to Sarah and explained his function at British Nuclear Power. He kept looking at Robert as if they were old school buddies

Sarah was expecting a Masonic salute at any moment. Which was odd, because Robert hadn't talked about James Wilson with any familiarity over the matter of the car crash. The good thing was that, unlike a lot of his generation, Wilson seemed to want to deal with her like a professional, and made coffee for them both.

Putting on a big and serious voice, he said, 'Philip Boyd was working at the very edges of our understanding of nuclear fusion. We think he may have come in contact with certain materials that caused his body to . . . react to the trauma of the accident in that . . . unusual way.'

He sat down on the sofa, right beside Sarah. For a moment she reacted, wanting to move away. He was so close that it was like he was making a pass at her. But his tone was entirely businesslike. The man had weird body-language issues.

'Like the driver who stole your car?' Sarah had made the connection almost at once. If that was some sort of bodily reaction, rather than a chemical poison . . . She frowned. No. She didn't believe that for a second. Radiation didn't do stuff like that. Even the arcane business involved in fusion couldn't fry people's insides suddenly, when they were far away from any radiation source.

'We don't know that, now, do we?' Wilson smiled genially.

'Well, I'm sure the lab cultures will help us explain the reaction.'

Wilson coughed politely and glanced at Robert again. 'I'm afraid, Miss Armstrong, your role in the post-mortem is over.'

Sarah saw that Robert was nodding sadly. 'Hang on! Two men implode after accidents and you want me to pretend it hasn't happened?'

'Sarah.' Robert started to make calming gestures.

'I'll have to insist,' added Wilson. He reached into his pocket and produced a piece of paper, which he laid out on the table in front of her.

She looked at it, incensed that Robert should have sold his soul to these people. Perhaps he hadn't. Perhaps she'd just been taken in all along by the charm of the white boys' club. 'What is this?'

'The Official Secrets Act,' said Wilson. 'You'll sign it, we'll witness it, and then we'll know where we stand.' He offered her his ornate fountain pen.

'And if somebody asks me about the post-mortem I conducted?'

'Deny everything.' Wilson met her angry gaze bluntly. 'Admit nothing.'

'What if I don't sign?'

Wilson sighed like she was a naughty child, and got up to wander to the window. He turned back to Robert. 'What's the going rate for a struck-off pathologist these days?'

Sarah stared at them, suddenly full of loathing for these dapper old men who smelt of tobacco and port. You laws do not apply to me, she thought. I will sign your rules, but I will no longer play by them.

She took a pen from Robert's desk and signed the Official Secrets Act, leaning on his telephone directory. As she looked up from her indignant flourish, she saw Wilson's eyes looking at her like those of a gnarled lizard regarding a fly.

Perhaps she'd given in a little too easily there.

Joanna led Blake and Melissa towards the door. She deliberately hung back with Blake as Melissa went through, nodding towards the other woman with a little conspiratorial nudge. 'What's going on, then? You and her started a little conspiracy of your own?'

'Too busy, too tired and too early,' Blake assured her.

'You missed one explanation off.'

'Did I?'

'Too smart,' Joanna purred. She let him through the door as he laughed.

As soon as the door closed behind him, he stopped laughing, and met Melissa's frosty gaze. 'I really hope not,' he said to her.

'Hope not what?'

He took her arm and led her out of the building. 'Nothing.'

11

THE CONQUEST OF THE SOUTH POLE

Blake and Melissa had been driving in silence for some time. He didn't really want to start a conversation in case it turned out to be about Joanna, about the archaeology of their relationship, about what was left. The truth was that there was quite a lot.

About a mile from the Nuclear Research Institute that was indicated on Gerald Ryle's business card, Melissa began just that conversation. 'After Joanna used the photograph without your permission . . . is that when it all went wrong for you?'

'That and a thousand other things.' He paused. He couldn't help but open up to her. 'Including the fact that I couldn't hold a camera for six months.'

'She left you after you left the business?'

'She said she didn't recognise me any more; that I was only half the man I was.' Blake smiled at the irony: that this quest should have come to him . . .

'Don't you ever feel angry?'

'Not for the last two weeks I haven't.' He'd said it before he understood it. Now he looked back to the country roads that curved and twisted in front of him, not wanting to give away any more.

She didn't make him.

Round the next bend came the entrance to the Nuclear Research Institute, a warren of high-tech buildings behind a security gate. It looked rather like a university campus. As Blake steered the car in, a lorry with the Zentex Software logo pulled out through the gates.

'Everybody uses them,' Blake noted.

'Um–hm,' agreed Melissa.

Sarah had assured Robert, after Wilson had left, that she was fine, that, although she was still angry, she understood the necessity of it all. She'd take his advice, take the rest of the day off, go home and relax with a hot bath and a good book.

She drove straight back to her office and picked up the phone. 'Hi, Gerry. Do you know if the Philip Boyd tissue cultures have been processed yet? No, there's no hurry. I need them back here, they weren't properly tagged. I'll come over and pick them up. Thanks.'

She hung up the phone and glanced behind her as a shadow passed down the corridor outside the room. So, she was now a whistle-blower. That hot bath and book looked like much the more comfortable option.

The Philip Gates was working at his desk when he heard the report on the television. He turned and used the remote control to increase the volume.

'Traditionally,' the reporter was saying, 'the whole of the Antarctic has been regarded as a virtual no–go area for industrial development, and an area of huge ecological importance. But after today's high-level conference, it would appear that, following forty years of co–operation, there are those now willing to take the risk.'

The Philip Gates tried out his smile again. The causality of this place had always interested him. It wasn't as simple as home – push and then watch things fall into place – but it had its own kind of action and reaction, a political kind. He felt the tug of the others and let himself join them.

'Britain now seems to be at the head of that group,' the reporter continued, as the Philip Gates body went limp, 'with its territorial claims fully supported by the US government, and rumours of further co-operation and profit sharing, if and when these proposals are put into operation.'

173

The Philip Gates felt the Leonard family were also watching the news. They were sitting in a line on their sofa, all different sizes. That always made all of them laugh, a visual joke. They were scanning the information quickly, processing it and cross-referencing it for the others.

'Outside the conference, a few official voices have been heard in protest. But ironically, it is the self same qualities which have made the Antarctic such a Mecca for international scientists which are now attracting the international fuel companies.'

The Philip Gates and the Leonard family felt the Mary Madigan MP join them. She was still sad. They saw, through her fingers, the image of the Elizabeth Madigan which was on her desk now. Disguise. Yes, it was an item of disguise. But it was also a confession of murder: the Mary Madigan MP's admission of responsibility in advance of when they would be able to practise justice and proper civilisation again.

'Supporters of the initiative insist that there is a huge geological heritage waiting beneath the ice cap, a heritage which can only benefit the planet as a whole, and which will service its fuel needs well into the next millennium.'

Millennium. They found some humour in that, too. But the feeling together was sombre again now, with the Mary Madigan MP part of them.

'In a world short on time, low on stocks, and hungry for energy, that is indeed a powerful argument. The pro-fuel lobby are offering computer projections and scientific theory to back up their claims, but their opponents disagree. In an impromptu meeting earlier today, Greenpeace and other environmental groups warned that we exploit this wilderness at our peril.'

They all understood that this was good.

The Philip Gates distantly heard a knock on his door, and fled the group. He was looking at nothing, his pupils rolled back, his body stiffened straight with dreaming effort, he knew.

174

He managed to return and blink and call for the policeman to come in.

And restrain the urge he felt to laugh and laugh at him for being a human.

Gerald Ryle was a gruff, white-bearded man in his late-fifties. He had an expression of academic concentration on his brow which suggested that he was always peering at his chin. He wore old tweed and a mis-attached identification tag, and Blake knew straight away that he was terribly human. He showed Blake and Melissa along busy corridors, past bulletin boards and people in labcoats arguing, across a bridge between glass complexes, and through a lab that contained banks of stainless steel high-tech machinery and rows of computer monitors. Melissa was a reporter, Blake a photographer, which, Blake had realised as he'd told the cover story to the security guard at the gate, was very nearly true.

'How long do you think you can carry on working here?' Melissa was asking Ryle, as Blake took a photo of the man.

He smiled, bemusedly. Indeed, he'd been bemused since they got here. 'I'm sorry?'

'You've threatened to go to the UN to get the Antarctic treaty restored,' Melissa explained. 'Yet this place is the leading research institute for Antarctic gas and oil. It can't be easy to stay in a place where you're so out of step.'

Ryle frowned, shaking his head at the thought, as if he couldn't understand why these two reporters were bothering with him. 'Science is a history of debates, disagreements. It's how we progress.'

'This is more than a disagreement, isn't it? According to what you said on television, all our futures are at stake.'

Ryle was looking tetchy now, irritated that his private battle had become something the press were interested in. They stopped outside his office. He waved a hand at

Blake as he lined up another shot, nearly batting his camera out of the way. 'Will you stop sticking that blasted thing in my face?'

'I'm sorry.' Blake abandoned the shot. 'I didn't realise it was annoying you.'

'I'm not comfortable with all this . . . this business.' Ryle led them inside and sat behind his desk. 'Can we just get it over with?'

'OK. We want to know if you've been threatened in any way,' said Blake.

'Threatened? How do you mean?'

'Has any pressure been brought on you by, say, James Wilson?'

Ryle looked flustered. That had been close to the mark. 'I really have no idea what you're talking about.'

'Philip Boyd?'

Ryle leapt to his feet, waving a finger impotently in Blake's face.

Bingo.

'How dare you come in here and talk about Philip like that? Have you people no respect?' A serious frown creased his brow. 'You're not from a newspaper at all, are you? Who are you?'

Blake looked skyward. He couldn't even impersonate a journalist these days. Maybe he should be grateful. 'Professor Ryle, we think you're in danger.'

'If you'll just let us explain –' began Melissa.

But Ryle had shut down completely. He waved and shunted Melissa and Blake out of his office, cutting off every sentence they began, like he was forcing himself not to think about what they were saying to him. 'I don't have time for this! Just get out! Get out!'

The door was slammed in their faces.

Sarah took delivery of Philip Boyd's tissue samples, scrubbed up, and started to work through them with as much haste as her careful disposition allowed. She'd accessed Boyd's unremarkable medical history, and so far everything about these samples matched everything she'd found out about the man. There was no trace of the chemical that she was sure had been used to assassinate him. Exposure to radiation, indeed! What sort of fool did they think she was? Robert certainly wouldn't have believed that story, which was why she hadn't tried to talk him round. He was implicated up to his neck, and, with Wilson, was going to be swimming in it to the same level, when she'd got some solid evidence. Official Secrets Act or no.

The tissue samples were each contained in plastic samples dishes. Sarah had got through ten of them so far, testing for chemicals foreign to normal biochemistry. She dropped a saline solution into each, then added a detector dye to the resulting liquid. She observed the results of each test under a microscope. A cool breeze from an open window was blowing across the table top, clearing the sweat from her brow. She was grateful for it. It made this seem less like defusing a bomb. She felt like something was about to go off in her face. Even if only politically.

No result on that last sample. She made a note, put it aside, and took the lid off the next. She added the saline solution off-handedly, luxuriating in the breeze passing over her, and nearly dropped the sample when she saw what was happening.

A trail of grey smoke was fizzing up from the tissue sample. She placed it quickly under the microscope, and watched the sample fade from sight, its organic structure collapsing like the floors of a house on fire.

She dived for the pipette rack, made sure that she'd used the right one, and held it up to the light, her mind already racing. 'Saline solution?' she whispered.

She had the horrible feeling that nobody was going to believe this.

Gerald Ryle drew his car up at the level crossing on the quiet country road just as the barriers were coming down.

177

He drummed his fingers on the wheel in frustration. Just what he didn't need today. He was probably on his way to a coronary. His battles were his own. He didn't know how the media had heard about his continuing disputes with James Wilson. Never mind with poor, poor Philip. But he knew that he didn't want matters of such weighty concern made into the stuff of tabloid headlines. It was probably the death that had attracted them, like flies to a . . . And if they hadn't been reporters, what were they? Hack writers, fumbling through the research for a sensational book? Secret-service spooks under Wilson's thumb, trying to see what he was saying to outsiders? Damn, but that train was taking a long time.

He noticed with irritation that the oil indicator on his dashboard had started to flash. But he'd only . . . Now they were all flashing. And his radio had come on, spinning through the stations as if the car were being bombarded by some sort of radiation. A complete failure of everything? This bloody heap had picked its time.

When the engine began to race, he actually looked to see if he'd pressed his foot on the accelerator pedal.

He hadn't.

It struck him that this might be a dangerous fault, being where he was. His hand went to the ignition key.

And somebody grabbed it and held it there. Ryle looked over his shoulder, crying out. He twisted in his seat. There was nobody there.

His other hand was grabbed, placed on to the door handle, and pushed down. He was shoved up on to his feet, out of his seat, tumbled out of the door, the engine still running.

The sun shone down and the birds sang in the trees as he was pulled and shoved by invisible hands, towards the railway line.

'No! No!' he shouted. It felt like there were many of them, intangible when he tried to grab for them, but with heavy hands that held him in place with tremendous effort. They swarmed about him invisibly, like gases in the air that would suddenly solidify at the point of each muscular movement to keep him marching like a puppet towards that terrible sound of the oncoming train.

Gerald Ryle believed in magic, now. He was certain these were ghosts, dead spirits come to prey on him. They slapped his head to make it duck under the barrier, then forced him on, leg after leg, like a mother making her unruly toddler walk, until he was standing right across the tracks. His feet were planted on either side, an ever-changing weight kept on them.

In the distance, the train was already visible, a solid brick of commuters and driver and glass and steel with a light in the middle. It blared.

He lurched his head around, and saw, far behind him, a gang of men in the red and yellow of railway workers trudging along the grassy banks towards him. 'Help me!' he screamed. 'Help me! Please! Somebody!'

His head was twisted back to the front, as if these poltergeists that fluttered the air around his face wanted him to see. He wondered if they would hold his eyelids open, if they would have to swish aside at the last moment. If he would have the courage and energy needed to jump then. If, there being ghosts, there was a God.

'Help me! No! Please! No!'

'What the bloody hell's he on?'

Mike Scanlon and his gang had just walked down the line from track works half a mile away. They were all looking forward to getting back to their depot, washing up and having a pint. They most definitely didn't want a loony standing in the middle of the line, about to inter-cept the commuter service. Mike and his crew, more than anyone else, knew the effects that a collision like that had. Not only a corpse on the track, but often an injured driver, or one who'd never be able to work again for fear

179

that somebody else would pull a stunt like this.

'Come on!' Mike shouted.

The four of them sprinted down the bank towards the man.

'Help me!' he was shouting. 'Please help me!' Which at least meant that he was stuck somehow, and not one of these wankers who liked to die at other people's expense.

Mike himself was the first to reach the man. He still had at least thirty seconds before the train was upon them. The driver must have seen them, because he was hitting the horn desperately. Mike grabbed the man round the shoulders, intending to haul him bodily off the track.

But he couldn't. He glanced at the man's feet, too fast to notice what was wrong. 'Come on, give us a hand!' he yelled as the others arrived. 'He's stuck or summat! Grab him! Grab him!'

They managed to fold him in half, so that, screaming, he was lying on the bank with his legs still pinned to the track. The train was close. Closer. They grabbed every bit of him, and, joining in his scream, with his fingers digging into their shoulders –

They pulled his feet free in a sudden jolt, like something had let go, just as the blurred bulk of the train impacted the air beside them. They watched it blaring past, all panting together.

'Thank you,' whispered the man, as he stared at the tail of the thing passing.

'What was it?' asked Mike. 'What was holding you?'

But the man just shook his head. He looked like he'd seen a ghost.

Ryle sat at his desk, looking into the black depths of his computer console, watching the details of his own face, staring back at him. He'd taken a taxi home the previous night. Had the AA collect his car with some spurious fault. Taxi in this morning. Had the driver lock him in the back. He was afraid with his skin, afraid all the way to his stomach. He flinched at every motion of the air around him now. He hadn't slept. He'd just sweated in his bed, beside the wife he hadn't said a word to. Because the words he wanted to say were mad. He'd thought he was going mad, and had begun to take comfort in that by this morning.

Until he'd come in here and found James Wilson sitting behind his desk, looking at him knowingly, approving of his fear.

'No,' he said to the man now. 'No. Absolutely not.'

'That isn't the answer I was looking for,' Wilson murmured. 'Perhaps you should have another try.'

'What's happened to you? Why are you bullying me like this?'

Wilson considered for a moment, as if about to offer a hypothetical reason, a plausible excuse that they could both live with. 'The Commission pays for your research, but you show no loyalty in return.'

'There's a difference between loyalty and . . . blind allegiance!'

Wilson suddenly became angry, as if incensed that Ryle was still offering resistance. 'You can't go on protesting a decision just because you lost the argument!'

'Really? I thought that's what scientists did. Carried on arguing. That is the scientific method, you know!'

Wilson fixed him with a cold stare, and delivered the words Ryle was dreading. 'Do you think what happened to you yesterday was the end? Do you really think it stops there?'

'Who told you about that?' Ryle didn't know what scared him most: the idea that his former colleague had murderous supernatural powers at his command, or the idea that he was confident enough to talk about them openly.

'The men who saved you said it was like trying to drag ten men back from that track.'

'How did you know?'

181

'The same way I know that your computer is going to go down for an hour in thirty seconds' time.' Wilson stood, and headed for the door.

Ryle could only appeal to the past, to how things used to be before the world had become so horrifying and his friend had become a gangster. 'What changed, James? Why are you acting like this?'

'It's you that's changed.' Wilson paused at the door. 'You can't see the truth when it's staring you in the face.' The thought seemed to amuse him. 'Not a great quality in a scientist. Goodbye, Gerald.'

He left. Ryle felt sick. That goodbye had sounded horribly final. He turned to look at his computer screen.

As he did so, the system crashed.

The screen went blank. For a moment, the Zentex logo in the corner persisted.

Then it vanished too.

Ryle started to cry.

Blake followed Sarah Armstrong as she led the way down the spiral stairs of her facility and through the antiseptic corridors, heading towards the mortuary. He had dropped Melissa off at her house after the visit to Ryle yesterday afternoon, and she had kissed him passionately and told him that she'd better pop in to the library tomorrow, feign illness, arrange some proper sick leave, do all that stuff. She had a life to keep up with that afternoon too. Cleaning. Cooking. Cats. Blake asked if he could see her that night, and she'd been coy, saying that she still needed sleep.

'You're still not sure,' he'd said. 'Ironic, considering that, after all these years, I am now.'

'Maybe I'm being careful for both of us.'

So he'd lifted her up from where she stood beside his car, and carried her to the door of her house. She'd unlocked the door, scrabbling quickly for her keys before the neighbours saw, and he'd carried her inside, thrown her on to her bed, kissed her again. And then left with a cheery whistle.

He'd spent the evening putting his notes in order and taking phone calls from her every half-hour. All conspiracy stuff. Nothing personal. They were expressing themselves almost entirely through paranoia, like two drug buddies flirting with their mutual addiction.

Alien invasion had never been so much fun.

Very late, he'd taken a call from Sarah, and been disappointed at first that it hadn't been Melissa inviting him over. She'd asked him to join her at the hospital early the next morning. Which was when Melissa was going to be excusing herself at the library. So he'd gone alone.

What Sarah told him when he got there made the hairs on the back of his neck literally stand on end. 'Saline solution?'

Sarah nodded, still bemused. 'I think that's what killed him.'

'He wasn't given any other medicines? Penicillin? Painkillers?'

'Not unless the paramedics are lying to cover their backs. And they've no reason to do that. He was picked up, seemed mildly concussed, no sign of any other injuries. They just followed standard practice. Oxygen, blood pressure reading, and put a line in to counter fluid loss.'

Blake didn't know what to say. He finally had a weapon. One so simple that it seemed to come straight out of one of those hokey alien–invasion movies of the fifties. 'Have you ever come across saline solution doing this before?'

They reached the basement labs. Sarah led Blake past the table where the bodies were taken apart.

'No. And I can't find any evidence of it happening anywhere else.' She looked at Blake as if she were certain that he knew more than he was saying. 'The first thing I did after that was check his blood for antigens. It didn't correspond to any group.' She let that sink in for a moment. 'After that I was prepared for more surprises.'

'What if he isn't human?' Blake tried to make it sound like a question. He failed.

'What?' Sarah stared at him.

'That's why he's reacted in this way,' Blake said. 'That's why his blood group doesn't exist. Because he isn't human.'

'This is some kind of wind-up, right?'

Blake realised that he hadn't been called here to see anything in particular, just to talk. Maybe to convince this dedicated woman that it wasn't just her. That somebody else was seeing the same things. 'Look at the evidence.'

'I am.' She paused. Then she went to her briefcase, which was sitting on a lab bench nearby, and pulled out the papers relevant to the case. 'I shouldn't be telling you this: they made me sign the Official Secrets Act. But I'm going to tell the world. When I can prove it. They're saying Boyd was exposed to some kind of radiation. Like they said about Wilson's car.'

'It's a cover-up,' Blake assured her. 'The reason he reacted the way he did is because he isn't human.' It felt good saying it outright. It felt good that Sarah looked steadily at him when he said it. It didn't sound so crazy any more.

Greg, the lab assistant who Blake had encountered the last time he'd met with Sarah, poked his head round the door. They both shut up, and Greg smiled as if he'd caught them having an affair.

'Are you Steve Blake?'

'Yeah.'

Greg pointed at a phone on the mortuary wall. 'There's a call for you on line one. Just pick it up.'

'Thanks.' Blake waited until the assistant had definitely departed and then went to pick up the phone. 'Hello?'

It was Melissa, all business. 'Steve, I just got back. Gerald Ryle called. Something's happened. He's gone into hiding.'

'What?'

'He wants to meet you.'

Blake glanced at where Sarah was still mulling over what he'd told her. 'Right now?'

'It seemed pretty urgent,' Melissa said. With a large dollop of understatement. 'You can pick me up on the way. If you want. I've got the directions.'

The directions led them out into the flatlands, to an isolated house that stood between two great old farms. Melissa tried out her fake sneeze on Blake. He asked about her colleague who thought they were having an affair.

'She doesn't think that any more,' Melissa told him, with a tiny smirk. 'She knows.'

'More than I do!'

Melissa pointed to the house. 'Isn't that the one we're looking for?'

Ryle answered the door behind a security chain, then led them quickly through the house to a wooden porch at the back. Beyond it were green meadows that stretched to the horizon. As they walked amongst green trees and sighing grass, Blake got the feeling that the academic was suffering from some sort of nervous complaint. He was visibly shaking, and kept looking in all directions, as if afraid of being attacked. He asked them for their real identities, and Blake told the truth. Ryle, despite his condition, seemed to accept that they were who they said they were, and told them the extraordinary story of what had happened to him at the railway line, and the threats from Wilson the next morning.

'Whatever the force that held me there on that railway line,' he said, 'it was greater than my will. My body was no longer my own. I can't explain why it was happening.'

'I think I can,' said Blake.

'That's good. That's very good. When you came to me

185

at the Institute what made you think I was in danger?'

'Your colleagues. You were making a lot of noise opposing the breakdown of the Antarctic treaty. That was inconvenient to a group of very powerful people.'

'We'd seen how they treated your colleagues when they made similar objections,' Melissa added.

Ryle nodded quickly, as if forcing himself to absorb things he would never previously have believed. 'You're suggesting that people I work with have been through a similar experience?'

Blake hesitated, remembering how Ryle had reacted to his mention of Philip Boyd when last they'd met. 'We're suggesting that they . . . didn't come through the other side like you did.'

Ryle took a moment to understand. He nodded grimly to himself. Of course, Blake realised, they weren't talking about quite the same thing. Ryle assumed that Boyd had been assassinated after crashing his aircraft. They knew he'd been replaced before that. But the end result was the same. Ryle came to his conclusion and stopped by a tree.

'I won't be any trouble to them any more. I intend to resign.'

Melissa looked horrified. 'No, you need to go back to work! Someone's got to –'

'No, no! You don't understand. It's a free-for-all now. The Antarctic treaty is history. I can't do anything more. They've already moved on to nuclear testing!'

'Nuclear?' Blake frowned. 'That doesn't make any sense. What would be the advantage of a power station down there?'

'Not power!' Ryle snorted. 'Weapons! They're going to test nuclear weapons in the Antarctic!'

Blake and Melissa looked at each other, equally horrified.

After a moment, Blake pulled out his mobile and called Joanna.

* * *

After they'd taken details and listened to Ryle's story all over again, mainly because he wanted to tell it once more, Blake had been left with no choice but to respond to the academic's urgent questions. He'd told him everything, with Melissa filling in her own experiences. To his relief, Ryle had accepted what he said.

'So what attacked me?' he asked.

'I think . . .' Blake took a deep breath. 'I think that, from what you've said, maybe the real form of these creatures we're dealing with . . .' He glanced at Melissa. 'I don't think they're solid like matter is. Maybe they're something close to a gas, at least, maybe that's the best definition in our terms. They run those human bodies they've made like we'd run a vehicle, by sitting inside their nervous systems. Obviously they can't escape easily: once they're in they're bonded to the body, or there'd have been no need to . . . Well, what happened to Philip Boyd and Elizabeth Madigan wouldn't have happened.' He walked around the garden, putting his thoughts together. 'I think you were attacked by a number of those creatures that exist on this planet without human hosts. Probably a great number of them. Individually, they're very weak, but if they all get together they can force matter to do what they want. Maybe these are aliens waiting for human bodies to be created for them. Maybe that's how they forced the people of Sweethope into the church. Maybe . . .' He stopped walking and looked at Melissa and Ryle. 'Maybe I sound like I'm mad as an otter.'

'You're not,' said Ryle. 'I'm convinced you're not.' He managed to share a smile with Melissa. 'Isn't that terrible?'

Blake and Melissa headed back to their car. Ryle followed them, his eyes darting to all points of the flat horizon, as if the distant buildings were going to leap at him.

'Must be nice to have friends you can run away to.'

Blake indicated the house with a nod.

'The house belongs to my brother. I just needed to feel safe.'

'You are safe.' Blake felt the need to reassure the disturbed man.

'It won't take the likes of Wilson long to find me if they look hard enough.'

'All the more reason for carrying on going to work, make out you've come to your senses. Keep your head down and don't agitate.' Blake saw the look of fear in the man's eyes and wished he had something more to offer him. If this was a shared nightmare, he himself had, for some reason, been spared the worst of it.

'Until when?' asked Ryle.

'Until you and I can get access to the media.'

They discussed this in the garden: the only solution was to convince more and more people, like Ryle and Sarah had been convinced.

'You really think that's the only way?'

'I know it is.'

Ryle sighed, and seemed to relax a little. 'All right.'

'I'll set it up.'

Blake shook Ryle's hand, and Melissa kissed him gently on the cheek.

Ryle watched them drive away, looking very alone in the landscape.

Melissa watched Blake drive, in silence. Now should be the time when they both felt most satisfied, vindicated. But the more people started to agree with them, the more frightening and real the shadow that was rising over them became. When it was something only the two of them could share, it was almost fantasy. Now it was becoming a blunt fact. Life during wartime.

It was selfish to want somebody when there was such a storm ahead. It was a bad idea to fall into bed with the first man who'd ever shared her quest.

Or maybe she was just putting everything she could in the way of a release which was devoutly to be wished. Maybe it was time she started to think that she deserved love again. Maybe she'd already grieved, in a strange way, for Philip. She decided to start their hobby conversation again. 'From what Ryle was saying it sounds as though they've started to accelerate. You're sure we can't get at the computer software?'

'How?' He sounded unusually bleak. 'Our only hope is if Joanna can set up this TV interview for Ryle. Then –' He yelled suddenly, and clutched his head.

'Steve!'

The car was swerving across the road, out of control. Melissa thought for a sickening moment that they were in the car with them, attacking Steve, moving the wheel. But then Steve managed to pull into a lay-by, still wincing with pain.

'I'm sorry!' he gasped, tossing his head from one side to the other as if to rid himself of the sensation. 'I think I need some air.'

They got out of the car, Steve still stumbling in agony, and climbed over a fence to enter a ploughed field. The sky was like something out of a Turner painting, all nebulous swirls and strokes of a deeper grey. Steve sat still on the damp, muddy ground for a few moments, trying to breathe normally.

After a while, the pain seemed to subside, and he looked up at Melissa, worried, but wanting to keep the worry from her. Why did men always want to do that? 'Nice field,' he said. 'Fancy a walk?'

Melissa kept her own council for the first five minutes of the walk. She kept looking at Steve to see if he was OK. He seemed to be. And he definitely wasn't going to share any pet theories about the cause of his headaches. Maybe that was a war survivor thing, too. Something that went beside the trust issues that he'd honoured her with.

She wanted to save him and be saved by him, but above all she wanted to talk to him. Lots and lots. So she returned to the grand idea that had come into her head when Steve had told her about his conversation with Dr Armstrong. The Ryle business made it seem all the more urgent.

'What if Joanna can't help us, Steve?'

He looked puzzled, as if he'd never considered the possibility that his ex-wife might not be able to solve everything. She launched into her plan, feeling more Enid Blyton than ever.

'We know what saline solution does to them. We know they suffer together. If we attack someone at the heart of things, someone we can get access to . . .' She took a deep breath. 'If Philip goes, then it might just cripple the whole network.'

Blake stared at her. 'You're suggesting we attack Gates?'

She was taken aback for a moment by his disbelief. Oh, let's not actually do anything practical! 'He's the perfect target,' she argued. 'And we know I can get close to him.'

He shook his head again, and she wanted to shake him.

'It's too dangerous. You're not thinking rationally,' he said. He must have seen the look on her face at the moment he used that word, because he started to stammer. 'Wait! I know how much you want to destroy him, Melissa. I know how badly you must want to kill your husband's murderer –'

Idiot! Fool! Here she had an idea that was going to save the human race, and he thought this was personal! 'This isn't about my past!'

'Isn't it?'

'No!' And suddenly she found that she'd been thinking about the things Ryle had said, and the nature of the being that was pushing around Philip's body, and she found that she was crying. 'Well, yes,' she said, bravely, ignoring her stupid tears. 'Yes it is! But –'

'Look, I know how you must feel –'

She broke away from him and ran, not wanting him to see the rage and the tears.

Nobody knew how she felt. Nobody could know. She'd had a comforting thought of finishing all this with a stroke, putting an end to all this fear, and her partner in all this wouldn't consider it. She ran, clods of earth flying from her heels, scrambled back over the fence and pulled at the door handle of the car. Locked. Of course it was locked.

She was ashamed that she was beating her fists uselessly on the door when Steve reached the fence. So when he got to her she turned and started to hit him instead. Because that was what a large man, the first large man for such a long time, was for. 'You don't know anything about me!' she screamed at him. 'You can't tell me what I feel!' All thought had vanished into the mass of long-suppressed horror that had risen in her throat. 'You can't tell me what I feel!'

She was hitting Philip, she knew. So she hit harder and harder.

Steve struggled to say something as he restrained her, comforted her with the mass of his hands, tried to hold her awkwardly, not knowing what he was to her now.

'Hold me,' she ordered, in a deep breath between sobs. 'Just hold me!'

And he held her, his face a mask of impenetrable sadness. The sky loomed up over them both, like a wave threatening to engulf them, and Melissa cried proper, open, tears, until all she could feel was Steve Blake and all she could taste was salt.

She continued crying, on and off, into the car, into Steve's house, and, at her urging and finally tugging by the sleeve, from his friendly sofa to his purely sexual bed.

They quickly undressed under the covers, glancing at each other from time to time, he not understanding at all

191

how she could be sobbing and smiling at him at the same time. He was wondering, Melissa could tell, if he should be doing something to help. He reached for her when they were naked, and then hesitated.

'No, don't,' she said to him. 'It's all right. Really, it's all right.'

And she took him in her arms, remembered how much she had loved that feeling, and began to show him the solution that sobbing and laughing together really required.

Melissa was certain, by the time she fell asleep, that she and Steven Blake were both human.

Melissa left Steve sleeping the next morning.

Love was good, and she couldn't contain a certain swagger of the hips as she quietly closed the door behind her and stepped out into the cool offshore breezes.

But she only had twenty-four hours to save the Earth.

Or something. At least she had a plan.

Dr Sarah Armstrong held two syringes in front of Melissa, and two phials of saline solution in her other hand. 'I'm going to pretend that I don't know how you intend to use these.'

Melissa smiled coyly. She'd called Dr Armstrong from her cottage after leaving Steve. The pathologist had sounded like she knew exactly what Melissa was after, from the moment she picked up the phone.

'You're really sure you know what you're doing?' she asked.

Melissa sighed. 'Yes. For the first time in the past five years.'

'That isn't what I asked.'

'Turning back isn't an option.' Melissa gave this good woman a gentle smile and hoped that, after the one strike Melissa was going to make, no horror would ever touch her. 'I don't think you'd be helping us if you thought it was.'

Dr Armstrong nodded, as if she were sizing Melissa up. Then she made her decision. She placed the phials in Melissa's palm. 'This is the strongest concentration that we use. If my theory is correct, one syringe should be enough to do the damage. That saline drip wasn't in very long.' She placed the syringes in the other palm. 'Either way, I don't recommend hanging around to see the result.'

Melissa put the weapons in her bag. She didn't really want to deal with the serious, sleepless look in Dr Armstrong's eyes because, this morning, she was on a roll of closure and destruction. But the pathologist stopped her before she could leave.

'Steve said something to me. He said these . . . These people, like Boyd and Wilson . . . He said they weren't human. Do you believe that?'

'I believed it long before Steve.'

'So . . . Does that mean that what you're doing isn't murder?'

She was asking the question for her own sake, Melissa realised. For her ethics.

Melissa met her gaze directly. She'd had years to think about this one. Maybe it was the sort of ethical question that would keep Steve awake at night, but she was going to make sure that he slept safely from now on.

'What I'm doing,' she told Dr Armstrong, 'is *necessary*.'

12

LOVING THE ALIEN

Blake had woken up scared. He'd thrashed about the bed like a becalmed crab, curling the sheets into weird shapes, before he realised what had been there the previous night that he was missing this morning. Melissa.

He fell, or stumbled, to his feet, managing to rid himself of the sheets, and quickly searched the artist's cottage.

He relaxed only when he found her note pinned by magnet to the fridge door:

'Off to get necessary things. See you afterwards. You talk in your sleep. "Oh, Joanna, oh." (Joke.) It was all lovely. Finally, for us both. More please. M.' And kisses and other symbols that Blake could only guess at.

He was still staring at the note when 'Oh, Joanna, oh' phoned him, and he found himself speaking to her naked.

She'd made progress with the mission he'd set her in that phone call from Ryle's cottage. She'd got him a slot on a national television show.

'You and Gerald Ryle have to be at the TV studio no later than 10.15 tonight. You go out live, so I hope you're feeling relaxed but confident, laid back but knowledgeable.'

Blake smiled. For the first morning in ages, he was feeling all those things. His head had stopped aching in the field and, since it was probably a stress thing, he was probably never going to get another headache again.

'And try not to bite your nails.'

'I'll do my best.'

'Have you ever seen Mark Knowles' programme?'

Blake stopped on his way back to the fridge. This had gone from being hopeful to being terrifying. 'Once or twice.'

Joanna sounded defensive. 'He's good, he's tough and he's sarcastic. He's something of a wet dream for the ABC1s, so expect a rough ride. I *have* told him you know what you're talking about.'

'Do *you* believe that?'

'You think I say what I actually believe?' She sounded unusually fond of him. 'What sort of madness is this?'

'Oh, cut the crap.' Blake was fond back. 'Do you think this conspiracy exists outside my head?'

'I wouldn't have got you on this show if I didn't. I think more of you than that. I always did.'

Blake looked at the receiver suspiciously. Could you tell when somebody had had sex just from their tone of voice?

He found Melissa at the library. She told him she'd been there all morning, catching up with her job. The other librarian gave Steve a little wave.

Melissa led him through into the display area at the back. The place where this had all begun. She seemed reticent somehow this morning, to Blake's irritation. He wanted to touch her, to throw an arm around her shoulders, but he didn't feel able to.

He told her about Joanna's call, feeling like the young suitor, trying to impress. 'I've arranged to pick up Ryle, just to be on the safe side. He still needs a bit of persuading.'

'I can't blame him. It's not just his reputation he's risking, is it?'

'Ryle's testimony is crucial. It really could be the only thing we need.'

She paused a long time. When she decided on what to say, it was with that precise tone, the survivor's tone, that

195

he'd so wanted to shake out of her. 'We have to do all we can. Attack them with everything. Exactly what they'll do to us if they get the opportunity.'

'Don't go,' he said.

She stared at him, shocked that he'd figured out exactly what she was planning to do. 'If I don't, then all we've learnt and done has been wasted.'

'I know –'

'Steve, I've called Philip. Made the reservations.'

He desperately searched her face for some chink in her armour. 'I'm still asking you not to.'

'And do what instead? Pray this'll all go away?'

He had a hundred different answers to that, the most obvious one being to expose this whole conspiracy on television. But, he had to admit, none of them would be as effective as what Melissa obviously planned to do.

She was still staring at him, shouting at him, obsessed and oblivious to the danger. 'You've got to remember why you started all this!'

He looked at her long and hard, managing not to kiss her. 'Because then I had nothing to lose.'

She turned away quickly, and Blake realised that she felt the same.

But she was going to do what she had to do.

Sarah had been working hard all day, trying to conceal the irritation she felt at having to do the everyday things of her business. At the end of the day, when her assistants had packed up and gone home, she flipped open the file she'd been covertly putting together, pulled open her cooling window, and sat down to what had now become her real work.

She worked her way through the post–mortem material, the accident report and Boyd's medical records, looking for anomalies.

She got to the list the paramedics had made, headed 'On-Site Drugs Administered'. She had to slap a hand down on it to stop it blowing away. A gust of wind from the window.

A sudden, worrying thought crossed Sarah's mind, and she opened her mouth. Her finger slid down the list of treatments and stopped. She had possibly just made the biggest mistake of her professional career. Or maybe the biggest mistake in the history of the world.

Melissa had returned to her house alone, and found her best dress at the back of her wardrobe, in the plastic from the dry cleaners. She'd applied her nail varnish without any thought in her head at all. Pinned her hair up emptily. Made her face up with no concern.

She'd looked at herself in the mirror when she'd finished, though, and wished that Steve was still with her.

Did she really have to kill someone all on her own?

She walked through the door of the restaurant wondering if this was the feeling absolute psychos got: the roller coaster ride of the power of life and death, with sex and glamour thrown in.

Philip was at their usual table, a glass of wine in his hand, and looked at her. He managed an approximation of an appreciative grin. She managed a horrifyingly sincere smile back.

It was just like when they used to date. This had always been Philip's favourite place in Norwich. 'Not poncy,' he'd say. 'They know what they're doing in that kitchen.' And she'd laughed at his habits, like they had all the time in the world.

'I thought for a moment you were going to stand me up,' he said.

'That was always more your trick than mine, wasn't it?' His work had resulted in a series of rain checks and apologetic phone calls. They'd always joked about that.

He didn't respond. 'Drink?'

'Yes. I think I need one.'

He ordered her usual, like he really was her ex-husband. 'Come on. I'm hardly going to bite.'

'I'm sure you're not.' She took a deep breath and began the roller coaster. 'I just know I've got a lot of apologising to do. That's all.'

Philip smiled at her like he was the happiest man on Earth.

Sarah put the phone down, frustrated. Steve Blake was out, so was that Melissa woman.

She had a terrible feeling that she'd sent at least one of them to their death.

They had the waiter bring more wine. He could still drink wine, then, Melissa noted, looking deep into those rough, hurt eyes. She was playing out her story. Letting the truth prop up the lies like any good actor would.

'The night Sweethope disappeared. That was the biggest thing that had ever happened to you. And I hadn't shared it with you.'

'And if you had? Do you really think it would have made a difference?'

He was still defensive, a little suspicious. This must be such a charade for whoever was in there. Such a weird thing for someone from somewhere else to understand: human fuss and love and all that.

She shrugged. 'I was jealous. I was outside all the fuss, the publicity. I felt . . . excluded. And I think that's when I started to make up stories.'

He was suddenly very serious. 'And how do I know you're not making up a story tonight?'

'What?' She suppressed a shriek at that piercing look. Thought of the hypodermics in her handbag.

'How do I know you've really changed your mind about me?' He toyed the air with his finger. Another familiar gesture.

She almost laughed with the relief. 'Because I'm not

198

afraid of you any more.' She emphasised the words, watching how the candlelight reflected in those eyes which were suddenly dull again. They didn't twinkle or gleam. They just absorbed light.

Philip raised his glass suddenly. 'Here's to new beginnings.'

She raised hers and they chinked. 'Cheers.' She felt like they were both observing each other. Maybe she was an interesting subject for study. The end result was that they were both looking at each other like kids out on a first date.

As with their adopted personalities, the lie had created an image that was close to being true.

Blake made his way to Ryle's safehouse feeling deeply disturbed. The sun was setting as he got there, tanning the fields. He felt itchy in his suit. He couldn't back out of his appointment at the TV studios. But he wished that he could also be near to Melissa, close enough to save her if Gates saw through her bluff.

Oh God, it was all happening at once. Please could he keep the first woman he'd let himself be close to for so many years?

Blake hit the horn twice, as arranged, and Ryle came out of the house looking like a man on his way to the gallows. He walked towards the car slowly and deliberately, as if every step was a big decision.

Blake got out of the car to shake his hand. 'Good to see you.'

'Wish I could say the same.' He was still clearly terrified.

'Has anybody tried to warn you off doing this?'

'No, no. They've been ominously quiet.'

Blake opened the car door for the scientist, and couldn't help but glance around the hedges and fields before getting in himself.

* * *

The bottle of wine was empty, and the coffees nearly finished. Philip was smiling at Melissa across the table, more and more gently, like he was discovering ancient memories in himself and liking them. Melissa had tried to put a wall between the two of them in her thoughts, but found that was useless. She was enjoying him again. Enjoying his attention. It was like she'd got her husband back through some sort of seance.

'I still can't quite get over the suddenness of the change,' he said.

'You've got Steve Blake to thank for that.'

Philip raised an eyebrow. 'That's a turn up. I thought he was busy pouring poison into your ear. His conspiracy theories are even more fanciful than yours.'

'Maybe it took someone as fanatical as Blake to make me see how far from the truth I'd really strayed.' She toyed with the glass, then looked at the floor, ashamed. 'It's a pretty unflattering reflection.'

'What made you so certain he was wrong?'

'All that stuff in the computer-software factory. I mean, if anyone was out to destroy him, then why didn't they do it there and then?'

She looked up into his eyes, and noticed the alien fluttering against them for a second. Then it was gone again.

'Exactly. Why didn't he just disappear in an accident? Or get blasted with laser beams? Or get whisked off in a flying saucer?'

'When he couldn't explain it I started to doubt myself. I didn't want to admit it at the time but, deep inside, I knew I was wrong.'

Philip leant back in his chair. So familiar a posture. 'The thing about the Steve Blakes of this world is that they're parasites. They bleed the hope out of anybody they come into contact with. And, worst of all, they don't even know when they're dancing to someone else's tune.'

'What do you mean?' The question came out a little too sharply.

Philip shrugged. 'It's my theory that Steve Blake's being used. Just as he was using you.'

'Now who's peddling conspiracies?' Melissa's mind was racing. Was it possible that this alien thing was boasting? That it had been seduced by the human emotions it must have now grown used to? Maybe she was stirring those up.

'You don't honestly believe Blake is working alone, do you? He's too lightweight. Too much of a loser. On his own, well, he'd just be a fly that needed swatting.'

Melissa trod carefully, certain that she was right. The thing was boasting of its power, using the words that Philip would have used. 'It only takes one fanatic to change history. That's what you always said.'

'This man isn't going to change anything!' he snapped.

He'd betrayed himself. Melissa saw him realise that, stop, make himself smile at her.

'Excuse me, I won't be a moment.' Melissa gestured vaguely and got up, heading for the ladies'.

She glanced back at Philip, and saw him smiling after her, the thing inside delighting in humanity like it was a hot bath. She nodded to herself. Yes. She was ready to do it now.

Unfortunately, Blake had to stop the car in front of the same level crossing where Ryle had had his experience. The headlights washed over the barriers as they waited for the train, and Blake turned to see how the scientist was doing. He was staring at the train, absorbed by his fear.

Blake decided to interrupt. 'I thought I might turn up tonight and find you gone.'

'It crossed my mind.'

'Well, I'm glad you stayed put. I know it might not feel like the right decision now, but I promise you it is.'

Ryle sighed, distracted. 'The end of the world is debated on an upmarket chat show. If that's really what we've come to it makes you wonder if we're worth saving, doesn't it?'

Out of the darkness roared a train. As it screamed by, Blake caught glimpses of a hundred people, sitting in a comfort they shouldn't have felt.

He looked back at Ryle. He looked relaxed now. Now that the train had gone by.

Melissa slumped against the wall when she got to the bathroom. 'I can do this,' she muttered to herself. 'I can do this.' She kept repeating it like a mantra. She went to the mirror, reached into her handbag, and took out one of the syringes. She tapped the shaft, tested the thing with a little squirt of water. It occurred to her that, in other circumstances, she would be nervous now, worried that somebody would come in and think she was a drug user. But she was above all that tonight.

She repeated the test with the second syringe. She didn't know if one would do the job, so she was prepared to use both. She put it beside the first one on the counter under the mirror.

She stared down at the sink, and took several deep breaths.

She picked up both syringes, and dropped them back into her bag.

She straightened up, checked her hair, scratched a mark from her nose, and shouldered her bag.

Then she headed for the door, calm and ready to save the world.

Philip paid the bill, and said that he'd walk Melissa to her car.

'I've never been one to refuse a police escort,' she flirted.

The night was still and quite warm. As they walked across the gardens, past the fountains and into the car park, Melissa seemed to hear everything much more sharply. The click of her heels on the tarmac. The retiring cries of distant seabirds. The low music from the restaurant.

To her shock, he hesitantly took her arm. 'You know what hurt me more than anything else about your breakdown? I realised you were in pain, but I couldn't get through to you. It was as if you'd become a different person.'

They'd reached her car now. She stopped before it, slipped from his arm. They were facing each other. She was shocked to find him moving forward, pressing her back against the bonnet.

'Don't look so scared,' he told her, with a gentle smile.

'Am I?' she whispered. This thing was actually interested. Beyond its disguise, it wanted her. Oh Christ.

It grabbed her and kissed her, roughly, its lips bruising hers.

Melissa tried to return the kiss, but failed. She thought about Steve, and about gases and explosives, and found herself struggling. She pulled away, and couldn't help wiping her lips with the back of her hand. She feigned nervousness and embarrassment. 'I'm sorry. I think this is maybe moving too fast for me. I'm sorry, Philip.'

'That's OK.' He spread his arms, looking every inch the guilty lover.

Melissa wrenched her gaze from him and tore open her bag. 'Bloody keys! Got to be in here somewhere.'

'You haven't changed. Here, let me.' He reached for the bag. This was something he used to do. Part of being Philip Gates, the personality that had seduced this thing into kissing her. All these years of living human life had made this one go native.

Melissa let him take the bag. She turned her face into his way and made the thing that looked like her husband kiss her again.

It was a deeper kiss this time, more sincere, in some insane way.

She took the bag from him. Fumbled into it. Her hands closed on the weapon.

She felt the yell of his exclaiming breath as she thrust

203

the hypodermic into the meat of his shoulder. She pumped the plunger a moment later.

'Why?' He staggered back from her, trying to reach over his shoulder in inhuman, toddler-boy gestures, and collapsed to his knees. He kept repeating that one word, sucking in huge, hurricane breaths.

Melissa hadn't thought about anything past this point. She watched his face contort in agony, and found herself terrified by it.

She could see it wasn't him. But this thing was suffering just like the man she'd loved.

It shouted, twisting and spasming.

It dived at her legs.

She kicked it away. Climbed into her car. Slammed the door. It reached, its hand shaking with effort, to the door handle, the hypodermic still jutting from its shoulder.

It shoved its face up against the side window and grunted at her. 'You think this is over? You think this is over? It's not over!'

Without fastening her seatbelt, she started the car, accelerated back, drove away.

She saw the body slump on to the tarmac just before she turned the corner.

13

RELEASE

Melissa's car sped along the country roads, all the fear that she'd held down welling up in her.

There was a car behind her. A police car: the rotating lights on its roof flamed into life.

She lost the will to run. Let them have her, then. She'd end up in a cell for killing her ex, not for saving the human race. Steve would visit. He'd be the only one to believe her. She slowed down, and flipped her headlights on.

The car pulled out in front of her, its siren wailing.

And sped straight past, on into the night, on its way to another emergency.

Melissa pulled off the road into a lay-by. She switched everything off and sat there, listening to the silence. It occurred to her to listen to the radio, to hear if everybody in the shadow cabinet had collapsed. But that would have been sickening, somehow, in a way that she couldn't understand.

So she just sat there and held on to the steering wheel for a very long time.

Blake and Ryle arrived at the Anglia television building with a few minutes to spare. An assistant floor manager, already miked up, clipboard at the ready, was waiting for them in reception, and stepped forward when he heard them announcing their names to the receptionist.

'Good evening, gentlemen.' He glanced at his watch, grimaced, and hustled them into a lift. His look indicated

205

what he wasn't going to say: that Blake was cutting it pretty bloody fine.

'I drove carefully in order to avoid being turned into an alien lifeform,' Blake whispered to him, straight-faced.

The floor manager smiled politely back.

When the lift doors opened, he led them at a trot along a plush corridor. 'Come on, you're both needed in make-up.'

There was a monitor in the make-up department. As Blake had his face slapped with goo, with extreme haste, he watched Mark Knowles doing the intro to his show. He looked like he was just about able to keep a straight face about being on TV, because, as he and the audience both knew but he would never boast about, it was all a bit beneath his intellect. The impressionist sketch of the Houses of Parliament in the background and the big round table seemed to mock serious-analysis programmes rather than copy them. Blake had always liked Knowles' show in the past, but now he felt horribly worried.

'Good luck,' he muttered to Ryle, as the scientist watched the make-up woman preparing her lotions.

Ryle managed a smile. 'Perhaps we don't need luck any more.'

'Good evening,' Knowles was saying. 'Later tonight we hear from two men who will be making claims that could rock the government. They have evidence of a conspiracy that threatens each and every one of us.' He flicked from mockingly serious to deeply ironic. 'Or . . . so they say.'

The audience chuckled.

Blake turned to where Ryle was protesting at the make-up. 'Don't fight it. You'll look weird without it,' he said. 'And tonight we're going to need all the credibility we can get.'

Melissa got home at around a quarter past nine, feeling exhausted. She went around the house, switching on all the lights. She wanted some confirmation now, some sense that the nightmare was over. But she hadn't wanted to tune into a news programme to see it. It would all be so fragmented and shadowy, a mysterious death here and there, important people going missing. It wouldn't feel like the end of an action movie, like closure. She'd make herself watch Steve's interview. He'd point the media in the right direction, because those he mentioned would all be dead.

She saw a light on her answerphone and hit the button. Then she headed for the drinks cabinet.

'This is Sarah Armstrong,' the voice said. 'If Steve or Melissa are there, could they call me as soon as possible? It's urgent. Please call.'

Melissa looked at the answerphone. Sarah had sounded terribly uncertain about something.

The James Wilson sat at its desk. It was looking at its computer monitor. It looked at the clock in the corner of the screen, and judged that it was the right time to begin.

It entered the Zentexnet with its own personal codes, and the modem connected to the remote service provider with a little cascade of sound that the James Wilson rather liked. It reminded it of home.

'Access requested'. The words appeared on the screen. In English, of course. A strange language would have allowed hackers and spies too big a clue. 'System code/name?' it asked.

The James Wilson typed in a series of numbers and letters.

'Location name required.'

'Sizewell,' the James Wilson typed in.

A graphic appeared. A map of a complex, with small red stars in key areas. The others had placed these responding units in exactly those places, over a long period of time. The units were, themselves, a part of the network.

They knew what they had to do. They were just waiting for the order to do it.

Blake and Ryle were sweating under the studio lights. Blake had never been keen about being on the other end of cameras. Now he was doing all the talking, not panicking, explaining his involvement in what had happened step by step. He couldn't see the audience: they were a shifting mass of shadow. He could only see Ryle, sitting silently and awkwardly beside him; the relaxed and confident shape of Mark Knowles; and the switching of the red light from camera to camera.

Knowles had actually been rather easy on them so far, introducing them quite soberly. Steve had forgotten that he was 'award-winning'. Either they'd really done their research, or Joanna had been especially sharp in her briefing.

'You're asking us to believe some incredible things here,' Knowles said, after Steve had finished his story.

The audience made an uncomfortable-audience sound. They were wound up, waiting for Knowles to deflate these weirdos with a single witty remark.

'I agree.' Blake nodded. 'I think they're incredible, too. Unfortunately they happen to be true.'

One of the Sweethope skeleton photos appeared on the monitor at Steve's feet. 'According to you, you took this photo underwater at Sweethope, off the Norfolk coast. How long ago?'

'Two weeks.'

'But it's not there now?'

'No. An explosion destroyed it straight after the dive.'

Knowles paused for just the right length of time. 'That was rather unlucky, wasn't it?'

Blake heard the audience titter and took a deep breath. He'd been waiting for the moment to play this card, knowing that it would slap down the funny stuff for a while. 'It was deliberately destroyed by a corrupt police

208

officer from Central Operations, called Chief Superintendent Philip Gates.' He'd avoided mentioning aliens so far, settling for calling the members of the conspiracy 'impostors'.

The audience actually applauded.

Knowles whistled. 'I wish I was your lawyer, Steve, because I think that allegation just earned him a fortune.'

The Anglia newsroom's evening shift, both of them, were sitting up in the gallery for *The Mark Knowles Show*, because Fullalove was interested in conspiracy theories. He wanted, Gallagher alleged, to be the next Woodward or Bernstein. What Gallagher wondered was why he'd chosen Norwich as the best place from which to explore the mean streets of official cover-ups.

Besides, it was a slow night. There were only half a dozen of the news crew down in the newsroom. Gallagher was typing up a Reuters piece on the Antarctic treaty for the overnight bulletins on the gallery PC when he took a phone call, cradling the receiver in the crook of his shoulder.

'Gallagher here.'

The director, who was busy switching cameras, conducting the vast bank of monitors and controls in front of him with violent swipes of his arms, shushed him.

But Gallagher had already stopped typing. He was listening to what the man on the other end of the phone was telling him. He gestured to Fullalove to come over, grabbed a pad and started to note the details. 'Yeah? My God! Right, I see.'

The others were paying as much attention as they could to the show in progress. He was getting irritated looks from all corners of the room now.

'OK, OK, ring me when you get there!' Gallagher put the phone down and turned to Fullalove, who was boggling over his shoulder at what he'd written on the pad. 'Get the overtime book out. We've got a big one breaking.'

'You're sure this isn't a con job?' Fullalove asked. 'Some firework fanatic's wet dream?'

'I doubt it. That was the County fire chief I was just speaking to –'

Alice dashed in from the coffee machine outside. 'Joe's going mad. They're calling the newsroom to full capacity.'

Davidson, the newsreader, ran in, pulling on his tie. 'Get two of them up here, fast!'

'What's going on?' bellowed the director over his shoulder.

'The big one,' Gallagher bellowed back. 'So give us a bit of slack, all right?'

Knowles had turned to Ryle. 'Steve's background is in newspapers. We're used to newspapers making things up. They do it every day. But scientists aren't in the habit of lying, are they, Mr Ryle?'

'No. No, we wouldn't knowingly falsify results.'

Ryle sounded to Blake like he was giving evidence, being exceedingly exact about what he said. It was a good image to project. The audience were interested in this. They might actually have swung them.

'So when I was told that you, a senior government science adviser, were willing to come on national television to back up Steve on the truth of this conspiracy, I sat up and took notice.'

'Back him up?' Ryle looked confused.

Blake stared at Ryle in shock.

Knowles frowned. 'I understood there had been an attempt on your life which convinced you –'

'What? Oh, you mean the other day! My car broke down at a level crossing. I foolishly tried to cross by foot. I would hardly call that an attempt on my life. Stupid, perhaps.'

The audience were confused. They'd lost the plot of who they were supposed to be cheering, who they were supposed to laugh at, who to believe.

'So let me get this right.' Knowles looked like a man who was feeling his reviews and ratings dip. 'You have doubts about Steve Blake's claims?'

'I have more than doubts.' Ryle laughed. 'I refute his claims completely.'

Blake opened his mouth in an exclamation of slow horror. He nearly slapped himself for being such a fool. But he had no test, no way of knowing who'd been replaced and who hadn't.

Trying to salvage something, Knowles turned quickly to Blake. 'Steve? This is a man who's on your side. Is this as staunch as your allies get?'

Blake knew the cause was lost, but he wasn't going to just throw in the towel and walk away. If he could just manage to keep the audience's attention, he had a real opportunity here. He looked daggers at Ryle. 'Well, obviously he's not an ally any more. You must see what's happened here. This isn't a setback to my claims. This is proof!'

Melissa had forced herself to watch Steve's TV interview. Now she sat in front of the television, flabbergasted, staring at the picture. 'Why didn't Ryle bleed?' she muttered desperately to herself. 'Why didn't Steve see him bleed?'

'Proof of what exactly?' Knowles was saying.

'Proof that renewal is an ongoing process!'

Joanna was watching the show with a big bag of crisps nearby. She found that she was eating faster and faster the longer the show went on. She'd had dreams about watching her ex drowning, but seeing it happening was nowhere near as entertaining as that. Poor Steve. But why had he gone in so unprepared, with a story which, to be finally, brutally, honest, was about as realistic as an episode of *Teletubbies*?

Steve was currently trying to define this thing called renewal, his hands hiding his face like he was deliberately impersonating a man who was lying, mad, or both. 'Replication, cloning, changing. The alteration or trans-ferring of —'

The phone rang. The sub-ed. on the other end didn't even give Joanna a chance to speak.

'What?' she shouted, at the news he was babbling to her. She killed the TV. 'Are you sure? How soon can we get someone there?'

The gallery above the studio was now a hive of activity. The entire news team were present, upsetting the pro-gramme staff with their elbows and their shouting and their vast coffee intake. Gallagher was typing out a script on a VDU, reacting automatically to all the notes and additions that were being thrust under his nose. Davidson, the newsreader, was reading it over his shoulder, mouth-ing the words, repeating anything complex.

'We have Mary Madigan for a quote on line three,' called Alice.

Fullalove put down the phone and called to Gallagher. 'We interrupt Knowles, yeah? The boss reckons CNN have got pictures.'

Gallagher didn't slow his typing. 'How can they have, unless they planted the frigging bomb?'

'I wouldn't put it past them,' murmured Davidson.

'CNN are offering them for two hundred thou.'

Gallagher laughed. 'Trust those bastards to get an exclusive on the end of the world!'

His own phone rang. It was CNN.

'Yes, yes. Yes. That's fine. I'm authorised. We can talk.'

'How soon are we going to get someone out there?' asked Davidson, preening himself ready to go on.

'You volunteering to go and bathe in fall-out, are you?' said Fullalove, ignoring Gallagher's frantic shush.

212

'Sure. I smoke Capstan Full Strength. Be like a health cure.'

Fullalove noticed that Gallagher was ranting down the phone, his gestures getting more and more frenetic. 'What are we going to do without pictures? I've got a feeling an artist's impression of a nuclear meltdown isn't going to play –'

Gallagher slammed down the phone. 'We've got them! They're piping them down.'

A few of the monitors flipped to the input coming down the line from CNN. Helicopter shots. The viewpoint hovered over something that initially looked like a volcanic eruption. An industrial installation of some sort, engulfed in flame. The sheer size of the blaze, the way the light of it blotted out the sky, hushed the entire gallery. Even the technicians who'd been trying to run *The Mark Knowles Show* paid attention when they saw the square block shapes and familiar logos of British Nuclear Power.

'It cost us an arm and a leg.' Gallagher smiled proudly. 'But, hey, no party without punch.'

'That's some punch,' whispered Fullalove.

Gallagher looked around him, taking in the faces of the journalists who were now all staring at the monitors, the lights of the flame colouring their faces. He'd never seen this lot look so concerned.

'They got you, didn't they?' Blake asked Ryle.

He had the increasing feeling that he was shouting into the wind, and had made up his mind to go out in as noisy a manner as possible. The ravings of a crank might just make the newspapers tomorrow. What made things worse was the sensation that some of the audience weren't really paying attention any more. There was a mutter running through them, as if they were whispering something to each other.

'I don't know what you're talking about,' countered Ryle.

'If we could get back to the subject under discussion –' Mark Knowles desperately attempted to hold his show together.

Blake ignored him. 'When did it happen? I should never have left you on your own.'

Knowles frowned, put a hand to his earpiece. Then raised his hand. The camera swung off Blake and Ryle and on to him.

'I'm sorry. We'll have to interrupt you for an important newsflash. Apparently there has been a major accident at Sizewell nuclear power station. John Davidson has the story.'

Blake noticed for the first time that a backcloth had been assembled nearby and a desk brought on before it. The cameras swung to cover the area as a smart, middle-aged man looked into the autocue.

Blake realised that nobody was looking at him any more.

Davidson had been practising his scales a moment before the camera cut to him. Now he had his serious voice on. He looked as imposing as a mountain. Good on him, Gallagher thought. The poor sods watching were going to need a bit of that authority-figure business to deal with this one. And depending on how fast they'd been, they might all be in line for some sort of award.

'Thank you, Mark. Yes, early reports are still coming in of a major incident at the Sizewell B reactor in Suffolk. Eyewitnesses talk about a huge fireball erupting into the sky at about 10.44 this evening. Nobody yet knows the cause of the explosion, but the police have not ruled out a terrorist attack. The risk from radioactive fall-out is thought to be minimal –'

The whole news team looked at each other with a 'Yeah, right' look.

'– as long as sensible precautions are taken. Police are advising those within a fifty-mile radius to stay indoors, but emphasise that the situation is containable.'

214

'Containable!' Fullalove muttered to Gallagher as soon as Davidson had finished.

'I love that word. Coffee?'

Blake and Ryle were hustled off the stage as Knowles got more instructions from the gallery. They'd got hold of somebody who could make a reasonably authoritative statement, and were going to interview them. Blake looked between the scenes of chaos on the monitors and Ryle's impassive face, as they arrived in the corner they'd been shoved into.

'You can tell me now. The bastards did finally get to you, didn't they?'

Ryle shrugged. 'Let's just say that I can see things for what they are.'

Blake pointed to the monitor. 'And this is part of it all, isn't it?'

'A small step in the right direction. This is your wake-up call.'

'What?'

But the thing that wore the face of Gerald Ryle just walked away, chuckling. Blake could hear the horror in that sound. He imagined what Ryle must have felt like when they finally got to him.

He turned back to the monitors, and watched the beginning of the end of the world, neatly framed as television news, as a distraction from the real issue that had now been buried.

Melissa was curled in a foetal ball by her sofa. The pictures of Sizewell burning had been bad enough. But a new detail had just been added. One that had made her legs crumple beneath her.

She just about managed to reach out for the phone when it started to ring. It was Steve. He'd seen it too.

Philip was walking across the shot, looking concerned, but very much alive.

'Are you watching this?' Steve asked. 'I thought he was dead! I thought you'd killed him!'

'So did I. Steve, listen.' She got to her feet, making herself get back to the fight again. 'Sarah Armstrong's been on the phone. She says she's got the answer. She's discovered where we're going wrong.'

Steve sounded bitter. 'We don't need her to tell us we've brought the sky down upon us.'

'You think they blew up Sizewell out of revenge?'

'I don't know. No. Maybe as a distraction. Listen, I'll meet you at Sarah's. As soon as I can.'

She started to ask when that would be, but he interrupted.

'I have to see someone first.'

'Who?' Melissa knew who it was going to be.

'Joanna. She's the only one who can help us now.'

And he put the phone down before Melissa could argue.

She set the receiver back in its cradle, and sat down, numbly watching her ex-husband walking back and forth in the frame. Back and forth, pretending to direct things.

Behind him, the burning nuclear power station billowed huge columns of black smoke into the air.

It looked like the funeral pyre for the human race.

14

'WE ARE YOUR DESTINY'

The Philip Gates sat in his car looking at the wreckage of Sizewell. Fire crews were rushing past, shepherding human beings from the outbuildings to ambulances. More fire engines and police cars were arriving all the time. The first volunteer crews in radiation suits were heading towards the main buildings at a march. They were knowingly shortening their lives. The shape of the installation was broken, remodelled into fire and clouds of smoke that knotted across the whole sky. The air smelt of chemical explosives. Not that the human beings would know that. What an unusual world, where bombs smelt like flowers.

The Philip Gates had started to understand how the human beings thought and acted. He had dreamt three times since making this body. That was why, as he watched the secondary explosions begin, he had to suppress the most extraordinary urge to laugh.

He leant forward to share the moment.

The Control was a handsome, dark-haired man, with hints of grey above a kindly face. He sat behind a large oak desk in a darkened room. On the desk were family photographs, his papers, his inhaler. He leant back and closed his eyes. He started to chuckle at the Philip Gates' experience. It was so beautiful, so cleansing.

He suggested that the human beings who had been exploring their system now knew a little too much.

The Philip Gates agreed. He was just starting to elaborate when he stopped.

The Control's pupils appeared once more, and he emitted a high, sharp note of exultation.

The Philip Gates had been disturbed by his driver, who'd opened the car door.

'What is it?' the Philip Gates asked.

'The press boys are ready for you now, sir.'

'All right. All right. Give me a moment, will you?'

'Yes, sir.' The driver closed the door again.

The Philip Gates took one last look at the destruction and smiled again. Then he adjusted his tie and got out to play, once more, the part that he had come to love.

At two o'clock in the morning, the newsroom of Joanna's newspaper was packed to bursting. Journalists were rushing back and forth, shoving past each other and reaching over each other as they worked at monitors, keyboards and phones. Blake slalomed through them. The motorway traffic had been increasing every minute, as more and more people tried to get out of the East. He'd rode the top of the wave, finding London to be just as jammed. He'd parked on a corner, on a double yellow line. There were journalists' cars all over the road, left there like discarded toys.

He saw Joanna from a distance. She was working the room, pacing from one corner to the other, smoking like she meant it. He called to her.

She looked up, startled, and then sighed. 'Steve. What are you doing here?'

'What do you think?' He made his way to her side, waving away the smoke. 'I'm offering you an exclusive.'

Joanna looked like she knew just which. She gave him a look of vast irony. 'This isn't a good time.'

'That's why I'm here.'

'I can't talk *now*! This is the biggest story in years!'

'And I can tell you why it's happening. And I can tell you who's behind it. And I can tell you it's going to keep on happening.'

Some of the journalists nearby had looked up. One or two of them, those who'd been around in the old days, had followed Steve's progress across the room, like he brought a headline and a front-page photo with him.

Joanna seemed to weigh their whole life together against her fraught condition and tomorrow morning's front page. 'I can give you five minutes.'

'That'll do for starters.'

'Make that three.' She steered him towards her glass-fronted inner office.

As they went, Blake felt the eyes of the others upon them. They could feel the story inside him, ready to blossom.

When they got inside, she shut the door behind them and dropped all the blinds. 'So?'

Melissa drove at speed towards Norwich. Her car's head-lights flickered over many, many vehicles going the other way, but she was the only one on this road.

She had to see Dr Armstrong. To find out what her mistake had been, and if she had a new theory or weapon in place of her old one. And to make sure she was OK. If they'd got to Ryle, maybe she ought to be picked up and taken to somewhere safe.

Melissa had kept the radio on, listening to the mounting panic of experts who, for once, had increasingly no idea of what was going to happen.

'This is surely the end of the nuclear era. The British public will not tolerate accidents like these. We are not in Russia –'

'It could be just as disastrous as Chernobyl. Though frankly, I think the British public will tolerate anything they're told to.'

Melissa saw lights ahead, and slowed. She drove past a checkpoint being set up. Cars going in her direction were soon going to be stopped. A Territorial Army van had its doors open, and TA members were dragging out sandbags.

'I'm sorry,' the radio man continued, through a lot of static that was in the air tonight. 'I'm going to have to interrupt to bring news of what look like two more copycat attacks at nuclear installations in the United States and India. We'll go direct to our American correspondent: Caroline Standing.'

Melissa bit her lip and shoved a cassette at random into the player.

'Don't fear the reaper,' it sang to her, as she drove on through the night. 'Baby take my hand.'

'You have to listen to me, Joanna!' Steve was pacing about the office like a caged animal.

'I watched your comeback, Steve, and I have to say I wasn't impressed.'

'The reason I was shamed on the Knowles TV programme was *precisely* because I was right!' he shouted. 'Can't you see that? Ryle has been renewed.'

'Do you expect me to believe that?'

'Take a close look at the copper in charge of the enquiry. It'll be Gates. And it'll be Gates because he can manage to bury the reasons it happened better than anyone else!'

She made a cutting motion through the air and glanced at her watch. 'This is as far as it goes, Steve.'

'When were my instincts ever wrong? Just tell me once!'

'That was then, Steve, that was before –'

'I'm the same person I always was! I have *not* changed! If you'd just wake up and see that!' As he yelled the words, he realised they were true.

'No.' She wasn't listening. 'Steve, do you realise how far I've travelled down the road for you? Because it's you?'

'So you were just doing me a favour? Humouring me?'

'I wanted to believe that you hadn't lost your touch. I wanted to believe we could work together again.'

'Same old Joanna. You never took a risk in your life

unless I'd taken ten times the risk first!' It was a huge release, saying these things. The world was crumbling around them, but they were finally talking. Blake was finally discovering who he was.

Which was probably why Charlotte chose just that moment to come in.

She glanced at him with a kind of swift, offhand loathing, and went to her mistress. 'The computers have gone down again.'

'Shit.' Joanna stood up. 'That's the last thing I need.'

'What software do you use?' Blake stopped her from moving off. 'Zentex?'

'Yes, like I told you, everyone does!'

'Exactly. Zentex is owned by the Leonards, more Sweethope survivors! Don't you remember how far we took this? Can't you see this is all linked?'

Joanna met Charlotte's angry gaze and made to go.

The voice from the television in the corner of the office stopped them both.

'The explosion succeeded because the computer-operated security system was sabotaged.' Philip Gates had stepped into a circle of flash bulbs and microphones.

Joanna stopped, her frown engaging with Blake's smile, again. 'So –'

'There is one man in particular we would like to assist us with our enquiries,' said Gates. 'We have a picture of him. His name is Steven Blake.'

Blake slowly turned his head to look at Joanna. Charlotte had vanished. He was acutely aware of the hundreds of drama-hungry people in the newsroom immediately outside this little glass cube.

Joanna was looking back at him like he was the bringer of all disaster and wonder at once. It was also a profoundly quizzical look, like she wanted to start asking him journalist questions.

He sighed. 'Oh come on. Do you really think I'd be responsible for that?'

221

Joanna looked at the screen, then looked back at him. As if she wasn't sure.

As Charlotte made her way to Charlie in the northern corner of the newsroom, she could hear that stern-looking policeman continuing his spiel. He was speaking from the CNN monitor on Charlie's desk.

'We would like to talk to this man as soon as possible in connection with this terrorist act. He is dangerous and might be armed. He shouldn't be approached.'

Charlotte arrived, and brightly tapped Charlie on the shoulder. 'Call security,' she said.

Charlie swivelled in his chair, to reveal that his fingers were already on the keys of the phone. He grinned at her.

As he did so, Jo stepped out of her office. That Blake man was beside her.

Charlotte carefully stepped between their eye-line and Charlie. This was for Joanna's own good.

Blake looked around at the whole roomful of people. Many of them were his former colleagues. Their expressions varied. Some had a look of staunch, hurt support, as if they were angry that Blake could be accused that way. Some were just gawping at him. Some couldn't meet his gaze.

He tried to say something meaningful to them. But the murmur that passed between them, and the aggression of their gaze, got to him, and he could only stammer. 'What? You think . . .? What, are you stupid?'

Then Joanna's arm was on his, and she was leading him, marching, her expression daring anybody to get in their way, towards the lifts. 'I am actively throwing away a story,' she told him, as the doors of the newsroom swished closed behind them. Blake could hear the noise from the newsroom becoming something like a shout. She pressed the lift button and waited with him, glancing back at the doors behind them from time to time, as if holding a great shout ready for the first rebellious journo that dared to come through them.

'Something tells me you're going to need a new secretary,' Blake said, loving her.

'I'm going to need a new career.' The lift wasn't responding, so she thumped it. 'Come on! Come on! I've got a lot of favours to call in.' Her eyes met his, serious for a moment. 'I believe you, you know. I finally do. I'm going to get someone to listen.'

'Just do what you can.'

'I'll do better than that. I promise.' Another thump. 'Come on!'

The indicator was moving at last. The lift was coming up from the ground floor. A long delay like that must have meant that it had waited for –

They realised at the same moment.

'Take the stairs!' Joanna shouted. 'Go on! Go!' But she grabbed him before he could move and kissed him.

Blake stared at her for a moment, taken aback.

'Be careful,' she whispered, her voice full of things that they'd messed up between them. Her face hardened again an instant later. 'Now move!'

Blake obeyed without a second thought. He sprinted through the door to the stairs.

Joanna stood by the lifts, her back against the wall, panting.

How was she going to explain this one to anybody apart from her therapist?

With a ping, the lift stopped, and two security guards ran out of it, looking around.

'Quick!' Joanna screamed at them. 'He's gone on to the roof! He's on the roof!'

They rushed out of an entirely different door to the one that her ex-husband had used. Joanna reconsidered. Even her therapist would wonder why she'd sacrificed a glittering career for principles which, previously, she'd thought to be non-existent.

She took a deep breath, rubbed off a rogue bit of lipstick, and turned to go and talk to her staff. She was going to try and sack Charlotte at least once before they gave her her job.

Blake raced down the stairs, tripping over his feet. He almost careered straight into the lobby of the building, but threw himself back at the last moment, ducking into the shadow of the swinging doors.

In the lobby in front of him, four more security men had run up to the lifts. A leader with a walkie-talkie slapped them on the shoulder and pushed the buttons for them. 'Third floor. Newsroom.'

They went.

Blake took his keys from his pocket, thumped open the door in front of him, and tiredly jangled past the security guard, heading past the familiar pot plants into the black- ness beyond. 'Goodnight!' he called over his shoulder.

'Goodnight, sir,' called the security guard. He didn't even look.

Blake found his car amongst all the other cars. He made himself avoid ducking behind it as a police car approached at speed, its lights flashing and siren blaring. Blake braced himself, but it went straight past, stopping at the steps of the newspaper building.

Blake slipped into his car just as the policemen ran into the building. As soon as they'd vanished, he screeched into a reverse and accelerated away across the city.

Melissa's car screeched to a halt in the car park of the Pathology Labs. There was only one other car there, which she took to be Dr Armstrong's. She'd switched quickly back to the news when she couldn't stand the message of the music any more, but the lyrics were still going through her head. Millions of people every day. Seasons don't fear the reaper.

She got out, then leapt back in to switch the radio off.

'In what is seen as the biggest act of co-ordinated terrorism ever recorded,' it was saying, 'no less than seven nuclear power stations have been simultaneously destroyed by a planted computer virus –'

The click left the car park silent, insects filling the cones of illumination from the lights. Distantly, an owl hooted.

Melissa licked her lips, and took quick small steps across the silence towards the building.

The doors were open, but nobody was behind the reception desk. Papers and forms had been left on the counter. A coat was draped over the receptionist's chair.

Melissa looked over the desk in the silence, bracing herself for a body. There wasn't one.

The thump of a door made her spin round.

Dr Armstrong appeared, looking wary and tired.

'Am I glad to see you,' said Melissa.

Blake sped down the empty lane of the motorway that led to Norfolk, glancing from time to time at the immense convoys of desperate people heading in the other direction.

He turned off at the usual exit, and slid down the darkness of the country roads, feeling a strange freedom in being a fugitive. At least it wasn't a game of disguises any more. They were fighting the real battle now.

He took a turn, then tried to accelerate and found that he couldn't.

The car's engine coughed and juddered, threatening to cut out. Blake looked round, wondering for a horrible moment if what had happened to Wilson and Ryle was about to happen to him.

Then he glanced at the petrol gauge. It was flat to the bottom of the red.

Ahead appeared a single light. A petrol station in the middle of nowhere.

Blake turned the wheel and let the engine die as the car rolled on to the forecourt.

He'd expected to have to yell and wake somebody up, or try and break into one of the pumps, but the place turned out to be open. Not only that, but it was one of those rare petrol stations which weren't self-service.

An angular, awkward-looking man in an oily cap and overalls had positively run out when Blake's car juddered to a halt. He introduced himself as Frank, and was at Blake's service. He'd had a lot of custom that night, yes sir, a bonanza, and he was looking forward to a lot more.

Blake got out of the car and watched Frank fill the tank. Then suddenly he was clutching his head again, as the familiar pain rushed up his spine and hit him between the eyes. He slumped against the warm bulk of the car, trying not to scream.

'You OK, sir?'

Blake was about to reply that, no, of course he wasn't bloody –

When the pain switched off again.

'Yeah.' He straightened up. 'Yeah. I'm . . . fine.'

Frank started to whistle. 'Who Wants To Be a Millionaire?' was the tune. 'You know,' he said. 'I think I know where we've been getting it wrong.'

'Who?' Blake frowned, not really wanting to talk.

'Us!' The garage owner made a grand gesture that encompassed the surrounding landscape and spilt a little petrol. 'You, me, mankind. Have we behaved for the group good, or have we only thought about ourselves?''

'These are pretty extreme circumstances.'

But Frank was well into his stride now. 'Take this place.' He screwed the petrol cap back on. 'If I'd gone off, like the others, what would have happened to you?'

'Good question,' Blake whispered.

'I mean, you'd have been stuck.' He looked up at the horizon again, at what looked like the fires of Sizewell, but were probably just the lights of the nearest town. 'Anyway, all this is going to change, liven up.'

'So you'll be staying put? Despite the fall-out and all that?'

'Too right. I'm going to be well set up here.' He cracked a toothy grin.

'Think you're going to stay busy after everybody's evacuated?'

'This place'll be my own regular little gold mine.'

Blake looked at the empty expanse of the road, wondering where he was going to sleep. 'So what happened to the group good all of a sudden?'

Frank took Blake's money, counted change out of a money belt and, while doing so, wagged his finger solemnly in Blake's direction. 'No, no, friend. You don't understand. I'm acting for myself, of course I am. Like everybody else. Except I've thought ahead. You think anyone'll want nuclear power after this? Can you imagine what this'll do to the fossil-fuel market?' He pointed proudly to his antique of a petrol pump. 'This stuff is going to be liquid gold.' He tapped his forehead. 'Foresight.'

Blake couldn't help but smile. 'I'm not sure this road's going to be that full of traffic. People get kind of edgy around radioactive leaks.'

'But not as edgy as they do on a Bank Holiday Monday when they have to keep the family happy.'

'I'm sorry?'

'Day-trippers!' He stared at Blake, flapping his arms to emphasise his big idea. 'I can't lose! They go to see the ruins of Pompeii, don't they? You think this is any different? All human life *was* here!'

Blake put a hand to his brow again. He was getting an ordinary headache now.

'You sure you're OK?'

227

'Fine.'

'You collect points, sir?'

'No. Not really.' Blake opened the door of his car and got back in.

As he accelerated away, he saw Frank in the rear-view mirror. The little man had taken a points book from his back pocket, and was eagerly using up Blake's discarded share.

The television images followed Melissa and Dr Armstrong into the pathology lab. They were playing on a set in the corner. There were now pictures from the various foreign installations that were on fire, as well as Sizewell.

Dr Armstrong took a seat, and Melissa did the same.

'I tried to get hold of you,' Dr Armstrong said, 'to warn you. I was checking the medical records of some other Sweethope survivors. Two of them died a year ago. Same story as Philip Boyd. Minor accident, no serious injuries, sudden collapse after treatment. But they weren't treated with saline solution.'

'So why did Boyd die?'

'Certainly the saline didn't do him any good. But I think what actually killed him was pure oxygen.'

'Oxygen?' Melissa stared at the woman. If only she'd known this a day ago. 'How?'

'I have no idea, but it certainly had an effect on the tissue samples. It was also the only substance I could find in common with the other victims. Oxygen is given as a matter of course by paramedics.'

Melissa had a sudden moment of realisation, and felt rather limited and human that it should have come to her this late. 'That's what Elizabeth Madigan was trying to tell us the day before she died!'

'I'm sorry?'

'One of them. Sort of. She said: "We cannot share your air, but we must breathe our own."'

Dr Armstrong looked across to where the television

228

was showing plumes of smoke filling the air.

Melissa followed her meaning. 'Maybe they can survive here because of the carbon in the air. What if they need an atmosphere with a lower oxygen content and even higher pollutants? Well, what we call pollutants. Maybe to them it's completely natural.'

'Well, they're going to be partying tonight then, aren't they?' Dr Armstrong slowly shook her head as the screen showed refugees in India running down the street from clouds of suffocating smoke that rolled behind them. She rubbed her brow. 'Look, I don't really know how safe we are here. Maybe we should go.'

'No. Steve will get here. I asked him to meet us.'

Dr Armstrong smiled sadly. 'I thought he was insane when I first met him.'

'Me too. That was part of the attraction.'

That was obviously news to the pathologist. She raised her eyebrows conspiratorially. 'Whatever it takes.'

'I thought he was insane for the same reasons I was,' Melissa continued. 'Because he'd seen that the world didn't fit together any more, that something was out of kilter.'

'So have you two got anything else in common, apart from a desire to save the world?'

Melissa closed her eyes, aware of how much she wanted to sleep. 'I don't know yet. Maybe I'll never get the chance to find out.'

The Philip Gates had attended to sending his police officers to control the press and sightseers. It was surprisingly easy to use these human beings to move the plan forward. They just agreed to every order he gave them. It was as if they'd become tired with their planet and wanted to hand it over.

He got back into his car, locked the door and relaxed in his seat. He closed his eyes, and let the body do what it would while he concentrated, feeling under the surface of

reality like his human hand would feel under a piece of
furniture.

He looked up suddenly and smiled. He'd found what
he had lost. He smiled wider. He really liked the feel of
that. He reached for the dashboard radio, and pressed the
send button. 'Gates to Alpha Unit. Gates to Alpha Unit.
Over.'

The radio bubbled into life. 'Alpha Unit receiving, sir.'

'Possible sighting of suspect Steven Blake.'

Blake was speeding along once more, listening to the
radio. The headache fluctuated. With his luck, he was
going to have a cerebral haemorrhage or something
before his species was wiped out.

'James Wilson of British Nuclear Power,' the newsreader
was saying, 'has repeated his claim that the media are
whipping the country into a state of mass psychosomatic
illness.'

Blake couldn't help but smile at that. The aliens were
surely taking the piss. They could afford to now, he
supposed. Or maybe they knew that that was the sort of
ridiculous pronouncement that the British expected from
their authorities.

There was a white car behind him. He paid sudden
attention to the image in his rear-view mirror. Was that a
police car? Hard to tell. Its emergency lights weren't on. It
was speeding at a steady distance behind him, but it wasn't
accelerating to intercept. Not yet, anyway.

Constables Condon and Lyons were experienced mobile
coppers who had been newly transferred to Special Ops.
So far, their policy had been strictly 'Ours is not to
reason why'. Their operations had been obscure and un-
explained, so far, but a bit trivial. It was quite something,
therefore, to find themselves shadowing the major suspect
in the biggest terrorist scare of their lifetime. Lyons kept
the patrol car at a distance from him while Condon kept

230

touch with the boss on the radio.

'We've picked up the suspect on the A11, sir. Pursuing
m. Do you want us to pull him over?'

'No. Just follow for now.'

'Affirmative.' Condon put down the radio and shrugged
Lyons. 'What you think? Is he meeting up with others, do
u reckon?'

Lyons looked dubious. 'If he is, then you'll hear me
outing for back-up, very loudly.'

ake was now certain that he was being shadowed by a
lice car. He slowed down at a major roundabout, and
ned the car for the first exit, signalling appropriately. He
d the same for the second, then went on to circle the
undabout again.

The police car did all of that too.

Blake understood what the point was then. They
anted his conspirators. Which meant Sarah and Melissa.

lorry joined the roundabout in front of him. He
dicated that he was going to take the next exit, then
noothly overtook the lorry as it lumbered around.
ccelerated. Sped off down the exit after that.

The police car didn't appear behind him.

Blake slammed the accelerator to the floor and grabbed
s road atlas from the glove compartment.

lpha Unit, sir.' The voice over the radio in the Philip
ates' car sounded worried. 'We lost him at the Postwick
undabout.'

The Philip Gates had his eyes closed. Beneath the lids,
: felt the body start to flicker the orbs, thinking it was
eaming. His hand just managed to close on the radio as
: felt round the edges of the dimension and got his . . .
s fingers, he thought of them as his fingers now, he was
used to this, into the right holes. 'You'll find him on
e B1065.'

'That takes him back on himself, sir.'

'B1065,' the Philip Gates repeated foggily, trying function in both dimensions. 'Heading north.'

Blake had improvised a route via B roads, across country. was just starting to feel very pleased with himself, as he sp along a dim road with high hedges, when he saw not but two police cars skid into the road behind him. 'C OK.' He gritted his teeth. 'Let's see what you know.'

He waited until they were on his tail, until he could their faces. Then he killed the headlights and brak suddenly into a forty-five degree turn into a side road.

They shot past, already braking.

Blake accelerated, did a fast turn around a bend, a swung his car down another narrow lane at an angle. sign saying WINDMILL LANE careered into view and th out again. The wheels were bouncing at speed over ha ened clumps of mud.

Blake felt almost exhilarated by the pursuit. He'd do this sort of stuff before, and felt sure the coppers after h hadn't. Indeed, last time he'd been in a car chase, pursuers had been shooting at him.

'You've missed him!' shouted the boss from the radio. ' took the Windmill Lane turning!'

Lyons looked archly at Condon. 'Very good, sir.'

The driver stopped the police car dead, and managed awkwardly co-ordinate three-point turns with the dri of the other car.

'How does Gates do that?' asked Condon. 'What's got, an eye in the sky or something?'

'He's top brass. Perhaps you have to be psychic now well as being a Mason.'

Blake thumped the steering wheel in frustration when lights of the police cars appeared behind him once mc winking through the trees. 'It can't be!'

He sent the car speeding across a crossroads, hoping

ome sort of traffic that would get between him and them. ut the countryside was deserted, thanks to the nuclear anic, a rally driver's paradise. He thought for a moment: iis car had been with him all the way, outside Joanna's uilding, Ryle's house –

'Stupid! Stupid!' He slapped the steering wheel again. They've bugged the car!'

A sign flashed into the headlights saying THOMPSON QUARRY. He swerved sideways into the woodland track iat led towards it.

Blake is off the road. He's turned off the road. Look out or a sign for Thompson Quarry.' Gates' voice crackled irough the leading police car once more.

The sign appeared immediately. Both cars braked, ame to a halt slightly past it, and had to reverse to turn. .gain, there was much spinning of steering wheels and esitant, urgent, co-ordination between drivers.

'This guy's better than Uri Geller,' muttered Condon as iey gingerly tried to accelerate up the rocky surface of ie country track.

'I hope he's good at bending metal, then,' said Lyons. This trick's playing merry hell with the suspension.'

Blake ran out of road, and spun the car to a halt with a wish of gravel right beside a flooded gravel pit. He opped the locks, kicked open the door and dived under ie vehicle, looking desperately for anything unfamiliar. Where is it? Come on, come on.'

Ten seconds, no sign of anything. Out of time. They iust have put it inside. He leapt up, went to the boot, ung it open. Ten seconds here. Diving gear. Photo- raphic equipment. Nothing.

The only sounds as he searched were the settling of ravel, the calls of disturbed animals and birds, and the rind on the water. Then another: the sounds of car ngines, bumping their way up the track behind him.

Blake straightened up. There was absolutely nowhe
to run now. They had him. He abandoned his searc
turned and watched the calming patterns of ripples on t
water, and wondered if he should, or ought, to put up ar
sort of fight.

'He is near the water. He's near water,' said Gates over tl
radio.

The police cars came to the top of the hill, the end
the track. The two coppers saw the dark shape of tl
suspect's car ahead, outlined against the background
water, shining in the moonlight.

'Strewth, he's right!' exclaimed Lyons.

'I wonder if he does racing tips?'

'Get him in on the lottery syndicate, eh?'

They came to a halt on the gravel beside the lake, tl
other car sealing off the exit to the road. Lyons ar
Condon got out, and walked across to the suspect's ca
their boots crunching in the gravel. They did the usu
search, inside, boot, under. No sign of him. And nothir
on the sheer walls of the quarry, either.

They looked at each other, then Lyons took out l
portable radio and hesitantly contacted Gates. 'We'
located the suspect's car, sir. There's . . . no sign of tl
suspect right now.'

The Philip Gates felt the shape of reality slip out of l
mental hands. There was no handhold any more. He w
shocked and puzzled. Where was the contact? His ey
flicked open. 'He must be there!' he shouted into tl
radio. 'Find him!'

They searched for a further half-hour, examining eve
inch of the quarry. Which was very easy, because ever
thing was visible. They swiftly found themselves goir
over the same ground again.

'He's pulled a fast one,' Lyons muttered to his mate. 'You tell the boss, OK?'

Condon sighed and did so. 'No sign at all, sir. He could be anywhere, sir.'

'He is at the quarry!' the shout came back.

Condon paused, then chose his words very carefully. 'Perhaps you could be a bit more specific, sir? Over.'

'Don't leave until you find him!'

The link cut out. The two policemen looked at each other again. They'd never heard the boss sound so angry. But more than that. It was weird, but he sounded almost like he was scared.

'So!' Lyons clapped his hands together then pulled his torch from his belt. 'You heard the man. We quarter the site, explore it, explore it again –'

'And repeat until breakfast. All in this wonderful atmosphere of nuclear fall-out.'

'Aw, I never wanted to have kids anyway.'

The two coppers fetched their comrades from the other car, and began to search the site yet again.

Steve Blake watched them silhouetted against the moon.

He was hanging like a foetus in black space, holding on to his diving tank, its mask over his face. He had his feet wrapped round a concrete block to keep him beneath the surface of the lake.

Torch beams played off the waters above his head. He was fully dressed, but it was still cold beyond any cold he had ever known. He looked at the gauge on the tank.

He hoped he could survive like this until they went away.

15

SOMEONE ON THE INSIDE

The taxi pulled up outside the Pathology Labs. Blak
lay in the seat at the back, looking exhausted an
wet. He'd stayed underwater for another twenty minute
until the policemen had left, and ten after that to mak
sure they didn't come back. Then he'd climbed out of th
lake, fumbled with the door handle of his car, his hand
too cold to open it, and finally settled on just dumping th
sub-aqua gear in the boot. He didn't want to use th
bugged car again anyway, he just wanted to sit in th
warm for a bit. He managed to do so, finally, and put th
heater on, rubbing his chest and arms violently.

Finally, when he was as thawed out as he was going t
get, he locked the car behind him and stumbled off dow
the track. He walked to the nearest village, where h
found an old lady who didn't 'believe in all that radio
active rubbish' up before dawn putting her washing out t
dry. He'd explained that his car had broken down, hopin
the newspapers hadn't been delivered yet, and tried t
give her some money, which she turned down, so that h
could call a taxi.

Now he hauled himself out of the cab, avoiding th
two suitcases by his feet. He'd made the driver wait
couple of hundred yards away from the artist's cottage i
Mayston while he sneaked around to see if he could ge
some of his clothes and equipment. But a police car ha
been waiting at the end of the road. So he'd had to tur
and go back to the cab. 'Toothbrush,' he'd said to th
driver, patting his pocket. The man hadn't seemed t

mind. It was terrible, Blake reflected, how this quest was costing him every detail of human life. These things weren't important against what he was trying to achieve, but he felt the loss of his possessions, his car, and the place he'd been sleeping.

'That'll be £81.50, mate,' said the taxi driver.

Blake frowned. 'Bit steep, isn't it?'

'Double rate after midnight and during national emergencies. Call it eighty pound.'

Blake handed over four twenty pound notes. 'Keep the change,' he muttered, wryly. 'Oh, and someone's left their suitcases in the back.'

'Those are mine, mate. I'm off out of it.'

The driver sped away so fast that Blake had to stumble back from the car. He watched it go for a moment, and then turned and trudged down the path towards the Pathology Labs. The sun was coming up on the eastern horizon. It looked red, as if stifled by smoke.

Blake hoped that Sarah had a kettle.

'Oxygen?!' Blake stared at the two women through the haze over his mug of coffee.

Sarah had indeed had a kettle, and had been filling him with hot drinks from the moment he arrived. Melissa had wanted to change his shirt, but there was nothing else he could wear. Besides, he had wanted to hear why her attack on Gates had failed.

'It makes sense, Steve,' explained Melissa. 'We had the right plan, but the wrong weapon. We were right, an attack on one weakens them all.'

Sarah looked dubious. 'I remain to be convinced about the psychic network.'

'How else do you explain the simultaneous nosebleeds when Elizabeth Madigan died?'

Melissa had the bit between her teeth again, Blake noted. Her failure with Gates hadn't set her back at all. He found that he was smiling admiringly at her.

'Coincidence? Mass hysteria?' Sarah didn't sound like she believed it, even as she said it.

'No,' said Blake. 'Exactly the same thing happened with Philip Boyd's death.'

'And it was happening right across the world,' said Melissa. 'I heard it on the radio. When one of them dies, they're all weakened.'

Blake saw that Sarah was still looking concerned, and shrugged. 'It's not much of an Achilles heel, but it's all we have. Maybe if enough of them die simultaneously, they all will.'

'Have you any idea how crazy that sounds?' Sarah asked.

It looked like a long time since she'd smiled. This hole in her rational universe was impossible for her to ignore, Blake guessed, but almost equally impossible to put up with.

'It's not just that,' said Melissa. 'What about the Zentex connection?'

Sarah shook her head violently. 'Software collapses from time to time. It can get infected with viruses. We all know that.'

'OK. So how do you explain the results of the post-mortem you did? The tissue cultures you examined?'

'I don't . . . yet.' Sarah looked as if she didn't really care what happened to the world any more as long as she got to crash out soon.

Blake could only agree with her. He yawned but, in the middle of the yawn, a thought struck him that closed his mouth suddenly. 'Oxygen. Of course. That's why they couldn't find me!'

'Have I missed something?' asked Sarah.

'When I hid from them I was underwater. I was breathing nitrox, high in pure oxygen. It must have interfered with their tracking device!'

Melissa was looking at him as if he were mad, again. 'Slow down, what tracking device?'

'Every move I've made, they've been there first. To begin with I thought it was the car that was bugged.' Blake bit his lip at the thought. 'But it has to be me.'

'They've bugged you?' Sarah looked him up and down, as if it wasn't safe to speak near him any more. 'What with?'

'I don't know! I think they've implanted something.'

'Without you knowing anything about it?'

Blake shrugged. 'You tell me.'

'When did you last use the oxygen?' asked Melissa.

'Three, four hours ago.'

Melissa went to the window. Blake watched her come to an uneasy conclusion. He was feeling slightly nauseous at the thought of a tiny mass of electronics under his skin. From the look on Melissa's face, she was about to say that he should take himself away from them, go far away. Either that, or that she was going to look for the bug surgically.

In the end, it turned out to be something far worse.

'A bug. An implant.' She was staring at the low, illuminated horizon, the dawn sky. 'Something electronic?'

'Well, it's possible –' Sarah began.

Melissa cut her off. 'But that doesn't explain why Steve could hide under the water. They'd still get the signals. Only . . . he was sipping oxygen, wasn't he?'

Sarah looked like she'd been hit over the head with a brick. Blake looked between the two women, hoping that he'd got this wrong. 'You mean it's not electronic, it's . . .'

Melissa sounded like she was making herself deliver this news. 'A piece of one of them. They normally make human bodies for themselves. Maybe a whole one and a whole human memory can't fit inside a human brain at the same time, otherwise they could take over living people, but . . . Maybe a little piece. Maybe a little, unconscious piece, linked to the whole consciousness of the aliens. That would be the perfect bug.'

239

Blake stared at her. 'You're right.' He touched his forehead, where Gates had touched him on the beach. Perhaps something gaseous had slipped through the pores of his skin. He felt violated. 'The oxygen knocked it out. Stopped the others from sensing it. Which means . . .' Blake leapt to his feet. 'They can pick me up again! They'll know where I am right now!'

Sarah rubbed her own brow, looking very tired. 'Slow down a bit, *who* will know? The police in general? Have they all been got at? Who's after you?'

Melissa turned from the window. Outside, the lights of two cars were approaching at speed. They pulled up just outside the lab. 'Philip Gates,' she said.

Blake tried not to think, just to react. He didn't know how much the thing inside his head was a part of him. He couldn't feel it. Thank God. He hoped that it wasn't party to his thoughts. 'There's no back way? A fire escape? Anything?'

Melissa looked like she was on the point of tears. She couldn't quite meet his gaze, as if he'd been taken by the things that had taken her husband. 'What's the point, Steve? We'll never get to my car now!'

Sarah pulled her car keys from her pocket and gave them to Blake. 'Use mine. It's parked around the side. Use the small door behind reception. And you'd better take this.' She ran across the lab and handed Blake a small oxygen cylinder.

Blake grabbed it like a drowning man, inhaled a deep, stunning, breath and held it.

'Take it easy!' Sarah cautioned, ushering them both towards the door. 'It won't last for ever!'

'Thanks,' said Blake.

'Don't waste your breath.'

Sarah slapped Blake on the shoulder as he took another long draught of the gas and rushed out of the door. Melissa followed.

*　*　*

The Philip Gates' smile suddenly dropped. Just when he was enjoying it again. He and the Ferguson and the human policemen who served them had stepped from their cars in the car park of the Pathology Lab, the Philip Gates with an absolute geographical feeling in his mind for where Steve Blake was. He'd taken it in his office an hour ago, and kept it steady, so he didn't have to concentrate on it.

Then, a moment ago, it had spasmed from his mental fingers again, jerked out of his grasp and vanished.

He yelled at the humans, noting the little tic of irritation on the Ferguson's face. 'Lock it down!' He gestured to the building. 'You know what he looks like!'

He led Ferguson and two of the policemen through the front doors as the others surrounded the building, checking for exits. 'Stay down here,' he told them, running to the lifts. 'Keep your eyes open.' He felt his mouth contort into a snarl, all by itself. 'I'll go up and collect.'

Blake had got the hang of this guards-in-reception business. This time, he peered out from the door of the stairwell. At the sight of Ferguson, he withdrew. 'No chance of getting out that way,' he whispered to Melissa. 'Or getting to Sarah's car.'

Melissa seemed more galvanised than ever now, as if trying to make up for her earlier despair. She pointed down one of the corridors that connected the Pathology Labs to the rest of the sprawling hospital complex. 'Down here.'

They sprinted through fire door after fire door, hearing the distant sounds of hospital life in the wards and kitchens. Was it Blake's imagination, or was there also always the sound of running boots, lacing through the complex, circling and closing on them?

They reached an exit to a parking bay. It looked like a clear run. No police. But they'd have to get round the building to Sarah's or Melissa's car. Blake took a quick gulp of oxygen from his cylinder. 'Bit like smoking ultra mild.'

'What now?' asked Melissa.

An ambulance was parked just across the bay. Blake tapped Melissa on the shoulder and indicated it. 'We get to fulfil a childhood fantasy of mine.'

'You must have had a funny childhood.'

They counted to three and sprinted out into the morning air.

Sarah did her best to look calm, undisturbed, and very, very normal. She'd selected the most banal of bookkeeping tasks, and was sitting at a workbench, pen tucked behind her ear, doing her best to concentrate on it. If she'd been trying any harder she would have been humming, she thought.

When Gates strode into the room, it was almost a relief. Don't look at him like he's something on your slab, she told herself. Pretend you don't know that he's a bioengineered vehicle from another world. 'Can I help you?' she managed.

He was looking round like he was surprised, gazing slowly around the room like he was sniffing the air. Which he probably was.

'Have you lost something?'

'Where are they?' he snarled.

She was going to enjoy this. 'Where are who?'

'They won't get far.'

She kept her expression neutral. Gates had turned and marched back to the door. Then he swept that missile-homing gaze round and pinned her with it again. Despite herself, she shivered.

'I'd really like to know why they came here at all,' he whispered. And stepped back towards Sarah.

The hospital's own security staff on the gate automatically raised the barrier for an ambulance speeding at full tilt, its sirens and lights blazing.

'Yes!' Melissa hissed as the hospital complex receded

swiftly behind them. She'd accelerated the vehicle right round the car park to get the velocity required to crash the barrier. Having it raised for them had been sheer luxury.

Blake emerged from where he'd been hiding in the back. He'd found another oxygen mask and cylinder.

Instead of kissing Melissa through the rubber, he ruffled her hair. Melissa turned back to the road and slowed right down, killing the lights.

Against all her expectations, they were going to make it.

Joanna tipped the taxi driver and trotted up the steps of the civil service building in Whitehall. The facility didn't have a name. She'd been given the address and made the appointment through Andrew at the Ministry. The civil service department that ran the place were called DI61. What they actually did was different depending on who you talked to. They were spookier than the Addams Family. Which meant that Joanna was probably on the right track.

She'd spent most of the previous evening lying to the police, talking to the investigating officers in front of her entire staff in the newsroom. Steve Blake had worked there, yes. But he hadn't been around for months. The call they'd got had been garbled and mistaken. Charlotte had stepped forward and taken responsibility for that, bless her. Joanna had done all that partly to project an image of unity, partly to dare any of her staff to contradict her. She was sure one of them would, but it would be after hours in an anonymous phone call to Scotland Yard. A call like that would require the gathering of further evidence. The net would be tightening about Joanna's throat right now. It might even close today. But for the moment she was free to work, and that was the most important thing.

As she entered the building, she realised that she was now pursuing a very Steve Blake sort of agenda. What happened to her career, her position, her old life, no longer

243

mattered. She was working for bigger things now, trying to save the world.

She hoped that Father Christmas was paying attention.

In a deeply panelled and polished waiting area, civil servants were gliding past with files, disks and papers. To Joanna's astonishment, military top brass from all three services were heading into a briefing room. They had three secretaries on the go, answering phones continually.

Well. This must be the place. The place where they dealt with alien invasions. Andrew had tipped her off that something was going down. The multiple reactor attacks had convinced the global intelligence community that what they had been denying for decades was finally happening.

A bad-tempered secretary looked up as Joanna approached her desk. 'Yes?'

Joanna doubled the look, sent it back at the secretary and watched her wilt under its flamethrower blast. 'Hello. I'm Joanna Ball.' A pause, like that would be enough. Then impatience. 'I phoned earlier, I've come to see Oliver James.'

Getting that name had taken favours to the point of her probably having to sleep with Andrew.

The secretary gave a little smile of triumph. 'I'm afraid Mr James is in a meeting at the moment, with another one lined up right behind.'

'He's expecting me.' Joanna trundled on the big guns. 'Gerald Cranleigh-Thomson has already called about me.'

The woman checked the list in front of her. 'It could be hours. Perhaps you could come back tomorrow?'

Joanna looked at the poor bitch like she was something she'd left on the side of her plate. 'I'll wait.' She sniffed.

She sat down, feeling less confident. Whatever was going on in this echoing hall was huge. Far bigger than Steve Blake. Far bigger than her.

She'd left the front page of the decade for this. God, why couldn't she just have stayed married to the man? She

244

thought about the past for a minute, and then wrinkled her nose at the sheer 'ick' factor of it. No, there was probably no need to go that far.

'I say,' she called to the secretary. 'Who's in charge of coffee around here?'

Gates was circling Sarah like he was wondering whether or not he could get away with arresting her. The thought worried the pathologist much more than she was letting on. She'd heard enough stories about people 'hanging themselves' in police custody. It had happened to a cousin of hers. No way was he going to get her legally. He was going to have to compromise himself if he wanted to drag her off, break the rules enough for her to be able to make a fuss to less obviously bent coppers.

So she played chess with those dangerous eyes, meeting his questions with reasonable answers. She hadn't even lied so far.

'So what is it you had to offer them?' he asked now.

'They came to me for explanations.'

'Of what?'

She took a deep breath, treading carefully. 'Of why a man should die and come back to life. Of how the death of one person could affect so many.' She allowed herself a puzzled little smile. If he was going to have her, she wanted him to reveal all first, to come out with all those alien secrets like the villain in a thirties serial. 'Above all, they wanted to know why someone's internal organs were burnt to a cinder when he suffered no apparent injury.'

'Ah yes, the autopsy. I believe the whole event is on video.'

'Standard practice.' And the stuff of a cult video release if I ever get out of this room. Better than that last alien autopsy. 'It's here if you want it.' She opened a drawer and handed Gates a copy of the video cassette. She'd carefully labelled it to look like the original. But she hadn't said that it was. 'There are also some tissue cultures.' She opened

245

another drawer and found the cultures. A single dish of transferred samples sat behind her battered old thesaurus on a distant shelf.

Gates looked surprised. 'I didn't know you'd taken them.'

'Normal procedures.'

'You have examined them purely in the interest of science, of course?' He came closer, his fingers kneading the air speculatively.

He looked like he was a predator, she thought. Had they made him that way, or was that what they were, or had the man this Gates was based on always been like that?

'All pretty inconclusive stuff,' she did her best to simper. 'I'm sure your boys could do better.' She pushed the sample cases in his direction. 'Will that be all?'

Their eyes met for a fraction too long, and Sarah knew that he wasn't going to be able to arrest her right now. She'd fended him off for the present.

'I'm sure it will. Until we question the suspects themselves.' He took the samples and headed for the door.

Sarah couldn't resist it. 'You'll never guess what they said about you!'

Gates stopped and turned back to gaze at her.

'They think you're an alien!' She made herself laugh, regretting this impulse already.

To her surprise, he threw his head back and bellowed with laughter, laughed so hard that he nearly dropped the samples. He put them aside and wiped his eyes with his gloves. 'The sooner we get those two safely out of harm's way . . .' he said, chuckling.

Sarah suddenly realised that there was a very obvious course of action open to her. A very dangerous one, too. But it would satisfy both her scientific curiosity and her anger at this terrible bully. She slipped an object into the pocket of her lab coat and moved closer to him, adopting a cheerful tone of offhand conversation.

She'd co-operated with the law, and been cleared of all wrongdoing. Now they could have a conversation. 'Their theories intrigue me. Science is full of imponderables. Even Isaac Newton described himself as a child playing on the shore.'

He was still laughing, wiping something from his mouth. 'Blake and his accomplice aren't exactly standing on the shoulders of giants. I'd hardly call their ravings "theories", would you?'

'Perhaps they're just searching for a way of explaining the inexplicable, like all good scientists.'

He looked at her like this was a crazy thought. She'd managed, through her co-operation, to slip back into the great mass of the public again, for this creature. Somebody to be fooled rather than dealt with.

'But you don't believe them?' he asked.

'Of course not.' She followed him to the door. 'But I do like to keep an open mind.' She stepped into his path, wondering at her own bravery. 'So I wonder, purely in the interests of science, would you mind taking a few breaths of this?'

She swung up the oxygen cylinder from her pocket to within an inch of his nose.

Give him credit, he didn't flinch. His eyes just did that predator thing again, narrowing to coldly calculating slits.

Go ahead, punk, Sarah thought proudly. They're never going to convict me of killing you like this. So make my day.

Joanna had realised, some minutes ago, that she was sitting directly under a portrait of the Queen. And, all things considered, Her Majesty was looking a lot better than she was. All this paranoid conspiracy excitement had made her look really raddled. It was all right for Steve. He didn't have a newspaper to run as well as Scooby Doo mysteries to investigate.

Maybe if she popped down the thrift shop and bought

a floral thing and a cardigan, started reading up on UFOs . . .

She stamped on the thought before it made her laugh out loud. As if.

Her mobile started to chirp. Loud against the silence, now that everybody important in the country had gone into their meetings.

She answered it. 'Hello? No. No, I can't get back. You'll have to hold the fort until I do. I've heard you boast about how much better you'd be at the job than me. Now's your chance! Oh and, Charlotte, no more calls.'

She hung up. All three secretaries were now looking at her like librarians. There was probably some sort of trade organisation for pretty young hushers and indexers and book pushers. Now that really was a conspiracy for you.

She switched off her mobile like she was carefully strangling a small bird, and glanced up at the Queen again.

The traffic patterns of East Anglia were still awry. Long stretches of empty road here, the most extraordinary congestion there. People were either fleeing or staying put, depending on how much faith they put in the official version of events. Melissa's ambulance encountered the end of a vast, slow-moving caravan of traffic within ten miles of the hospital. It looked to have been going all day and night. Some of the vehicles seemed to contain their owners' entire possessions. Some displayed eccentric anti-radiation devices. There was even a Volkswagen Beetle wrapped in silver foil. Cold inside that, Melissa thought.

Steve was standing beside her now, taking a squirt of oxygen every now and then.

'We should turn around,' she told him. 'The longer it takes us to get to London, the more likely they are to track us down. I don't think this lot are in any mood to pay attention to an ambulance siren.'

'We have to get to Joanna,' he insisted. 'She promised

248

to go to the top. They'll believe her.'

Melissa very quietly raised an eyebrow to herself. He'd been itching to call Joanna ever since they'd got into the ambulance.

Steve heard her, in that way men did. 'She promised!'

Melissa shrugged. 'I don't trust her.' All right? Just a feeling. Ignore me.

Steve had the gall to laugh. 'What?'

'Why do you think she's doing this?'

'Oh, come on.' He laughed until he realised that she wasn't going to break down, like one of his mates down the pub, and be jollied into laughing along. 'This isn't about *us*!'

Melissa remained silent. The slow train of traffic was getting on her nerves, and she didn't want to start a row with Steve. It was just that, with her having held this quest in trust so long, his faith in the magical power of his ex-wife to solve everything was . . . Quite unreasonable of her to think so, maybe, but . . . bloody irritating.

'This traffic!' Steve echoed her thoughts, lost for something to say. 'Turn off here!'

Melissa stared at the road ahead. There was nothing. 'Where?'

'Here!' He was definitely in the mood for a row. A narrow country road had appeared around the bend, and was coming up at the tortoise pace of the convoy. He must have known it was there. Melissa sighed and turned off.

Beside the road was a public phone box.

Of course. How very convenient.

The phone box turned out, to Melissa's guilty joy, to have been vandalised. Bare wires trailed from the handset. For a moment, Melissa had a vision of an England where the aliens were in charge, hunting down the remnants of humanity. Things would slowly fall apart, and there would be more and more refugee convoys, more and more discarded machines.

'Stupid kids!' Steve threw down the receiver.

'What now?' Melissa tried to sound positive.

'We find another one.'

They drove along the empty roads, the ones that led away from civilisation, away from the warmth of other people. That was the great English disaster all over, Melissa thought. That need for a perfect countryside unsullied by other people and their opinions. It didn't matter what did it, Triffids or a plague. There was something about the English that craved emptiness in their own meadows. That must be what drove Englishmen to go and lose themselves in deserts. Perhaps it was a memory of centuries ago, when you could walk through the fields of the Black Death and pick blackberries, without new towns or pollution or America.

She shivered. That would only last a moment for her. She needed the warmth of other people.

She squeezed Steve's arm to tell him he was OK really. Even if he wasn't able to rely on her to save him from his English-male disasters.

They pulled up outside a boarded-up railway station in the middle of nowhere. The place had been abandoned long before the crisis, long before the aliens came. It was the victim of cuts to branchlines, prey to the ravages of Railtrack. There was a dusty door to an ancient shop set into the white bricks of the station buildings. The sort of place that would have sold newspapers to fewer and fewer commuters, and died the death of places beloved but largely private, as empty as the dreams of the men who got on board there. The shop looked like it had persisted longer than the station had, in the way of a futile gesture. Recent magazines could be glimpsed through the glass of the door. The owner had abandoned this futile gesture, to flee the rumours of nuclear fall-out. Melissa wondered if that had been a relief.

She also wondered if they were being exposed to

radiation at the moment, and if that would hamper her ability to have children.

She didn't want to wonder that, so she went to the door and hammered on it. 'Hello? Hello?'

'Nobody home,' said Steve, looking around the old building, sadly. He pointed to the roof suddenly. 'The phone's connected. That's all we need to know.'

So he felt for where the lock was inside the door, took a run-up at it, and kicked at the door until it exploded inwards.

Melissa had never seen anybody do that before. She supposed that you were allowed to break into places that people had left behind.

She followed Steve inside.

The shop had been abandoned in a hurry, thought Melissa. The till hung open like a toothless mouth, empty of cash. Sunlight illuminated the darkness in shafts, catching dust motes floating in the beams like little stars.

Steve went straight to the phone behind the counter. He smiled and nodded at the dialling tone, then tapped out a number. He paused as it rang, then, to Melissa's surprise, he handed the phone to her.

'You'd better do this.'

She was about to ask him why, when the number answered. 'Hello, I need to speak to Joanna Ball. OK. I see. My name is Melissa. Old friend of hers. Oh yes, from way back, darling. Can you tell her to call me on this number?' She rubbed the dust off the phone with a finger and read the number. 'Soon as she can. Yes, it's very important.' She hung up and looked at Steve rather smugly. 'She's going to ring back.'

He laughed. 'I gathered. Thanks for making the call.'

Melissa had got it by now. 'We could hardly have you saying "I'm Britain's most wanted and here's my daytime number", could we?' She went and hugged him.

He leant heavily on her and they swayed back against the counter.

'I've had it.'

'Why don't you sleep in the ambulance? Use the oxygen. I'll wake you when she calls.'

Steve yawned and stretched theatrically. 'I might just do that.' He ruffled her hair and headed for the door.

Melissa wandered to the magazine racks and started leafing through *Attitude* and *Loaded*, *Dreamwatch* and *Vanity Fair*. 'Is this how you imagined the world would end?'

He stopped by the door, framed in the light, looking like a huge, awkward soft toy in silhouette. 'Holed up in the backwoods of Norfolk? No. I can safely say this isn't what I had planned.'

She half looked up at him, pretending to be interested in a free gift of moisturiser. 'And did you see yourself clutching a camera rather than an oxygen cylinder?'

'Taking photographs of the end of the world? Yeah, that's about my measure.'

She didn't want this conversation to stop or continue. 'The you that was, or the you that you are now?'

He didn't move into the light. 'Same thing.'

She shook her head firmly. 'No. I don't think so. I couldn't have –' She stopped herself. She'd nearly said it out loud.

He moved back from the door, a strange, quizzical look on his face. That was what he did best, quizzical looks. 'You couldn't have what?'

'Nothing.'

He came and touched her on the shoulder, hesitated a little. He wanted her to say it first. 'You couldn't have what?'

She turned a little out of his reach, looked the other way. And said it very simply. 'I couldn't have fallen in love with the Steve Blake you used to be.'

There was silence. Then more silence. She swallowed

back her terrible, defeated feeling. Then, brave, she turned back quickly, grabbed a handful of magazines, made to go to the counter to read them.

'Forget I said anything,' she called brightly to him, holding up a hand. 'It's OK. You go and rest. We can just leave it.'

Steve was staring at her, his face lost in shadow. 'You didn't mean it?'

She looked up, on the verge of anger. 'Of course I meant it. I wouldn't have said it if I didn't mean it. I don't say things I don't mean!'

He looked back and forth, as if he were trying to find the right words for one thing or the other. He had that look on his face again, like somebody had slapped him with a fish. He'd looked just like that when they'd made love, astonished by how passionate she'd been. That had given her considerable satisfaction at the time.

She dropped the magazine, and all pretence. 'I don't want poetry, I don't want flowers, but I would like you to tell me how you feel.'

'I would have thought that was obvious.'

She bit her lip against a grin. 'Erm, no. I'm not an emotional psychic. Men do go to bed with women they don't love, or so I'm told.'

'I want to spend the rest of my life with you,' he whispered. He moved into the light and looked straight at her.

'I'm sorry?' She was astonished at the passion in his voice.

'I want to spend the rest of my life with you. I'm crazy about you!' He approached until his brow was touching hers. She put a hand against his chest.

'Now don't exaggerate. You hardly know me.'

They both laughed.

'You really know how to take a compliment, don't you?' he said.

'Oh, it's part of my charm.' She slipped her hands

253

around the back of his head and rolled her face into his and kissed him deeply, igniting once more that strength and passion in which she found such an echo of herself.

She pulled away, swept the magazines from the counter, and judo-rolled him on to it. 'The rest of your life?' She looked down at his continual puzzlement, laughing and shaking her head. 'What an unusual man you are.'

He raised a finger. 'Erm, oxygen?'

'In a minute,' Melissa told him.

Joanna was glad that she was wearing such fantastic shoes today, because she'd just spent half an hour staring at them. She'd been mentally clothes shopping, called up the newsroom and got them to read out every detail of the changes to the final edition, chosen the provisional lead for tomorrow. Then she'd checked on Charlotte via every department head. A star was born, it would seem. They were all glowing. They were probably preparing the speeches about how much fun it had been working with Joanna.

She had quickly run out of anything meaningful to do.

Which was exactly the point at which one of the secretaries hopped up and tapped over to her. 'He's ready to see you now,' she said.

A cluster of RAF squadron leaders had just emerged from an office across the echoing hall. The last one of them caught the secretary's eye and left the door open. Inside, Joanna glimpsed the rich-red interior of a very plush office. She got to her feet and followed the secretary.

The Philip Gates pulled his gloves back on as he walked down the spiral staircase on the outer wall of the Pathology Lab. He felt very good. The structure of his body was reacting, like it had when the human Melissa had aroused him. The body's glands were distributing adrenaline. It was hard not to shout or laugh.

The Ferguson and the human policemen were waiting for him. 'Let's get moving,' he said.

'Is he back on line?' the Ferguson asked, frowning at the mixed impulses they could both feel.

'Not yet.' The Philip Gates led the way back to the vehicles. 'But he's doing his best. He wants to be found.'

He could see the human policemen exchange puzzled glances at that. They thought he was talking about their suspect, rather than the fraction of a being he knew well that lay inside him.

Right at this moment, the Philip Gates didn't care what they thought. He got behind the wheel of his own car and drove off very fast, jerking the music on the car radio up to maximum.

He was here.

He was here. That was very nearly all he could think.

He was the Steven Blake ... No, he was not. The Steven Blake, the name centre, was just beside him, but he was not knotted into it. He could only exist and, frustrated, call to be freed. Call to be given his identity back with the extra mass of memory that would take. Maybe, because of his familiarity, he would be given control over the memory of Steven Blake and a copy of this body.

He hoped not. He wished to be free.

He was here.

Steven Blake was asleep in the back of the vehicle. His dreams were deep and disturbing. The driver was reading definitions straight out of Steven Blake's memory: he'd allowed the oxygen mask to drop from his face, the cylinder had leaked oxygen. And now it was almost all gone.

Which was why the driver was aware, now.

He was here.

'Steve? Steve?' Blake came round to the feeling of Melissa's cooling hand on his brow. He'd only been asleep for an hour. And he'd had a dream about being on Mayston beach again.

No, that had been Melissa's hand. He glanced at the empty oxygen cylinder and mask and sat up. Melissa looked like she'd been sleeping herself, probably across the counter of the shop. He rubbed the back of his head. 'Did Joanna call?'

'Just now. She's found a way out for us. She's told us what to do.'

Blake blinked at Melissa's smile and rubbed his head again. He felt like he'd had his brain extracted through his nose.

Joey Foster liked his job as security guard at the Pathology Labs, and had been worried that morning, when he came on his shift, to see police cars screaming out of the hospital gates. The receptionist, who'd just come on herself, had assured him that they'd just been pursuing that terrorist that everyone was talking about. They hadn't found him here.

Joey had sighed with relief. In his four years here, he'd never had an incident. Corpses didn't have issues like that, and the more fractious areas of the hospital, like casualty, weren't his department. A lot of his mates had taken leave suddenly when the reactor blew, but Joey was made of sterner stuff. He figured he'd been around the X-ray department for so long that all his sperm had two heads by now anyway.

He whistled as he made his usual first patrol of the corridors, wondering why that black girl, the pathologist, wasn't about yet. She was usually first in, last out, bustling between her office and the cutting-up-bits room. Maybe she'd got the heebies about the radiation as well.

'We interrupt this broadcast to bring you more news of the Sizewell incident . . .'

He heard the radio from the office up ahead and smiled to himself. No, she was about. A real trooper, that one.

He ducked his head around the door. No sign of her. Or anybody. Well, her little ducklings didn't usually get in until lunch time. He clicked his tongue at her for leaving the radio on.

'Police have now confirmed that computer equipment controlling the plant was sabotaged . . .'

He went over to switch if off.

'And that continuing problems in the existing digital systems will delay the clean-up operation for some weeks . . .'

He saw the shape crumpled in a corner and for a moment thought that it was a sack of something that somebody had dumped there. His senses caught up with him a moment later.

It was Sarah. She was crushed into the corner at a strange angle, her limbs jutting everywhere, like every part of her had been broken. Her face wore a look of stunned surprise.

Shaking, Joey got to his feet, crossed himself, and ran to tell somebody.

16

THE ESTABLISHMENT CLUB

Blake drove the ambulance while Melissa consulted the map on her lap. Joanna had given her a set of precise directions, which she'd scrawled on it.

'I think we should have taken a left back there,' she said.

Blake had kept looking in his mirrors as they'd zipped from empty road to empty road but, even though he'd run out of oxygen, there had been no sign of pursuit. 'You sure? I thought this base was supposed to be in the Sleaford direction.'

'It's not easy when the destination isn't actually on the map.'

'It must be!' Blake gestured to the wetlands all around them. 'Every place has a name.'

'Oh, here it is!' Melissa pretended to find it. 'It's marked "Secret Military Base"!'

Blake looked at her sighingly for a moment, but her sympathetic smile melted his heart. He brought the ambulance to a halt and turned it round.

Joanna had somehow got to the man who was in charge of the British government department that dealt with UFOs and similar things, Melissa had told him. She'd been as surprised as they were that such a department really did exist. She'd named a few friends, put their evidence in front of him, and he'd asked for Blake and Melissa to come in out of the cold immediately. Various governments were communicating on the subject of the aliens, and an effort was going to be made to do something about them. Everything Steve had discovered could be valuable.

'I have to admit,' Melissa had said. 'This Joanna of yours can come in useful sometimes.'

'She's not mine,' Blake had said. 'You are.'

But he shared the sentiment. He felt like his quest was nearly over. He could soon go back to being one of the little people, and let the men from the Ministry take over. A very English thought, but it wasn't until he thought it that Blake realised how much he'd missed that comfortable feeling.

They drove along another twisting path, until Melissa saw a signpost, turned the map in all directions and started swearing.

They stopped to take a look at the map and Melissa's written notes together.

'That's where we went wrong,' said Melissa, pointing to a biro-covered turning.

'You're not geographically challenged, by any chance?'

She began to fold up the map, the point decided. She had a dangerous look on her face.

'Did Joanna say how she got through to the people we're going to talk to?'

'She didn't go into detail. But she was pretty euphoric.'

'She must have signed up the serial rights for fifty pence. That's the only thing that makes her euphoric.' He changed the subject back to the dangerous one. 'Are you sure this is the right road for this turning of yours?'

There was a sudden blast of sound and a flash of movement overhead. Three USAF F-111s had appeared over the hedge, so low that Blake and Melissa ducked. As the roar and the red of the afterburners faded over the next field, Blake noticed that their undercarriages were down. They were descending close by like giant crows. Under their wings Blake recognised the weight of a full nuclear payload.

Melissa pointed. 'Look! Over there. That must be it!'

Two fields away, by the sea, there was a cluster of square, black buildings. A rotating aerial atop a tower. And in the sky overhead . . . Blake looked up and up. Black military shapes were circling in holding patterns, rank after rank of them.

'You know,' he said, holding up a finger like he'd just had an idea, 'I think you may be right.'

Blake drove the ambulance right up to the gates of the RAF base which was not on any map, nor even named by any sign. They stopped beside the checkpoint at the door. An RAF regiment soldier got out of his office, which looked to be a hive of activity, actually unslung his rifle, which Blake noticed was loaded, and marched over to them.

'Are you as scared as I am?'

'They're on our side.'

'Answer the question.'

'Petrified.'

'What's your business?' the soldier asked.

'We were told to come here,' Blake began, fishing in the pocket of his jacket in a way which, he just knew as he started it, had made the soldier stiffen to alertness. He carefully extracted his press card, which he handed to the man.

The soldier looked between Blake and the photo on the card. In the circumstances, that was a pretty useless gesture, but maybe the idea was that an alien would panic. Or maybe they were sweeping the vehicle with some sort of alien detector.

'One moment, sir,' said the soldier. He disappeared back inside the gatehouse with the card. Beside the barrier, a few feet away, two more armed soldiers were paying attention, unslinging their weapons.

The soldier in the command post looked down at a monitor of some kind. Probably that anti-alien thing. Then he opened his door again, and made his way back to the ambulance, a little less wound up, Blake thought. 'Go through. You're expected.' He nodded to the opposite gatehouse, and the barrier rose ahead of them. The two soldiers beside it shouldered their arms once more. 'Follow the signs to Sector C, please, sir.'

Blake nodded gratefully to him, put the ambulance in gear again and drove through the gates.

'Hear that?' he said to Melissa. 'He called me sir.'

The base was full to the brim with soldiers, RAF personnel and armaments of all kinds. They followed a convoy of cruise missiles for a while. Squads of various regiments in full kit jogged past, training. Blake thought they were all looking very grim. Like they were heading for combat. That struck him as unusual. Surely the aliens hadn't suddenly opened up a war front somewhere? Oh well, the human race will fight a war the way they want to fight it. He imagined the soldiers bursting into offices and town halls all over the country, and shivered. It was going to get like a police state very quickly. Let's hope they did have a test for aliens, otherwise a lot of other people were going to get rounded up, and a lot of inconvenient people accidentally shot, and the whole invasion would become a worldwide coup. Whoever ended up on the right side of that would be, he suspected, very hard to tell apart from the aliens these soldiers would originally be hunting.

He smiled grimly to himself. The official acceptance that he'd craved so long had arrived, and he immediately found himself doubting it. That was probably part of what (a) being British, (b) being human and (c) going on a quest, were all about.

He brought the ambulance to a halt before another barrier. Within the large complex stood a much smaller one, newly erected, by the look of it. A hard point, the final redoubt. The guards on this one had the bulky, untroubled look of special forces about them.

The barrier here swung up immediately, and one of the guards waved them down. SAS cap badge, noticed Blake.

'Please follow me to the security check.'

He'd stopped being sir, he noted. The soldier walked in front of the ambulance, and indicated a parking space inside the compound. He waited until they got out, and then led them towards a card-controlled turnstile inside the door of what appeared to be the entrance to an underground bunker, swiping his own card through a black box beside it. They went through, each with a solid clunk of the turnstile. The solider didn't follow, but pressed the button on an entry phone beside the turnstile.

'Mr Blake has arrived.'

Blake didn't like the finality of that. He led Melissa into the lift that stood behind the turnstiles and pressed the only button available.

The lift travelled a long way down before its doors opened to allow Blake and Melissa into a vast, high-tech foyer. Blake realised that this had been where his taxes had been going all these years. There were blast doors in all directions, a real warren. Thick metal bulkheads were painted in civilised colours, and concealed lighting gave a very good impression of daylight. A solitary guard sat behind a vast security desk. He probably had a bazooka underneath it. There were security cameras everywhere. There'd even been one in the lift, which had limited the conversation to brave little smiles and hand-holding. Blake felt like turning right round and heading for the surface again. These guys obviously had everything in hand. But Melissa's restrained little smile convinced him to stay. She'd been dreaming about this sort of acceptance for years, about there being somebody with a big base to save her world from the aliens. So he approached the desk.

But, as he did so, a familiar voice rang out. 'There you are! I thought you'd got lost!'

Joanna marched in, surrounded by three soldiers, her own detail, no doubt, assigned to cater to her every vhim. She threw her arms around Blake and hugged him, vhich surprised him for a moment. But then he found hat he was hugging her back. They had, for once, come hrough for each other.

Joanna made to shake Melissa's hand, but Melissa kissed ner cheek, looking very happy. 'Thanks for getting us nere,' she said.

Jo smiled like Mother Teresa and glanced at Blake. When they said you'd arrived, I had to come and meet ou. These are the boys.' She flicked a finger towards the grim-looking soldiers. 'You look absolutely terrible.'

'Thanks,' said Blake, as she led them back through one of the blast doors, along a corridor that was lined with plush ministerial doors. He took Melissa's hand. Suddenly, ne felt completely at home.

'Don't say I never do anything for you, will you? Come on. We can't afford to waste any time.'

They headed down a central staircase, passing military personnel, and civilians with clipboards. Some of them looked like scientists, others like office staff. Blake clicked his fingers. 'I know what this reminds me of: *Men in Black*!'

Joanna raised an eyebrow. 'Hardly. Through here.' She ed them into an office complex, where there were maps and illuminated diagrams and rows of PCs. 'I moved neaven and earth to get through to this guy.'

'Hmm. You owed me those, didn't you?'

'I just missed the biggest news story of the century to save your skin. I'm probably now an ex-editor. Once I ound the guy in question, he put me straight on to n RAF Hercules and brought me here. I think it was either that or shoot me. So do try and show a bit more gratitude.'

Blake stared at an illuminated map of Antarctica as they marched past. It was covered in tiny red markers. 'How lid you get them to believe you? About the conspiracy, I mean.'

'I didn't have to. Turns out the M.o.D. had been monitoring Gates for the past six months.'

'What?' Blake felt as if all his glory had been snatched from him. 'If they knew, why didn't they act?'

'Apparently, they decided to use him to smoke out anyone else involved.'

'And they did nothing?'

'They didn't expect the Sizewell attack to come so early. They think that was down to you.'

'Glad I could help.'

They came to another blast door at the end of the office space.

Joanna keyed in an entry code that she'd obviously had difficulty memorising. 'It wasn't much help.'

Blake didn't understand quite what she meant or how to reply. He settled on humility. 'I know.'

The door opened and they stepped through. The military escort didn't follow.

They were in a suite of private rooms. The small office space and power desk immediately told Blake that this was where the boss lived. A boss who, despite the vast funds obviously at their command, didn't have time for ostentation. The name plaque on the desk said OLIVER JAMES. No rank, no title. Serious spook, then. From an inner room came the sound of running water.

Joanna settled herself on a chair. 'You can start to relax now, Steve. It's nearly over.'

'Who have you signed up to ghost my story?' They flopped into a sofa next to her. Melissa's hand strayed to Blake's. He hesitated for a moment, but Joanna was giving out none of her tigerish body language. It was OK. It was all going to be OK.

Joanna smiled. 'I thought you could give me first option on that.' She looked tired herself. Something behind her eyes seemed deeply different, as if this experience had been an awakening to her. 'It's good to have you back.'

'Please, do take a seat!' called a rich, fruity voice from the bathroom, redundantly. 'I'll be with you in a minute.'

Blake was about to share a tension-releasing laugh with the two women, but suddenly his head felt like it was splitting open again.

'Steve? Steve?!' Melissa put a hand on his shoulder, concerned.

'It's nothing. The headache's back with interest.'

He winced as it faded, and glanced up to see an unguarded look on Joanna's face. She looked incredibly interested in Blake's headache. Oh God, this was the side-effect of some weapon, wasn't it? He was going to end up being poked about by military scientists.

Oliver James strode into the room, a very tall man in a dark suit. He had a pleasant, ruggerish look about him that said that long ago he'd seen combat.

They all stood, automatically.

He shook Blake heartily by the hand. 'I'm delighted to meet you!' He waved for them all to sit down again, and went to perch on the edge of his desk, sizing them up like somebody who was finally seeing in the flesh people who he'd known the look of for ages. 'We've been monitoring your efforts for some time, and I have to say I'm impressed. The nation will owe you a debt of gratitude when all this blows over.'

'Thanks.' Blake sighed. 'It's good to be somewhere safe.'

'Oh, it doesn't get much safer.'

Melissa was shifting in her seat, looking uncomfortable. 'Could you tell us who you are exactly? Joanna –' she glanced at her, using her first name without prejudice for the first time Blake could remember '– seemed rather hazy.'

'Ah, yes.' James drummed his fingers on the desk. 'My job isn't the sort you go shouting about. I'm Military Intelligence, man and boy, head of Special Operations. Which was specially set up to deal with this little lot. I was brought in six months ago to look at the Gates situation a Central Ops and found, as you are aware, that there wa more to the whole thing than a police cover-up. Mucl more.'

'I see.' Melissa was nodding, happier now.

'It must be very hard for you, Melissa. A persona tragedy as well.' He raised a big hand. 'I only know the basic facts, of course.'

'It's been difficult, yes.'

Blake stood, and started to pace about the room. He couldn't settle. As James and Melissa bonded, he went and leant heavily on the wall, checked out the display case o shooting trophies, wandered around behind the desk.

And stopped suddenly. He was aware of Joanna's eye upon him. She'd been watching him, every pace. He'c thought that it was a sort of Utopian, all's-well-that-end's-well, new and hopeful look.

That was until he'd seen the shape in the dust behine James's desktop diary.

He managed to swing back and wander in the othe direction, to flop on the sofa beside a bright-eyed and galvanised Melissa. He glanced at Joanna again, and chewed on his knuckle.

James addressed him. 'Now, given the seriousness o the situation, we need all the information we can get or Gates and the others. Whatever you tell us will help u immensely to devise our future strategy.'

Blake suddenly wanted to ask him what sort of strategy he meant. They weren't by any chance planning an assaul on Antarctica, were they? An assault with the potential to quickly go nuclear? 'Well,' he muttered, vaguely. 'Where to start, really . . . It's not easy to put things in place.' He winced again, as once more that unheard communicatior raced through him, made his nervous system cry out.

James settled behind his desk. 'Whenever you're ready Steven. In your own good time.'

'I'm trying to get this right.' Blake looked around the

266

room, wondering about exits. He felt like a rat at the bottom of a very big trap. 'It's important to me that I get this right.'

Joanna looked impatient. 'Come on, Steve. You've told it often enough!'

James hushed her. 'I understand, Steve. It's all a bit of a shift in perspective, isn't it? Let me try and fill in with some of what we know already. We know that the invasion is international, that the Sweethope incident was replicated in one form or another in various parts of the world.'

Melissa looked up at that and nodded excitedly. She was well into this, Blake thought. How the hell were they going to get out?

James took a deep breath, as if making a revelation. 'We believe that the invaders are not . . . exactly human.'

Blake nodded. 'We agree so far.' They were so far down, and the security in this place was extraordinary.

'We know that they are experts at infiltrating human technology and that they seem to have a collective mentality which may give them certain shared weaknesses.'

That admission made Blake pause. Maybe his paranoia had finally overcome him. Maybe he was fighting long after the need for fighting had ceased. He needed to know more. 'So what's it all for? What are they doing here?'

James took a paper map from a drawer and rolled it out on to his desk. 'Infiltrating key posts so they can stage a major nuclear detonation in the Antarctic, so we think. There's lots of activity going on down there. Satellite surveillance indicates troop movements. This detonation would, of course, begin the collapse of the ozone layer, and thus perhaps melt both ice caps. An irradiated flood would destroy our civilisation and make space for them.'

Blake leaned forward. He didn't have to feign his interest. 'And you know who they are, do you?'

'In a way, we all do.' Perhaps he caught the nervous smile on Blake's features. At any rate, his tone changed.

267

'They're our past, catching up with us. We think they'v[e] been here before.'

'When?'

'Oh, about four billion years ago.'

Blake stared at him.

'Their biological make-up is remarkably similar to tha[t] of the first lifeforms on earth. Or so the science bo[ds] tell me. They're gaseous, or at least that's the close[st] comparison. They thrive on hard radiation. Give it ou[t] And we think they've got some sort of extra-dimension[al] aspect. Here but not here, if you see what I mean. Whe[n] oxygen changed the atmosphere of Earth, all those yea[rs] ago, they couldn't survive.'

'But they can now?'

'Twentieth-century pollution seems to have done th[e] trick. We've invited them back, so to speak. They're no[t] comfortable here yet. Even in the human bodies the[y] make for themselves. But these are chaps who can cro[ss] interstellar space on their own, so they're willing to put u[p] with slumming it a bit.'

Blake slowly opened and then closed his mouth agai[n] He took a long sidelong glance at Melissa. She wasn[t] looking quite as happy any more either. This level [of] knowledge was way beyond anything the M.o.D. coul[d] have found out. 'If I could iron the whole thing out in m[y] head . . .' he began, again. 'I don't know –' He sudden[ly] pointed to a coffee percolator on the other side of th[e] room. 'Is that coffee? Do you think I could have some?'

Melissa had been listening to the conversation, gettin[g] more and more nervous. She'd started out wonderin[g] why on earth Steven should be stalling. But that feelin[g] had gradually been replaced by a sensation of creepin[g] discomfort. She leapt up at the mention of coffee. 'I'[ll] get it.'

She went over to the percolator on the side tabl[e] found a cup and a jug of milk and started preparing th[e] brew. Steve was rubbing his face and looking all round the room. He was clearly looking for ways out. It was clear to her anyway. And if it was clear to her, then it ought to be clear to Joanna as well. But why was he bothering? Was it his political principles, or did he honestly think that —

A flash of motion caught her attention. While her conscious mind had been engaged with thoughts of Steve's paranoia, she'd noticed the bank of monitors that formed part of the wall over the side table. They showed the images from some of the many security cameras outside. The motion that she'd seen had been familiar, domestic. Her eyes darted around the display. And saw the motion again.

Philip was walking into the complex. Being saluted by the guards. At his left and right marched Gerald Ryle and James Wilson.

Controlling the terrible fear that surged inside her, a fear that seemed as ancient as that of the fly in the spider's mandibles, she clenched her muscles and her teeth and made herself pick up the cafetière without shaking.

She turned and carried it back towards Steve and the others. 'Well, who's for —'

And as she passed the desk she spun and flung the coffee straight into Oliver James's face.

He screamed and bellowed, grabbing for his eyes and collapsing across the desk.

'Gates is here, Steve!' Melissa screamed. 'It's a trap!'

Steve leapt to his feet, grabbed her hand and sprinted for the door. He turned back when he realised that Joanna wasn't following them. Melissa didn't know what he thought, how sure he was.

But she saw the expression on his face as Joanna calmly walked over to the desk, where James was struggling to his feet, and pressed a red security button.

'Joanna?' he whispered, as if he couldn't believe it. 'No . . .'

A siren squealed into life. Joanna turned to them,

sucked in a breath through her teeth, and shrugged.

Melissa grabbed Steve's hand and pulled him through the door.

Blake slammed a series of security bolts behind them. They were in a narrow corridor that led to a single lift. A bolt hole, it looked like. He couldn't get over it. He thought that Joanna had seemed strange, but he hadn't really known, even when he'd felt the alien communication in his head, even when he'd started feeling like he was trapped under his own personal Jeep.

Even when he'd looked behind James's desk diary, and seen the outline of an inhaler, left behind in the dust by some fallible, human cleaning lady.

He hadn't been able to tell if his ex was real or fake.

The door vibrated under a vast impact. Blake could hear a screeching. It sounded like James was throwing his whole body weight against it. The bolts sang with the impact.

Melissa had left his side, and was hitting the button to summon the lift.

'Steve!' shouted Joanna, muffled through the door. 'Come on, Steve! Let us in! We only want to talk!'

The wood around the bolts began to splinter.

The lift doors opened.

Blake and Melissa dived inside. They gazed at the wall for a moment. There was only one button.

Melissa hit it.

The lift doors began to close.

Oliver James burst through the door, splintering it into fragments. His eyes were blank and shining white. He seemed to be thrusting forward on instinct alone. His big hands ripped the air as he thundered, screeching, towards them.

The lift doors closed just before he hit.

A concussion sounded from them.

Then it was far above them.

Then it was gone.

Blake took Melissa in his arms and held her.

The Oliver James stepped back from the lift doors and shut off the pain from his reddened face. He'd make a new one soon. He closed down the adrenal glands of the body and was calm. As soldiers and workers ran into the corridor in emergency response, he became one with the others, and turned to speak to them. 'They're going down. I repeat, they're in the lift and they're going down.'

The Philip Gates, the Gerald Ryle and the James Wilson stopped in reception and turned on the spot, feeling the direction that the Oliver James was pointing them in.

'They're heading for the bunker,' said the Philip Gates. He turned to the human soldier on the reception desk and pointed at him. 'Total shutdown! Total shutdown!'

'Total shutdown, sir.' The human nodded calmly.

The Oliver James had briefed the military on the special status of people like the Philip Gates. But it was still astonishing, the way they all obeyed.

'And put the whole base on Alpha Alert.'

The soldier switched on a microphone. 'Alpha Alert. This is an Alpha Alert!'

The Philip Gates looked back to the others of his kind and enjoyed his smile once again. 'No way out.'

The three bodies set off as one, marching at speed past the sirens and slamming doors and running human soldiers. They were heading for the stairs. They knew where they were. This base was almost as familiar as their home.

Blake and Melissa rode the lift to the very bottom of the shaft. It felt like they were descending into the depths of the Earth. Finally, the doors in front of them slid open. They stepped cautiously out into a narrow, gunmetal corridor.

271

'We must be in the basement by now,' murmured Blake. 'Come on!'

They looked around the corridor. A door at each end. The whole area seemed disused compared to the base above their heads. They spontaneously ran to the door on their right, and found that it was locked.

'Got any more ideas?' asked Melissa.

'Yes, actually, just one.' Blake led her off in the opposite direction.

At least that door wasn't locked.

The Philip Gates and his people walked down the service stairs into the basement level, eased the blast door closed behind them, and activated the coded lock. They knew from the Oliver James that the lift would not be allowed to move upwards. Now it was just them and the human. 'I said he wanted to be caught,' said the Philip Gates.

Blake and Melissa ran into a storage area. Row upon row of drums and cylinders and machines, and shelves with tools and equipment.

'You still need ordnance if you want to take over the planet,' muttered Blake. He went to a side door and tried it. It was locked, and a quick tapping of various obvious combinations didn't do any good. 'This door's sealed. We'll have to find another way out.'

He hit some more keys, just for luck, and obviously activated some sort of descriptive function. The word SEALED flashed up on the panel above the lock in nasty red letters. 'There's no way out. I think we're trapped in this bunker.'

He turned to Melissa, but she was looking back over her shoulder. From nearby came the sound of certain, confident, steady, footsteps.

They didn't say anything. They took the only route open to them, further into the bunker.

They ran down corridor after corridor, but found that

there was always only one door they could open, only one way they could go. They were being manipulated along like lab rats. And always right behind them were the sounds of the footsteps, slow and purposeful, as if they had all the time in the world. Under Blake and Melissa's feet was an ordinary dusty floor, like that of any warehouse. Above their heads was a tangle of pipes, like you'd find in the basement of any hotel. Only this wasn't a familiar place, built by their own civilisation. This was the heart of the end of the world, built with their civilisation's help with the aim of destroying it.

They turned a corner and ran into a pair of heavy double doors, secured by a padlock on a chain. Melissa turned, her breathing hard, and stared back into the dusty gloom. Behind them came the footsteps. They were heading up the corridor towards them.

On the wall beside the doors was a firepoint. A hose, an alarm, an axe.

Blake broke the brackets and grabbed the axe.

He swung it with desperate, dreamlike strength, and brought it down on the chain, splitting it open with one blow.

The doors swung back.

Blake and Melissa ran through. And stopped.

In front of them stood Oliver James, his eyes still shining white, his face a mass of blistered skin. Beside him were Joanna, and two soldiers, their weapons trained in their direction. The look on all their faces was the same, one of elementary patience. They'd been standing here, just waiting for them to arrive.

Blake and Melissa spun around. Walking up the corridor behind them came Philip Gates, Gerald Ryle and James Wilson.

'Steve,' whispered Melissa, her voice very calm now. 'This is it. There's no way out.'

Blake held the axe to his body, feeling its comforting weight. He glanced quickly between the two lines of

273

persecutors. 'There has to be. There must be.'

Oliver James raised his voice. 'I'm afraid not, Steven. This is as far as it goes. I'm what our people here call Control.'

Gates pointed to the axe. 'Very primitive, Steve. Very early *Homo sapiens*.'

'Stay back!' Blake found himself yelling, beyond all ability to reason with these creatures. 'Stay back!'

'What are you going to do with an axe, Steve?' asked Gates. 'Kill us all? Come on. Let's not make this any messier than it need be.' He stepped forward, his arms spread wide. 'We don't want to hurt you. We don't enjoy hurting you. We have several very gentle means of execution.'

Blake swung the axe in a jerky little chop. 'Get back!'

'Is this what it's come to? After all the invention, all the progress, all the arrogance, you're reduced to facing your nemesis with an axe!' Gates laughed. The others didn't join in. 'It seems to me that we came just in time. Mankind has run out of ideas.'

Blake shook his head. 'You can't win.'

Oliver James spoke up again. He sounded impatient, rather than gloating. 'We already have. You know why? Because your pollution drew us here. It made this world a place where we can breathe. Now, by starting a hot nuclear war in the Antarctic, we can make sure it's a place where we can thrive. There was a vestigial plan amongst the governments of the world in case this sort of thing ever happened. We discovered it. Took it over. Got hold of such a budget! I think you'd find that ironic as well, wouldn't you, that we're pretending to go to war on ourselves?'

Blake felt like he was in a nightmare. He could feel the warmth of Melissa pressed against his back. The last two humans awaiting the end. 'No . . .' he whispered.

'And you were so close, Steven,' James continued. 'So very, very close. If only you'd realised. We are not infallible. We can be beaten.'

'But instead of beating us,' Gates chimed in, 'you chose to help us.'

'No!'

'Yes. Oh, yes.' James nodded.

'You know it's true,' said Gates. 'You were set up for this whole experience, Steve. As what's called a random walker. You were sent to ferret through our system, to discover its weak points. And you uncovered so many individuals who were dangerous to us. Cartwright, Ryle, Joanna. You led us to every one of them. Even Sarah Armstrong.'

Melissa gasped. 'What have you done to Sarah?'

But Blake wasn't listening any more. He was tottering on his feet, trying to hold on to the axe, as wave upon wave of psychic alien laughter throbbed through his head. The empty space in his brain was echoing to it, trying to answer it.

'Ever wondered about those headaches, Steve?' asked Gates.

'Painful,' added James. 'But necessary.'

'You see, Steve —' Gates pulled his glove from his hand and held up his palm '— you've already been one of us.'

'You can't make me believe that.' Blake straightened up, fighting the pain.

James held up his hand too. 'It's a kind of immortality, you know. Your memory lives on. It's confined, of course, used by one of us as a source of information and persona. But one day we may allow you to be free again. One day when this world is ours. Come on, Steven!' He sounded like a jolly uncle or team captain. 'Come to us!'

Gates pointed to Melissa. 'But she doesn't come with you! She's not tactically significant. And we . . . I will have payback for what she did to me!'

Blake looked at Melissa. She smiled back at him, absolutely certain of death now, and brave in the face of it. Blake thought that she would probably prefer to die

275

rather than have her memory used by these things. He turned back to the aliens.

'Never,' he said.

Gates relaxed again, his breathing slowing. 'You really have very little choice.'

'Even if you kill me it won't be over,' Blake told him. 'If I can figure you out, so can others.'

'You can't fight evolution, Steve. That's all this is. And right now, it's almost over. This is the end game.'

James nodded. 'Spot on. You keep trying to assign moral values to us, like we're characters in one of your stories. But we're just not in the same frame as you. We're not good. We're not bad.' He shrugged his big shoulders. 'We're your destiny.'

'No.' Blake glanced upwards, looking all around for some exit, some way out. 'You can't win!'

Gates pulled off his other glove. He wasn't really paying much attention to Blake any more. 'We already have. You know what defeated you in the end? Your people's imagination. You couldn't believe an invasion like this could happen. It's too much of a fiction. What did you expect? Little green men?' He smiled again, and Blake thought the smile had something sad about it, as if the alien inside Gates was suddenly aware of some awful truth about itself. 'We're just like you.'

James took a step forward. 'It's our turn now.'

'Join us, Steve,' Joanna said, following him. 'Come and join me.' She held out her hand.

From the other direction, Gates closed in on Melissa. Blake could feel her breathing speed up. Feel her determination not to cry out, not to give them any satisfaction.

They closed in on all sides of the two humans.

When he knew Gates and Ryle and Wilson were coming after them, Steve Blake had decided that there was only one thing he could do, for himself and for all humanity. Now he was going to do it. He waited until the

276

aliens, if he could call them that, were close. Until he just about still had room.

Then he swung the axe.

'Never!' he shouted. 'Never!''

The axe embedded itself in a large pipe in the ceiling. He just hoped that it was the pipe he thought it was.

He looked Gates in the eyes.

And saw that it was.

'No!' shouted the thing in the shape of a policeman.

Before anyone could move, Blake tugged the axe out and swung again.

The pipe split in two.

And a jet of pure oxygen blasted out of it.

Everybody around Blake and Melissa fell, jerking and spasming, as if the creatures inside these human bodies couldn't control them any more. Only Gates remained on his feet. He took a step back, and for a moment Blake feared that he would run. But it seemed that the alien's feet were failing him. It was all he could do to remain upright. The expression on his face contorted into a mask of anger and fear.

Blake watched, the adrenaline surging through him pumping the scene into slow motion, as Gates reached into his jacket, and, as if the movement were his last, as if it required all his concentration, he pulled out an automatic pistol.

He was aiming it at Melissa.

She stared, her mouth open in a terrible question of 'why'.

Blake put one foot in front of the other, pushed himself forward. He wondered, as he spread his body wide in front of the woman he loved, if it was the alien or the memory of her dead husband who was going to kill Melissa.

Gates fired the gun.

The bullet plucked Blake off his feet. Spun him about the axis of his left shoulder. He slid on to the ground with a slap of blood against the wall.

Gates tumbled into a twitching, helpless, heap.

Blake looked up at Melissa's face as it swam into view above him. 'Is . . .?' he whispered, feeling certain that he was going to die. The pain had swamped him completely.

'Melissa!'

The scream made her turn.

Blake could only look as Gates came crawling in their direction. Smoke was curling from his mouth and nostrils. His eyes were blazing white. He reached a shuddering hand towards Blake. 'Melissa?' he pleaded.

She cradled Blake in her arms, and pulled the axe to them protectively. 'Don't come near him! Get away from him!'

'Melissa. Melis . . .' Gates reached out his hand again. And then fell. Flames flickered between his teeth, and blood flowed freely from his nose, forming a pool around his face. His head lay awkwardly on the concrete, his eyes fading into pure white.

Melissa cradled Blake in her arms. He felt her warmth and strength.

And he finally allowed the darkness to overtake him.

Mary Madigan lay dead across her desk. Her palm was open before her. In it lay her mother's wedding ring.

The Nuclear Research Institute was full of bodies. Secretaries ran through the corridors that were littered with them, their hands over their faces, fearing contamination.

Ferguson was crumpled in the front of a crashed police car. The young constable beside him was trying to explain the accident over the radio.

Across the world, in centres of power, at the UN, in parliaments and courts and secret complexes, the bodies lay bleeding. Everywhere, the representatives of the next level of power stared at the bodies, and wondered what they should do next.

The Zentex complex ground to a halt at the news that something had happened to the Leonard family. The workers formed an uneasy, muttering crowd around their house, waiting for some announcement about their future.

It never came.

Melissa walked beside the stretcher as the military surgeons wheeled Steve out of the bunker. He wore an oxygen mask and was attached to a life-sustaining drip. Dressings covered his shoulder wound. But Melissa was sure that, under all that, he was sleeping peacefully. Hundreds of bodies were being recovered, from all over the complex.

A high-ranking soldier, who looked like he'd just arrived, marched up to her as Blake was being transferred to the back of the ambulance. 'Do I take it,' he asked her, his moustache visibly bristling, 'that what we think just happened is what actually happened?'

Melissa brushed the hair back from her face and thought about it, aware of how absurd she must look, her cardigan sopped with blood. 'All I can say is that the man in that ambulance isn't any sort of terrorist, and that he just saved the planet for you.'

'Oh, we're aware of that. We've been reading Dr Armstrong's report. Couldn't avoid it, really. It was posted right across the internet a few hours before she died.'

'And?' Melissa looked suspiciously at him.

The man raised an ironic eyebrow. 'And you're both free to go, Miss Prentice.' He folded his swagger stick under his arm and moved off, looking around for his unit. 'Captain! Be careful with those bodies!'

Melissa got into the back of the ambulance to hold Steve's hand. As the vehicle drove off, she watched the base and the soldiers and the drifting smoke of genocide vanish into the distance.

She didn't know what she and Steve Blake were going to do next. But she knew they were going to do it together.

He opened his eyes and smiled at her. 'Melissa?'

She squeezed his hand a little tighter. 'The genuine article.'

279

EPILOGUE

UNTITLED

Graham shouldered down the door of the Leonards' house. Pat followed him inside, pushing through the security guards who'd called them and were insisting on seeing for themselves.

Patrick and Pauline Leonard were lying on the carpet in twisted positions, blood all around them. Pat knew instantly that they were dead, but Graham bent and checked for vital signs anyway.

He shook his head. 'Nothing.'

Pat headed upstairs at a run. She leant heavily on the banister rail when she saw the little girl lying on the landing. 'One more up here!' She must have been about nine. Blood everywhere again. This must be Fiona Leonard. God, had they taken something and given it to her too? She checked for signs. None. They weren't going to get anything out of –

A child's cry came from across the hallway.

'We've got a survivor!' Pat shouted, and ran into the bedroom.

She found the youngest, four-year-old David, slumped against the wall, like a puppet who'd had his strings cut. His nose was pulsing with blood. But he was wailing at the top of his voice. Pat went to him, reaching into her medical kit.

'It's all right, darling,' she hushed him. 'It's all right.'

She'd checked him over by the time the others entered. She turned to Graham with a smile. 'He just needs cleaning up and he'll be right as rain. Won't you, chicken?' She ruffled his hair.

The David Leonard didn't know who he was any more. He couldn't remember why he was here, or what he was supposed to do. But he could feel that there was somebody who knew, way up above his head, far far away.

He allowed the human beings to carry him past the bodies of his fellows, and went along with them, shielding his eyes.

He knew he was different from them, and he knew that he hated them. And that was all.

For the moment.

As they carried him out of the house, the workers who surrounded the place cheered. Past them, on the horizon narrowly glimpsed between buildings, the sun was setting.

The David Leonard inverted his eyes and watched it rise instead.